UNITY PENFOLD

MARGARET TABOR was born in London in 1934, the daughter of David Tabor, a wine merchant, and his wife, Minnie. Her parents named her Margaret, but she was universally known as Shosh, her infant mangling of Shoshana, the name she wished she had been given. A keen theatergoer as a teenager, she rejected the idea of Oxford University and instead went on to train as a stage manager at the Central School of Speech and Drama in 1953. She was very active backstage in the 1960s London theater scene, later working in the production office at Theatre Projects on such productions as *A Funny Thing Happened on the Way to the Forum*, *Fiddler on the Roof*, and *Cabaret*. In 1958 she married fellow stage manager David London, with whom she had two children. After their divorce in 1965, she married the actor Peter Copley.

She published three novels, all with elements of horror or the supernatural, under her maiden name: *The Baker's Daughter* (1979), *Unity Penfold* (1980) (also published as *Nightmare Street* and *Eclipse*), and *The Understudy* (1983).

In 1981 she and her husband moved to Bristol, where they became well known in the local theater community. In later life she became a much sought-after script editor for her writer friends. She died on Boxing Day in 2020.

I0633322

MARGARET TABOR

UNITY PENFOLD

VALANCOURT BOOKS

Unity Penfold by Margaret Tabor
Originally published in Great Britain by Heinemann in 1980
Published in the U.S.A. as *Nightmare Street* by Pocket Books in 1982
First Valancourt Books edition 2024

The Valancourt Books name and logo are federally registered trademarks of Valancourt Books, LLC. All rights reserved.

Published by Valancourt Books, Richmond, Virginia
http://www.valancourtbooks.com

ISBN 978-1-960241-25-2 (paperback)
Also available as an electronic book.

Set in Dante MT

To Gid.

I borrowed the name, though none of the qualities, of a young friend for one of my leading characters. As this act of petty larceny seemed to amuse rather than distress him during his final illness, I have retained it. This book is also to the memory of Face-Alan Wilkinson.

CONTENTS

Part One

Face and Unity

'I went home and it wasn't there.'

She told me this as she huddled, white faced and tiny, against a stone parapet in Euston Station as the concourse slowly filled with police.

'Why are they here?' she whispered as they invaded the space, silent and ruthless, men with a purpose but no hurry.

I shrugged. 'Trying to prove that blue is beautiful? Jesus O'Reilly! There's enough of 'em. Must have called in the cavalry.' I watched them a trifle warily as they quietly stationed themselves in regular batches around the perimeter of the concourse.

I put away my guitar. Folk songs and fuzz are antipathetic, though it had been my strumming that had brought her toward me, her face and hair wild and dirty, her age unguessable under the soiled layer of fatigue. She was wearing the anonymous and ubiquitous uniform of jeans and sweat shirt.

She plucked at my sleeve and repeated, 'I'd gone home and it wasn't there.'

I stared at her, hoping to gauge the nature of her nuttiness. She was a nothing, an urban derelict, desperate and destroyed, another random wanderer in the late evening traffic of a main line railway station.

'What's your name?' I asked gently.

She looked at me as if I'd asked an obscene question. She lost strength and crouched further down into the safe shadow of the parapet that flanked the stairway down to the nether regions of taxi stands and Tube stations.

'My name? Yes, I suppose everybody has a name.' A cough, midway between a laugh and a groan, shivered through her frail body. 'Yesterday,' she said emphatically, her eyes daring me to interrupt, 'yesterday, I was called Unity Penfold.'

The groaning laugh turned predictably into a dry sobbing that soon fell away into apathy.

I settled down beside her on the stone floor and leaned my head back against the rough, chipped mosaic that had looked good once, long ago, in the architect's office.

'Want to talk?'

'Will you tell them?' She nodded at the deepening blue ranks.

'I'm well known for bad habits, but confiding in coppers is not one of them. Full of prejudices, me. I don't even have one as a best friend.'

The laugh failed, but the attempt gave her the impetus to speak. Once started it spilled out, a cornucopia of facts and memories, trivia and heartbreak, a whole lifetime in vivid capsules. She spoke fast, telling her tale in fervid whispers, the episodes lacking sequence, flashing back and forth, as she tried to stuff the sum of her experience into a small pocket of time. There was a tassel on my guitar case and she used it, plaiting and twisting the threads, drawing the energy to speak from her frantic fingers. She needed to talk and I listened. Whether her story was truth or mere madness, I couldn't tell; but as she spoke, the activity of the huge concourse gradually stilled as the weight of the increasing police presence pushed everything into the edgy, waiting silence that comes before a storm.

Yesterday afternoon she had walked home, she said, jaunty from a day's outing, lunch with Klaus Narraway and an unexpected encounter with a girlfriend whom she had supposed to be abroad. As she swung around the corner into the quiet street near Primrose Hill where she lived, she was eager to tell her husband the bundle of gossip she had collected, make up to her kids for bad-tempered tears that morning. Then it struck. The street, familiar and reassuring, had pulverized her into shock with the peaceful normality of its appearance, for without warning, without trumpets, fire or flood, her home had gone.

Vanished.

The neighboring houses had smugly joined sides to obliterate it. The street had folded like a paper ribbon to cancel her existence.

She had been born a year after the end of Hitler's war, which made her thirty-two. There was a tradition of Quakerish names in her family. There were even two maiden aunts, Charity and Mercy, 'like the Misses Pecksniff. I always liked Martin Chuzzlewitt because of them, though my aunts were nice and jolly and not at all like their namesakes. But they are dead now. No way to reach them. To ask for the help they'd love to give . . .'

They had adored her father, a younger brother. He was an academic, Dr. Samuel Penfold, an expert following his scholarship down some unreachable tendril of Mediaeval Studies. She had grown up in a quiet village outside Oxford in an atmosphere of lavender and muted voices. Susan, her mother, was fragile, there were no other children; and Unity soon learned to obey without argument the gentle persuasive voice that masked an indomitable rectitude. It was a diet of high thoughts, clean living, no extravagances, and the affection offered, though genuine, was undemonstrative. The child Unity was fed, not on love and the rough and tumble of siblings but on good manners, self-control and books. Books supplied all her wants, filled in the emotional gaps and fueled her imagination. Whenever she could, she would wander along the curling, country lanes living out in her mind the fabulous adventures that she had plundered from her father's bookshelves. Adventures happened to magical and exciting beings; they could never happen to her. But there was fostered in her a fervent desire to imitate them, to live a portion of these adventures somehow, somewhere, however vicariously, to become, just briefly, an echo of a God. With a practicality that was remarkable at the age of nine, she worked out that the only way to achieve this miracle was to become an actress. Television was banned in her own household, but tea with schoolfriends had provided tantalizing glimpses of the small, gray screens of the period, and the occasional, often illegal, visits to the cinema had confirmed her resolve.

To Susan's horror, whenever the fatuous inquiry of visitor or relative forced Unity to answer the inevitable, 'What are you going to be when you grow up, dear?,' she had answered staunchly in the teeth of her mother's disapproval, 'An actress, of course.'

'I had to fight for it. Mother refused to discuss it. Father laughed and said I'd grow out of it. They loved me, of course, and I adored them, especially my father. But we had no meeting ground. They couldn't recognize as serious an ambition so alien to themselves. I won in the end. You see, I had Klaus on my side.'

Samuel Penfold's high-minded intellectualism went hand in hand, as it often does, with an implacable hatred of tyranny. Recruited by way of the Old Boys' circuit of the University, he had joined one of the many undercover, yet largely amateur, agencies trying to circumscribe the worst tragedies that arose with the growth of Nazism. During the late thirties he made frequent journeys to Europe that were never discussed in the household. He returned gray and grim from these excursions; and, when some time after the war was over and a decoration discreetly came his way, Unity, then a toddler, was told little about it and could only guess, as understanding came with age, the extent of her father's courage.

In 1938, Dr. Penfold strode back from Germany and into Susan's twilit sitting room leading by the hand a gawky waif who looked smaller and bleaker than his ten years. This child rarely spoke and when he did could only manage a mixture of German and Yiddish. He had been labeled and packaged by his despairing parents and surrendered to a mere acquaintance in whose goodwill they would rather trust than take the risk of keeping the boy in the hope of outrunning the approaching holocaust.

Dr. Penfold did well. He donated the lad to a childless couple who cherished the starveling and whose care and concern were amply repaid by the pride they earned from his rapid growth and a rich harvest of scholarships and academic honors. His pseudo parents had died when he left University and had bequeathed him their name, their Berkshire cottage and a small income. His real parents had never been traced.

'I love Klaus. He was eighteen when I was born. His accent has all gone. Just a few guttural r's. He was the nearest thing to a brother. He'd take me on picnics at weekends when he was up at Oxford getting all those letters after his name. He invented a private world, just for us, when I was five or so. I still half believe in it. My parents adored him too. They listened to him when

he insisted that I should be allowed to go to Drama School. He
was always there. Always on my side. That's why when they said
that he'd gone. Gone ...' She stopped talking and her face went
blank with pain. 'Gone ... Klaus. He wouldn't do that, you see.
Wouldn't go away without saying. He's always there to help me.
He came back all the way from Paris to be with me when my
father died ...'

She lifted up her head in that archetypal gesture of despair
and I saw fresh tears start down her grubby cheeks following the
course left by a previous bout of crying like spring waters filling
up a dried out river bed.

'What then?' I asked, prodding her back to her story. 'What
happened then?'

Drama School. A jumble of memories. Two names recurring,
escaping from the narrative again and again like a talisman, a
magic incantation, as if by reciting the names she was affirming a
creed. Pippa Waters and Ned Roland.

'They were third year when I was just a first year. After they finished the course, they took out a tour of *Maria Marten*, around all
the clubs and working men's halls in South Wales. Ned directed
it. He was Ned Taylor then, but when he joined Equity he had
to change it as they already had a Ned Taylor on their books.
Pippa played the lead and adapted the original script. Gave the
production political overtones. It was just before all the student
riots ... Peace and Love ... ironic, really. They were looking for a
dogsbody and took me along. I was co-opted as an A.S.M.'

Her simplicity and keenness had enchanted Ned and amused
Pippa. Pippa, tall, spindly and plain but with a frenetic energy that
promised everything. Unity spent the summer with them, bump-
ing along in the back of a Minibus from gig to gig, dossing down
in school halls or cheap lodgings; working till they reached the
dawn exhaustion of total inefficiency. They became inseparable,
a gang of three, with Unity little more than a schoolgirl dazzled
by being treated as an equal by the grown-ups. If Pippa exploited
her willingness to please and Ned was beginning his life-long
devotion to her elfin charm, she was too bemused to notice.

They played games in the tedious gaps between activity and
the rare moments of rest. 'Titles' was invented by Pippa. One had

to make up the title of the most spectacular flop in which they would ever be likely to appear. Marks were awarded up to 100. Ned had scored a winning 99 one morning when, after a sleepless night, he struggled under the weight of two Patt 23's and the folding frame of a rostrum.

' "Epitaph for a Dustbin," ' he announced in sepulchral tones, twisting his face with the easy mobility of the character actor.

'Define,' Pippa demanded without looking up from a duel with a recalcitrant sewing machine.

'The theater is dying. We have been told often enough. The dead need an epitaph. The theater is also a repository—brief chroniclers etc.—we collect and reflect the discarded refuse of society. Attitudes, fashions, passing fads. We are a mirror. And a waste-paper basket. "Epitaph for a Dustbin." Elegy for the theater. It can't win.' A few days later, Unity picked at some greasy chips in an all night caff and delivered herself of her first offering, carefully hoarded until the moment was propitious.

' "The Guelph who was a Ghibelline." '

Ned blinked. 'Sounds good. What does it mean?'

'I've no idea.' Unity was flushed with audacity. 'It's a mystery play. Historical. It's bound to fail.'

Pippa laughed noisily through a mouth full of bacon and beans.

'You're not just a pretty face.' She studied Unity's eagerness with slow concentration. 'You'll do,' she said finally. 'Very well indeed, if my opinion is to be asked on the subject. I'll give that ninety-seven. Ned will think I'm mean not to give full marks. But that's his problem. And yours.'

Unity blushed.

They played 'Botticelli,' a long and arduous guessing game with no surrender that lasted for days till they had exhausted the alphabet and each other. Then they started that cruel game where one of them thought of a person and the other two had to guess whom from a series of images. At first they stuck to strangers, but their list of mutual acquaintances was small and they were forced to use intimates.

'What day of the week?' Unity asked, chasing an elusive subject.

'A wet Sunday,' Pippa sniggered.

'What animal?'

'A little dog. A small, wagging, eager, persistent doggie, patiently waiting for scraps and affection,' Pippa said firmly, looking at nothing.

'Why, it's Ned!' And was ashamed. At Pippa for the description and herself for guessing correctly.

She married him, of course. One further year at Drama School and then a year with a good Rep, living for a brief spell the reality of her hedgerow fantasies. Ned had meanwhile carved himself a career in television, an existence as structured as an accountant's.

'A nine to five actor,' Pippa said scornfully, erupting occasionally into their placid lives. She had filled out so that her long legs were now balanced by a fine bust and her straggly hair had been teased, penned and colored to a flowing pre-Raphaelite glory that emphasized high cheekbones, huge eyes and sultry lips that owed far more to paint than to nature. In the intense flowering of the Fringe Theater of the late Sixties, she had given a string of brilliant performances, fulfilling her early promise with flamboyant ease.

Then Chris was born. And two years later, Tim. She could afford help, nannies for the boys; but nobody asked for her. Ned's career had flourished as predictably as Pippa's, but along another path. Unity's had foundered. She had faded too soon from the scene to have made her mark as a juvenile, and was now competing, an unknown, against hardened warriors for the leading parts; and she was not old enough, plain enough or experienced enough for the cameo character parts she was put up for.

She started to cry, which earned her a curious glance from a passing cop.

'Keep going,' I urged.

'I'm not blaming Ned. It's not his fault. I love him. I need him. But he's gone away as well and I don't know where he . . .' Her voice faded out again.

'Go on.'

She wiped her eyes with the back of her sleeve, smearing the dirt over more of her face. The unnatural silence of the station made her self-conscious, but she pulled another thread from the tassel and continued. Slowly at first but soon gaining pace to the full, breathy speed of before.

A year ago, when Tim the younger boy was five and going to full-time school, the depression had come, caught her by the throat and dragged her out of the sunlight. Ned and the boys had held on to her valiantly, but the blackness took her until she cried all day at the very pain of her painless existence. She had love, security, hope and pleasure, a future to plan and no fear for tomorrow. But it wasn't enough. She wanted an identity. She needed to be Unity Penfold, not Mrs. Ned Roland. She wanted for herself the flattering stir that accompanied Ned or Pippa as they ventured into public territory, the thrust of autograph books and the watchful eyes.

Ned's agent, Jamie Marriot, put her on his books. He sent her to countless and fruitless interviews and dutifully put her name forward for unsuitable parts. One commercial, two days on a second feature film, and a voice-over for Schools Television were all that resulted. A pitiful handful of jobs and blank unreasonable and unreasoning despair.

Euston was peaceful again. The police phalanx was still, ranged around the concourse with that patient, unconcerned nonchalance of the professional fighter. The few members of the public who eyed the indicator board tried to maintain the unanxious lack of interest of the habitual traveler; but most of the passing human traffic was strained and unrelaxed, awkwardly aware of the police presence. It was becoming clear that the happening, the event that called for such a massive display of law was geared to an arrival or a departure. I scanned the flickering, electronic letters of the board from my perch behind the parapet and followed the disorder of Unity's narrative.

Yesterday.

The dark stain of the morning's awakening receded during the day. It became, as usual, a memory, distant but containable. An experience that was recognizable but no longer mine. Like a situation presented in fiction or on TV. Tomorrow, I promised myself, I would defeat it, banish the useless and suffocating blanket that fell upon me daily as I emerged from the womb safety of sleep.

Ned understood. He always does. Dredging up sympathy from the still center of his love, his kindness, his reticence; he understood but I fought him as he tried to pry me loose from my self-imposed and self-indulgent misery.

He brought me breakfast on a tray. Coffee and toast and a bedraggled crocus in an eggcup, a loving token that smelled sootily of the dank garden.

'You spoil me, Ned. You feed my guilt.'

He said gently, 'Don't mind the guilt. Don't mind anything, please. You are letting all this happen. Doing it to yourself, Newt. You know and I know that it will only take one little incident, one spark of hope and you'll be singing like a lark. Get away from us all. Force yourself out of the house. You'll enjoy it. Go out. Lunch with friends.'

'I can't. I can't go anywhere.'

'You must. You have to. I'll make you.'

I argued, sulked and resisted. I clung to my depression as if I feared that by being coaxed out of it I would be invalidating its reality.

'Take the chance now,' he begged. 'Next week I'll be rehearsing again.'

I didn't want to go out. To go out would mean having to make an effort, fake an appearance. I would have to outstare the pitying glances that went with inquiries about work and progress in general. Outside, the world judged worth in terms of distance. Signposts passed. Achievement equated with mileage.

'All my friends are working. I will not go and hang around theaters or studios like a bird looking for crumbs.'

'Then go and lunch with Klaus. Research biologists are not noted for their theatrical chatter.'

I clung to him. 'Oh, Ned. Ned, I wish I were some use to you.'

'Newt, darling. You can never be useless to me. Please, just go out and break the cycle. I'll deal with the boys.'

The Land Ecology Research Institute is part of London University. It backs on to Gower Street and offends the weathered gray stone of the area with its brash, new walls of yellow brick, studded with ill-proportioned windows. Once inside the reception hall, however, the outer vulgarity gives way to the

comfortable reticence of carpets, discreet lighting and air condi-
tioning.

'Dr. Narraway, please.'

'Is he expecting you?'

'Yes, I'm Unity Penfold.'

The receptionist purred into her house phone.

Klaus met me as I left the lift. His long, white coat flapped
around his ungainly figure, his thick glasses were pushed up to
rest absurdly on his domed forehead.

'Ah, Unity, it is good to see you. My dear, I wish you would
remember an old friend more often. It rescues him from boredom.'

He beamed at me and I stifled a desire to pirouette for him. He
has that effect. He makes me feel beautiful, theatrical and intelligent. He also makes me behave like a little girl.

I kissed his cheek.

'Where are you taking me to lunch?'

He has an adventurous taste in food. Barbara, his wife, lives
in the Berkshire cottage and divides her time between running a
pony club and keeping house for two hefty teenage daughters and
Klaus, when he can tear himself away from his laboratory. The
cooking that Barbara provides is as sensible and sturdy as she is
herself; and, if Klaus had a secret, I would guess it to be a secret
yearning for the exotic in both women and food. He has never
said anything about the women. He has a bachelor flat in town to
which I've never been invited and Ned jokes about sexual explorations privately pursued. Certainly, he hunts after outlandish dishes
with a dedication that is hard to fathom. When I was a student, he
would drag me for miles to find a Burmese curry or a properly
prepared bouillabaisse.

'You chose the wrong day to phone. I have to be in conference
all afternoon so there is not enough time to take you to a Kurdish
restaurant that I've found in Balham. All is goat—meat, cheese,
yoghurt, butter. Very strong. Pungent. Another day perhaps. A
treat for you. But first, you must phone Ned. He wants to talk to
you before I take you to Gianni's. Safe, a little passé, but we can
trust him.'

I was thankful to be rescued from the goat. Ned had news of
Pippa.

'No, not a script,' he said hastily, guessing my hopes. 'But Pippa is back from her tour a week early and longing to talk to you. I thought you might like to pop in and see her after lunch. It's on your way home.'

Klaus and Gianni greeted each other happily in a spate of multilingual insults. I disappointed them by my lack of appetite. It put a damper on their elaborate plans for the menu.

'You might as well have Barbara's cooking. Soup and salad. I will allow no such nonsense,' he protested. 'And that reminds me. You never visit us any more. It is a sadness for all of us. The girls would love to see you.'

I accepted the rebuke. 'I know. I've been naughty and neglectful. There have been difficulties ... nothing serious, but you know how it is.'

He smiled. 'And you will tell me only if you want to. But not very difficult I trust. You look tired.'

'I refuse to make the conventional retort of "you mean I look old," but you do mean that, all the same.'

'Old!' He laughed with boyish delight. 'No, I do not mean old. I am precise by nature and would say that, if it were true. An *old* ...' he underlined the word, '... an old friend's privilege. But you do look tired. So, eat slowly and drink carefully. It would be a sad waste indeed to repudiate the gift of health and leisure by spurning the blessing of a good meal. Now, do you want to tell me what draws the skin so tightly over your cheeks and shadows the smile in your eyes. It is not Ned, is it?'

I patted his hand. 'No, dear Klaus. Take the belligerent expression off your face. It is not Ned. You don't have to fight a duel for me. Ned is fine. A jewel. A husband in a million, and that is part of the problem. Every damned little thing is fine. Kids, finances, I might even get a job—one day. And yet,' I tried to blink back the stinging tears, 'and yet I wake each morning in weeping, sick despair. It's a vicious circle finally. The more I cry, the more useless I feel. The more useless and ungrateful I feel, the more I cry and the less I can cope with.'

He tried to interrupt, but I forestalled him. 'Don't talk to me of clinical depression and pills, please. I neither believe one to be the cause, nor the other the cure. I know what I need. But I lack the guts, courage, call it what you like, to go out and get it. I want to be me. To be whole. To collect all my scattered bits and get it together, in that good and useful phrase of modern slang. Centered. Together. That's all.'

Klaus said, 'I beg you, don't despise medical assistance. Nor Gianni's miraculous soufflé . . .'

'No,' I interrupted him this time, my mood already lightened by the glass of wine, 'don't you see? It really is not medical. I've almost forgotten it all by now. Anything can tip the balance. A song, a phone call, a job, of course . . . I swing back and forth. Born under the sign of Gemini. The twins, two people. It all lies in the stars. "There was a star danced and I was born . . ." Oh, if I could play Beatrice. Astrology is the answer. It has made of me an emotional tennis ball.'

I prattled on, getting pleasure from Klaus's elaborate pantomime of disapproval.

'In the laboratory my bunnies don't behave any differently because of their birthdays. Only if I feed them on different diets and chemicals. Then the difference can be measured, the changes tabulated.'

He poured more wine, gently removing my protesting hand from the rim of my glass, 'You see, I feed you an intoxicant, alcohol, and you look more cheerful. You smile freely, you like to tease me with your nonsense. You have color in your cheeks. That is a scientific fact and more believable than the mumbo jumbo of the fashionable astrologers.'

'So, I'll have to become an alcoholic.'

He laughed. 'That is not your fate. What a theatrical remark! No, you are destined to remain an enchantress . . .'

'A ragamuffin. Look at me, I can't even dress like a lady.'

'A sprite. Peter Pan, who never grows old . . .'

'Oh, Klaus, you are such a tonic for me.'

After lunch, we walked up Gower Street and crossed the Euston Road. Pippa lived in the straggle of near derelict houses that were all that remained of the northern end of the old quarter. When the new clearway had dissected Gower Street, it left behind a small area marooned in the hinterland behind Euston Station.

Klaus came with me. He had an errand to fulfill. His daughters had begged him for days to venture out of his Rabbit Warren, as they called the laboratory, and patronize Laurence Corner, a miraculous depository of all that was secondhand in military clothing and equipment.

'I wouldn't dare to return without rugby shirts. I suspect that they are obtained from the prison service as they have six digit numbers stencilled on the front and are hideously stained. However, they are all the rage in Berkshire and Angela and Carol have demanded them with menaces.'

As we parted in front of the shop, he kissed my hand. 'Come again soon. Whenever you feel depressed. Maybe you will not be strong enough for the goat. I'll find you nectar and ambrosia instead.'

Pippa lives in the next street behind a wine red door, the only one in sight that is freshly painted. A flight of stairs leads up from a small hallway. From the other side of a closed door on the ground floor there is always the clatter of a typewriter. It's the office of a seedy model agency, not all of whose business is legitimate. 'Very handy,' Pippa would say. 'When I'm an old whore, I'll be living over the shop.'

I ran up the stairs and banged on Pippa's door.

'Pippa? Hey, open up. It's me.'

She appeared, her head wrapped in a towel. The rest of her was in a wild mixture of harem pants and a Shetland sweater.

'Hi, Newt, you're early. Ned gave me the impression you'd be later. Come in, do. Chaos as usual.'

'What happened to the tour?'

'All fucked up, darling. I'll tell when I've dried my hair. Do you want a drink? There's some Genever in my suitcase. Contraband. I had to vamp the customs man as I was also carrying about four litres of brandy for my father and Willis.'

'Pippa, you are incorrigible.'

'Oh, I hope so.' She shifted a litter of clothing from the divan. 'Well, do you want some mother's ruin?'

'No thanks. I've just lunched with Klaus and he filled me with wine.'

'Did he? He has a letch for you, that one. One day, he'll pounce. And you'll be offended, you silly mouse.'

Our friendship is based on incompatibility. I envy the way she cuts a relentless path through life leaving a wake of lovers, husbands, triumphs, and defeats, old clothes and enemies with a single-minded purpose from which she will not be deflected. And she, I suspect, nurses a secret admiration for the domesticity and peace that a husband and children provide. It would stifle her but she likes to live it vicariously.

'How is Willis?' I asked.

'Pissed, I expect. When I left him in Amsterdam yesterday, he was well on the way.'

'You left him behind?'

'Of course, darling. I only travel with sober men. I can't stand it when they puke.' She tossed a packet of cigarettes at me. 'I suppose you're still not smoking, you little prig. How is the lovely Ned?'

'Kinder to me than I deserve.'

'Since the moment he looked gaga at you nine hundred years ago in the Co-op hall in Pontypool, I could have told you that you would be able to trample him underfoot. He adores you, you lucky bitch. I wish I could command such devotion.'

'But, you see . . .'

'But, but, but . . . Newt, I promise you, you don't know just how lucky you are.'

The kettle boiled in her tiny cupboard kitchen, which she had painted in bright red gloss. She handed me a cup of sad-looking coffee. She caught my glance and grinned. 'Pretty grim, isn't it? There's no milk I'm afraid, but I'm putting gin in mine. Sure you won't?'

I shook my head and settled back on the divan. 'Tell me all.'

She had turned down a TV series to go on this tour with a new production by a notorious experimental director who rejected everything from scenery to language. It was a tale of rage and temperament, missed trains and lost deposits, an abduction, a suicide, a vendetta and finally, an outraged public, closed theaters and angry authorities.

'So what could I do but a moonlight flit before the two sides met up? Luckily, I had kept my hot little hand tight around my return ticket. I grabbed the booze and ran.'

There's a logic, I thought through my laughter, to send Pippa on such a rampage: I could never survive it. Watching her verbal acrobatics as she sketched and, no doubt, embellished the highlights of the tour, I felt a small, comforting nudge in my mind that told me that I would never, given the choice, have chosen Pippa's path rather than my own. Delighted with this discovery, I sat back to enjoy Pippa and, when I left to battle with the early rush hour, the pendulum had swung way up, and I started home exhilarated and at peace.

My bus died at Camden Town. It came to halt in a flurry of honking and banter, good-humored because of the spring sunshine. One week earlier and the same incident would have been the cause of bad temper and sullenness as the passengers were turfed off while the Asian bus conductor charmingly told the blatant lie, 'Another one soon. Oh, yes, coming very soon.'

So I walked, the exercise on top of the wine and laughter produced what I hoped was a becoming flush to my cheeks. I carried no handbag: I had stuffed some notes and loose change in my jeans, so I put my hands in my pockets and swung past Camden Lock, the flattering reflection in the occasional shop window taking ten years off my age, though plate glass is notoriously lacking in discernment. Ned would want to hear of Pippa's plight. I rehearsed the telling in my head and a neat turn of phrase popped up that lifted me further into my euphoric mood. A great giggle began at the absurdity of my depressing morning and I tried to gather it up, feed it, hold on to it for protection when the pendulum would swing down again for the next disintegration.

Past the Roundhouse, over the canal and into Regent's Park Road, still smiling at strangers, still admiring the image that I thought I presented. With thespian vanity, I saw myself in camera, a long tracking shot that followed me along the street like the loving camera work that tracked the young Julie Christie through the streets of 'Billy Liar.' I heard the director's voice:

'Lovely, Unity, just the quality I want. Jaunty, confident, brave . . . for we are not as young as we were, are we . . . victorious over difficulties . . .'

Even my fantasies let in the bad news, but the dig about my age amused rather than depressed me. It was true, and I could be, would be victorious.

With jaunty, brave and confident step, I walked to 4, King Henry's Crescent.

It was not there!

I had been too involved in my daydream, missed the turning, walked too far. I ran back to the corner. The street sign with the familiar chip in the bottom of the K, the other houses, the post box, the street lamps, all are as they were this morning. No number 4. No house. Not even a gap. The familiar adjacent houses had swung closer, leaving a garage between . . .

Shock waves like nausea. Ripples of panic.

Dizziness. The air somersaults. Take a deep breath . . . force calm . . . there's a reason . . . a mental aberration . . . moment of forgetfulness . . . too much wine.

Fear of insanity . . . amnesia. Should sit down, head between knees. Ned would know what to do. Ned?

'Ned!' I screamed. In the quiet afternoon, a street sweeper watched me with a lack of curiosity that said that the employees of the London Borough of Camden had seen it all before. He was the only person in sight, idling away till knocking-off time. I went to him, forcing a deprecating grin.

'Can you tell me where number 4 is?' I asked, my casual tones ringing loud and false.

'Can't.'

'But . . .'

'Ain't no number 4, that's why,' he said with satisfaction.

'But there must be,' I insisted with manic calm. 'Look, the numbers go up to 12 at least. Over there.'

He didn't follow my pointing finger. 'The way this 'ere crescent's numbered it don't make no difference. It's a right old mess. Drives the postman barmy.'

'But there's always been a number 4.'

'Not in my day. Not since the war, anyhow.' He leaned against his broom, ready for a chat. 'I reckon there used to be 'ouses on that side only, ran 1 to 14. Then Jerry dropped a few bombs and the Council built them new flats in the gaps. Then they put up that new estate on the other side. There used to be marshaling yards there for the railway when the Roundhouse was used for the big engines. Some bright spark tried to arrange the new 'ouses to be numbered alternate like, same as in the other streets. What a ruddy mess. No, there ain't no number 4.'

Another somersault. I held on. 'Where would number 4 have been?'

I thought I sounded reasonable, but my voice must have betrayed me for he moved off, nettled by my disbelief.

'Couldn't say. Ask somebody else. Kids'll be out of school any minute and the little blighters'll run right through this lot if I don't get it into me cart. 'Ere, you don't look very well, miss.'

The boys?

Whispering outside the door as I struggled to stay asleep, to delay the moment when the depression and bleakness would rise up like pregnancy sickness.

Ned's distant voice. 'Shut up, Tim! What do you want, anyway? I told you to let Mummy sleep.'

Chris's voice in a self-important whisper. 'I told him, Dad, but he won't listen.' And then Tim, slighter and wispier. 'But I've got to ask her if I can be a Viking.'

Chris's voice rose to full volume in contempt. 'You're a bloody liar, Tim. You've never been asked to be a Viking.'

'Yes, I have. Promise. Mr. Prentice said I could be a Viking if my Mum made me a headdress. I've got to ask her.'

Ned again. 'O.K., boys, breakfast is ready. I'll ask Mummy later. Come on down now. And be quiet.'

I heard Chris scamper down the stairs, and Tim calling after him, perplexed. 'But Ol' Prentice said I've got to let him know today.' Then getting no answer, he followed, jumping disconsolately two steps at a time. I heard him grumble, 'What's wrong with Mummy anyway?'

The day had aborted, the machinery of our daily lives had foundered on my inability to accept the totally acceptable. Tears ran into my pillow.

The boys!

Whatever had happened, whatever catastrophe my lunacy had precipitated, the boys must not be alarmed. I'd phone the school and try and catch them, before they left, arrange to meet them at the Tube station. I didn't see the illogic of my reasoning, that they were hardly likely to return home to a house that didn't exist, I thought only of their bewilderment and insecurity as they faced its inexplicable disappearance. I thought of Tim's freckled innocence and Chris, more ponderous and thoughtful with his father's good nature . . . I ran to the phone box in the next street.

I felt in my pockets for the correct coin. Three pound notes, some silver, a few coppers, a small comb and my front door key. I looked at the key in surprise but it reassured me in a curious way. It seemed so normal. It told me that I was just suffering from a momentary blankness, a residue of depression topped up by an unaccustomed lunch-time drink.

The telephone box was filthy; but, with rare luck, it was working and the correct phone directory, L–R, was more or less intact. I looked up the number and dialed.

'Regent's Park School, good afternoon. We are just about to close. Is it urgent?'

'Oh, good afternoon. This is Mrs. Roland. There's been a slight mishap, nothing serious, but I'd like to get a message through to my boys, please, if it's possible to catch them before they leave.'

'I'll put you through to the secretary.'

Silence.

'Yes?'

'I wonder if you can help me. I want to get a message through to my boys. It's rather urgent.'

'What's the name, please?'

'Roland.'

'Roland, let me see. I don't remember any Rolands. Are they new?'

'Chris has been there two years. Tim started last autumn. Look, can you send somebody . . .'

'How strange! I can't see any Rolands on our list at all. Are you sure you've got the right school? You don't want the Regent Academy, do you?' A tone of slight disapproval crept in. 'That's quite another establishment.'

'No. No, I know I've got the right school. Please, I know this sounds silly, but I must meet them before they come home . . .'

'Can you tell me their form teachers?'

'Tim is in Mr. Prentice's class, and Chris is with Mrs. Gilmore.'

'Hold on a moment. I'll check.'

The line went quiet and I could hear the approaching rasp of the street sweeper's broom. I turned my face to hide from his now inquisitive gaze and the sweat began to trickle from my forehead. I leaned against the pane of glass to cool my cheeks.

'Hello. Mrs. Roland, are you still there?'

'Yes.'

'I really don't understand this, Mrs. Roland. I think you must have made a mistake somewhere, though I must confess I don't see how. I've checked with both Mr. Prentice and Mrs. Gilmore. Neither of them has any recollection of any child called Roland, Tim or Chris. Hello? Are you still there?'

My own voice didn't belong to me any more. 'But you have teachers called Mr. Prentice who takes the first year and Mrs. Gilmore who takes a class of older children?'

'Yes.'

'Then I can't be mistaken. Please, if you are determined to be so unhelpful, would you put me through to the Headmaster?'

'I'm sorry, Mrs. Roland, I can't do that. And I'm sorry to say this, but the facts speak for themselves. It sounds remarkably as if you've lost custody of your boys and you are trying to gain illegal access . . .'

'What are you talking about? I can't think . . .'

'So, in the circumstances, I can't help you any further. You'll have to contact the local Education Officer. In any case, I think you would be well advised to go through the proper channels. Perhaps your husband's solicitors . . .'

Ned?

Warm and loving in the soft dark. A being, a presence to keep the nightmares away, to have, to hold. The private closeness, the shared burdens. A chunky man with a clown's face and no taste for the intangible. Orderly and giving. A talent for tenderness.

'Darling Newt. Look at you. Slim as a reed, a mere slip of a thing, and not a day over twenty-five. Mother of two—a likely tale.'

'Don't tease, Ned. I'm old and wasted. Unwanted by the Great British Public. An old woman of thirty-three.'

'Not till June. Don't wish your life away. It's too precious to me.'

'But my life is a mess. I am ashamed because I have nothing to complain about. Nothing at all, and yet I'm sick at heart.'

'I know.' He turned away, still generous enough to try and conceal his hurt. 'I know that we, the boys and I, are not enough. I wish we could be, but we're not.'

'I need work as well. A job. To be me. I know you understand that, but, oh God, Ned, I'm such a dreary lady for you. I don't know how you stand it. And sometimes I feel the boys slipping away from me . . . You are good and kind and I'm nothing but a mess.'

A nestling comfort, a caress and an old, old joke.

'A norrible mess?'

'A nawful mess.'

'Then why do you feel so soft, smell so sweet, give me so much joy . . . ?'

Ned!

Trembling, sweat and tears chasing each other down my face. I grabbed the phone book again. Ned was somewhere. I was having a bout of amnesia. I would remember soon. I needed to be reminded, that was all. It happened all the time. One heard tales of blacking out.

I rifled through the flimsy, dog-eared pages. Roberts-Rodway-Rogers-Rohan-Roland. About a dozen Rolands. I scanned them carefully. I'd forgotten whether he had made the entry N for Ned or E for Edward. But there was neither N nor E. No Ned Roland. My husband, whose existence was being denied by the Post Office . . .

Where was he? Where? Working, perhaps. On location? Who would know?

Jamie. Jamie Marriot. Thank God for the 'Post Office Tele-communications Section 103 London Postal Area Alphabetical Telephone Directory L–R.' I rushed back through this blessed bible.

'Marriot Management.'

'May I speak to Jamie Marriot, please. It's urgent.'

'Who's speaking?'

'Unity Penfold.'

'Who?'

I comforted myself with the thought that she was new to the job. 'Mrs. Ned Roland,' I said in defeat.

'Putting you through.'

'Hello. Marriot here.'

'Oh, Jamie, thank God. Look, I know this sounds idiotic, but I can't remember where Ned is.'

'Sorry, I don't follow. Ned who?'

'Jamie, don't be ridiculous. This is Unity speaking. My Ned. Ned Roland.'

'Are you like Equity? Sorry, love, but I've never heard of Ned Roland.'

'Jamie, for God's sake, stop playing games. You're his agent, aren't you? Please! Where is Ned?'

'Ned Roland, you said?'

'Dear God!'

'Hang on a sec.' His hand must have partially covered the mouthpiece but I heard him say, 'I've got a right one here. Hey, Linda, stop doing that for a moment. Listen, petal, we don't have a Ned Roland on our books, do we? No, I thought not. Wonder if he's in *Spotlight*. Look him up, will you.' He hummed impatiently.

'Jamie,' I pleaded, but my appeal and his silence were inter-rupted by the warning pips from the phone and I had no more coins available.

'Please, Jamie,' I shouted through the pips, 'call me back on this number,' but my feverishly recited digits fell into a dead receiver.

There was nothing to do but stand in the phone box that smelled of stale air, staler urine and the sweat of fear without thought or will or motion. I think I was waiting for the world to make sense again. A lad whistling past on a skateboard roused me from a near catatonic state.

I thought it all out very carefully as if my mental muscles were brittle and might break with any effort. I would walk out of the phone box and down King Henry's Crescent and number 4 would be there because it couldn't be anywhere else. And Ned and the boys would be there. And I would know that I had had one of those weird experiences that would make a good yarn for a dinner party.

Three deep, deep breaths. A quick tug with the comb at my untidy hair. Of such gestures, normality is made. One. Two. Three . . . Hey Presto!

But there was no house, no number 4. The numbering which had always been eccentric was now demurely conventional. Odd numbers on one side of the road, even numbers on the other. Number 5 stood primly in place next to number 3. Number 3 had just been sold and was aswarm with the same army of builders that were there this morning. But number 5? Marion Hill, of course. Her son was in Tim's class. She might know something, have a message for me, let me rest for a while.

I almost laughed with relief that so simple a source of help had not occurred to me before.

I ran up the front door steps and rang impatiently at the bell. She opened the door immediately and looked at me blankly, her pale, nervous face peering around the cautious angle that she allowed herself.

'Hi,' I said, 'has Oliver got back from school?'

'Yes, but I . . .'

'Oh, good,' I said, with a sense of something being right at last. I tried to pass by her and go into the hallway, but she barred my way firmly.

'Look, Marion, I haven't the plague. I just want to ask Oliver if he knows what's happened to Tim.'

'Who?'

'Who? The world's gone mad. Tim. My Tim. Did he walk home with Oliver?'

Her uneasy expression was easily read. It was the look of

somebody who has been accosted by an eccentric stranger with whom it is impossible to deal without making a scene.

'I don't know who you mean,' she whispered.

'Marion, for God's sake, don't be so thick. You might as well say that you don't know who I am.'

'I don't,' she said.

'I'm Unity,' I insisted, though I knew it was hopeless. 'I'm Tim's mother. I live next door.' I pointed.

'It's been empty for months.'

'No, not that one. The one in between with the blue door. It's gone somehow. I don't understand either, but that is where I live. You know I do.'

She was terrified now. My weight was the only thing that prevented her shutting the door in my face. She gave a nervous glance behind her as if to reassure herself that Oliver was safely stowed inside.

'Marion, let me use the phone at least. Please. I've got to get help and I haven't the right coins. Please. Listen, I can prove that I've been here often. I know where the phone is. It's on the bookcase to the right of the dining room door. There's a print above it of some mill workers. Marion, you've got to listen. How could I know that? Marion . . .' She was staring wildly. I put out my hand to shake her by the shoulders. She screamed and pushed my arm aside.

'You're crazy. Go away. Crazy. I've never seen you before in my life. Go away.'

Her terror gave her the strength to slam the door. I could hear her pushing the bolts inside and I could imagine her, trembling and tearful, leaning back against the barred door and considering whether to call the police.

Halt the threatening chaos. Keep a semblance of calm by concentrating on practical matters. Three £1 notes, a fifty-pence piece and some odd pennies. I could get money in the morning as soon as the banks opened, but meanwhile I had neither check book nor banker's card. I hadn't needed them for a lunch date.

Klaus?

Klaus! I was startled that I'd not thought of him before. It was worth a taxi, just to catch him before he went home, just for the reassurance of his exasperated teasing. It was his wine that had caused the confusion. The very least he could do was unravel, untangle the knot and give me back to myself.

For the second time that day, I pushed open the glass door of The Land Ecology Research Institute. A janitor confronted me.

'I'm looking for Dr. Narraway, please.'

'Is he expecting you?'

'Not exactly, but he'll be very pleased to see me.'

'Wait a moment. Take a seat. We're closing up really. He might have gone home.'

I sat and pretended to flip through the scientific journals arranged in neat display on a low table. I had the notion that by displaying an outer coherence an inner truth would follow. The receptionist was about to leave, her coat flung over her shoulders. She answered the janitor's inquiry with resigned patience while shutting down her switchboard. The conference over, the janitor came back to me.

'Who did you say you wanted, miss?'

'Dr. Narraway.'

'We don't seem to have no Dr. Narraway here. Are you sure you've come to the right building? It's easy to get confused with all these University centers and institutes.'

'Of course, I'm sure. I was here today at lunchtime. I went with him to his laboratory. It's on the third floor and to the right as you leave the lift.'

'Just a minute, miss.'

He went back to the desk. There was more conferring and the receptionist put her intercom back into commission. The janitor ran his finger slowly down a directory. I waited till their attention was fully held and then ran to the lift. As the automatic doors slid shut, I heard the janitor shout after me and saw the receptionist reach for a red telephone.

I beat them in the race to the third floor. The laboratory door had a glass window. Through it I could see the long benches, some lab assistants and, at the far end, in his little cubicle of an office, I could see Klaus, his white coated back bending over some papers on his desk.

My legs sagged as gratitude overwhelmed me. Longing for the safety that his presence promised, I found a last burst of speed and ran through the lab to his cubicle. A stranger turned around, his white coat a mocking parody of Klaus's. He looked at me with polite astonishment and sat down at his desk. My flight through their quiet world had collected a train of lab assistants who crowded in the doorway behind me as I confronted the impostor.

'I want Klaus,' I said frantically. 'This is his office. Dr. Klaus Narraway. I had lunch with him today. I know he's here. There's no use in trying to fob me off. I'll ... I'll break the place up, if you don't let me see him.'

'My dear young lady,' Klaus's inadequate understudy favored the pompous approach. 'You may certainly have Klaus, who or what he may be but, alas, it is not in my power to provide you with him as I am unacquainted with the gentleman in question.'

There were no words. The nightmare was complete. Time slowed to a sequence of stills, mug shots outside a cinema.

The seated scientist with well-bred insolence tapping his pen against the side of his nose.

The lab assistants, three men and a girl, who gawped at the door.

The girl had rabbitty teeth, in sympathy with her experimental creatures, and a fading love bite on her unattractive neck.

Two of the men exchanged glances with the greed of those with dull lives who hunger for the heady breath of scandal for titillation.

The third was openly enjoying the prospect of another's discomfiture, whether it was to be mine or, better still, his boss's.

The tableau was broken by the janitor.

'Dr. Hilliard,' he called from behind the massed assistants, 'Dr. Hilliard, the lady slipped by when I wasn't looking.' He broke through the cordon. 'I'm ever so sorry but I couldn't stop her.'

'That's all right, Hughes. I've no doubt you did your best.' He rose to his feet. 'However, this young woman is clearly confused and it is our duty to offer help. It can serve no purpose to confront her like a criminal. Go back to your work, please, gentlemen. Anne, be so good as to fetch a glass of water for Miss ... ?' He looked an inquiry at me. His assumption seemed to be that women who went in frantic search for missing men must, of necessity, be single.

'Penfold,' I supplied faintly, but I felt the scene slip from my grasp.

'Hughes, a chair!' I heard Dr. Hilliard's command and the world went black.

Ned? Klaus? Chris? Tim?

To which limbo, into what darkness had they been dragged from me? Where could I find them? How could I reach them? Ned, help me. Help me. Please.

I kept my eyes shut in the comparative safety of the blackness as meaning returned. I was slumped on a chair, my head resting against a starched fabric that smelled of hospitals and through which an indefinite female odor led me to suspect that my supporter was the rabbitty Anne. My respite from consciousness must have been brief for I could hear Hughes's voice, a mixture of anxiety and justification.

'I don't know what we could have done. She just ran past. Mind you, sir, she don't half look peaky. A bit touched, I should think, poor thing. Should I send over to the hospital, sir?'

'I think she's coming around.' Dr. Hilliard had moved away. 'Try her with a sip of that water, Anne.'

The paper cup was thrust between my lips and I had to open my eyes to prevent being choked. Anne's face was peering at me, repressed excitement ill-concealed under a sickly show of concern. I would provide a good story to relay to the giver of adolescent bites.

'Thank you.' I pushed the cup aside and sat upright, acting a superficial calm. My speech was carefully modulated.

'Dr. Hilliard, I understand that I've intruded into your laboratory and that I have somehow made a foolish mistake. I was under the impression that I was in this very office earlier today. I have clearly had a lapse of memory and I apologize. If you can help by telling where I can contact Dr. Narraway, I would be more than grateful.'

Dr. Hilliard beamed at me. I had become rational. I had displayed decent signals of social acceptability by offering an apology in correct language.

'That's better, Mrs. Penfold.' He had observed my wedding ring. 'But, please, don't apologize. Mistakes can happen to the best of us. We will find your missing friend. Hughes, fetch me the University Directories and the Medical Register. In the flurry of your precipitate—er—visit, I can't recall the name of the gentleman we seek?'

'Dr. Klaus Narraway.' I enunciated as if speaking to the deaf.

'Narraway. Most unusual name. Narraway. Do you know, I believe it is ringing a tiny bell. Wait here, young lady, and I'll consult a colleague.'

He bustled out of the laboratory. His voice and fruity laugh could be heard in the corridor. Anne and I were left alone with nothing to say. After a while, the fruity laugh stopped and he came back to the office.

'Never forget a name. I've solved your mystery. Your friend Narraway. My colleague filled in a few details. Reminded me of a brilliant thesis he wrote in the late forties. Quite remarkable paper. Very able man. Then he took off. Extraordinary. Married a foreign girl, Indian or Nepalese. Went off to do research and teach in Africa or South America. Such a waste, really. Why are you smiling?'

It was Klaus's other life, the exotic might-have-been that always tinged his dreams.

'It sounds so like him,' I said illogically.

'My dear Mrs. Penfold, if you knew him at all, you must have been in your cradle. Extraordinary his name coming up like that. I must look up his paper again.'

He had been ushering me through the lab. By the lift he shook my hand murmuring inconsequential remarks about pressure of work. Some twinge of conscience made him pause, alerted perhaps by my stricken face. I was terrified of being thrust out into the alien world again.

'Can I persuade you to follow Hughes's excellent advice and pop over to the hospital? They'll give you something. It wouldn't do, you know, to faint again on the streets.'

He allowed himself to be reassured by my forced social smile and was happy enough to return to his work and forget me.

There was one other chance, one final straw to clutch. I didn't dare to hope as I crossed the Euston Road and, for the second time that day, walked by Laurence Corner to Pippa's flat. I remembered walking there earlier with Klaus on his way to buy rugby shirts for his girls. I thought of the girls, their flushed healthy faces, the bouncing young bosoms in the pale, blue shirts. I wondered where they were, or whether their blameless young existences had been blotted out forever by the Nepalese lady.

Neither Pippa nor the model agency was there, of course. The house was derelict and due for demolition.

That seemed to be it. Her words petered out as the concourse became charged with static, the expectancy of action. Too many police by now, too much weight. It was useless to attempt a count. While Unity was talking, more had filtered in. Not that she noticed. The telling of her tale had altered her physical shape. She was shrunken, almost wizened, her energy depleted, her stock of vitality used up. Under her fashionable mop of dark curls, her age was showing, her brown eyes which had been quaint, round and startled like a painted doll, had sunk back into dried up prunes, pushing her delicate nose into unnatural prominence. There had been a spot on her lip and she had worried at it, an unwitting outlet for her bewilderment, and now a trickle of blood was mingling with the grime.

Some senior cops strolled by like sheepdogs patrolling their flock. They stopped by our parapet. One of them looked at his watch, checked it against the station indicator and nodded. A few yards away, a policeman talked into a hand held walkie-talkie. A few seconds later, he stopped talking and shook his head. The inspector jabbed his thumb toward the ground. In reply, the young cop spread the fingers of each hand and added a three. Thirteen minutes to zero. The battle groups relaxed. The sheepdogs strolled on. Whatever was brewing, it had to be big. That quantity of law said so, and I've bummed around fast and far enough to know that when the storm broke, it could be strong enough to sweep Unity and me apart and I wanted some answers first.

It would be easy to stick her in a category—nutter—and leave her to stew, but there was the ring of truth in her voice and the details were consistent enough to be genuine. Most nutters shift ground and contradict themselves when the facts prove inconvenient. Her story, though crazy, carried its own logic. Curiosity is a basic evolutionary device. Nothing venture, nothing win. Mine was insatiable.

'What the hell did you do then?'

She started out of her stillness as if she'd received a small electric shock. Perhaps she'd been asleep.

'Do,' she said bitterly, 'what is there to do when you've been . . .' she searched for a word, 'lost . . . cancelled.'

She said that she had walked all night, pounding a beat between the known outposts of her confusion. Gower Street, Pippa's flat and, always, back home, back to King Henry's Crescent, always in the desperate hope that this time, this moment as she turned the corner, the house would be there in its rightful place and the long nightmare would be over. Dawn found her cold and shivering. April gives sweat shirt days, but the nights have frost in them. She wandered into an all night café and ordered a large breakfast in the company of long distance lorry drivers. It had used up most of her precious money and when the food was in front of her, she couldn't eat it, though she drank the hot tea greedily and ordered more.

When the banks opened, she was waiting outside. She took without question, accepted meekly, the fact that neither she nor Ned had an account that could be traced. I reckoned she'd have been surprised by then to find anything else. Nor did she argue when a phone call to her doctor proved equally fruitless.

The concept of any personal future was beyond her. Her immediate concern was to keep clear of authority in any of its myriad manifestations. Her fear was, reasonably, that her story would be unbelieved and unbelievable. She would be labeled 'for the bin' and sent away.

'If I go anywhere, police, doctors, welfare people, I'll have to tell them who I am and when they find out I don't exist they'll lock me up. I've got no means of support. I don't understand the Social Security system . . . you need cards, numbers, an identity . . .'

A huge shiver ran through her. It consumed her totally for a few seconds and then subsided into a steady trembling.

'Have you eaten anything?' I asked.

She shook her head. 'I can't. I've tried but it's no use. Tea, that's all.'

'You should do better than that.'

'Cold. Very cold. Walking and walking. Then it started to rain. I went back to the laboratory just now. The windows of the third floor were still alight. I wanted to go in again but I didn't dare. I was freezing. I thought of Euston. You can always sit in a station. Nobody notices ...' She looked about her but couldn't see or sense the high tension electricity. 'It's warm here, at least.'

The trembling dissolved back into tears. 'On the way here. As you turn out of Gower Street and turn right, there's a building. Do you know what it's called? It has stained glass windows and it's the headquarters of a trade union—the railwaymen, I think. It's called ...' She began a giggle that glinted with hysteria. 'It's called Unity House. Unity House. Don't you think that's funny? Very, very funny.' The giggling stopped abruptly.

The police were on the alert. I checked on my watch. Eleven minutes, two to go and they wanted to be very ready.

'I came here because it was warm. Somewhere to go. You were singing ... I liked your face. Not blank like the others. Brown and sort of watchful ... I liked the song too.'

Waiting, unworried, for a night train to Scotland, to try my luck up north, I had strummed a little. Not to busk, for once, just for myself. A sad, aware, little tune.

> *We were young, we were merry,*
> *we were very, very wise,*
> *And the door stood open at our feast,*
> *When there passed us a woman*
> *with the West in her eyes,*
> *And a man with his back to the East.*

She had stood right in front of me, her dark eyes staring. I hadn't noticed her before.

'Who wrote that?'

'Some old sheila from the last century wrote the wordies.' I always overdo the Aussie when I play. It pleases the punters. 'The tune by yours truly, Phil Mallet, known to his friends as Face.'

The storm broke with the tinkle of breaking glass, the only low decibel sound I know of that can carry any distance in a crowd. A warning bell that galvanized the concourse. The police stopped gossiping, the public stood still, ill at ease and puzzled. The breaking glass was a call to arms. The heavies moved like fast, silent tanks through the ranks of their own men, homing in on the tiny disturbance with ruthless intent.

Right. The big fight had started. The bell had rung. Seconds out.

'Now listen carefully, Unity.' I got up and knelt by her side. 'I reckon there's going to be one hell of a shindy, a real beaut. Keep close to the parapet whatever happens. Keep close and we'll talk more later.'

She woke up to the atmosphere. 'What is it? What's going on?'

'Not a clue. Stay safe.'

Then we heard it. The tribal chant, the battle cry. Three long, singing syllables from a thousand male throats, a downward inflection in a minor key. It screamed defiance, a paean, that started in the corner by the bookstall and flashed across the whole area in a wild diagonal of fighting, yelling men.

'LIV—VER—POOL!'

'LIV—VER—POOL!'

A few ignorant passengers smiled in premature relief. The mystery was explained: it was only an away match for Liverpool. Mid week, 7:30 kick off—must be the Cup. Night specials to take the supporters back home. But the smiles soon faded under the threat of the constant scuffles, the broken bottles, the heaving crowds on the brink of uncontrol and, above all, the heavy brooding presence of the police that stepped on any exuberance, however innocent, almost before it happened and whose own aggression in the teeth of a potential threat brewed its own violence. Who were the hunters and who the hunted? It was hard to tell.

'ARS—SEN—AL!'

'UP THE GUNNERS!'

There was a screaming counter attack along the other diagonal. Another running thread of young men ricocheted against the first. It bothered me as they fell to the ground in small scrimmages that both sides sported red and white colors. My football phase was passed in Melbourne and I am pig ignorant of the British soccer scene. I watched the coincidentally matched combatants as they were pushed back by the thin, blue lines of bobbies. The spirit of Empire not dead, it seemed, only transformed and repigmented.

It was a panorama of sporadic incidents, little explosions, flaring tensions, violence held in check by the threat of police violence. The fuzz out to squash trouble before it began, pouncing fast on any sign of partisan activity, a moment's exhilaration. In reply the supporters became truculent, oppressed and, naturally, on the offensive. The whole station was polarized into armed camps, each ready and waiting for the other to break. And in the middle, the no-man's-land, stood the paying customers.

I heard an American voice asking a sergeant in a querulous voice about the huddle of blue raincoats in a corner perpetrating some pretty heavy action—crowd control, I think is the correct term—against some struggling creatures on the ground.

'No trouble, madam,' he said, in that reassuring voice with which they are issued on getting promoted. 'A few soccer fans. They get a bit excited sometimes. Everything is under control,' and then, when the American lady had taken her indignation elsewhere, I saw the same sergeant pushing in front of him a scrawny youth who would be hard put to it to make six stone weakling-of-the-year. Each shove sent the youth reeling and the Sergeant punctuated each blow with, 'Move, you bastard, move, or I'll break your fucking ankle.'

The Arsenal attack had finished, the attackers removed or cordoned off, but among the Liverpool supporters little skirmishes erupted, swelled and died down. It was impossible to move in the station at all. The special trains were delayed or not yet prepared to be boarded by rampaging fans. The P.A. system squawked an occasional apology but it was inaudible in the swaying, undulating mob. Once or twice small bands of barely adolescent boys with unbroken voices and eyes that knew all the questions burrowed through the mob and yelled a reedy, nasal, 'LIVER-POOL!,' that faded away if the police made any move toward them. The enforced containment of fans and cops within such a limited precinct had the effect of raising the climate some few degrees centigrade. There wasn't a storm brewing now, it was a typhoon. But not yet. Everybody was still waiting. A pseudo silence fell over the station, nothing now but the occasional noise of breaking glass from the older boys who had made for the station bars, and it was from there that the bubble finally popped.

I didn't see or hear the trigger, but suddenly the seething mass burst like a volcano. The army of red bedecked youths stampeded through the concourse. Passengers, luggage, police were all ignored. The lucky bystander found that the tide divided around him and left him standing, a bewildered rock in a sea of turmoil. The unlucky one was swept away, without choice, into the maelstrom.

A tidal wave carried me off. I fought against it. My guitar was leaning up against the chipped mosaic and I had no other way of earning my living. Nothing like the fear of starvation to give a man strength; but, if you can't lick 'em you have to join 'em, and the only way I could keep on my feet was to trot along with them.

It was very nasty for a while. People falling, fights on the ground, whistles and truncheons, faces speckled with blood and the smell of panic. I was thrown off the merry-go-round by Platform 13. I'm big enough to look over most crowds, but this one was jumping too high and too fast. I found a litter bin and leaped up on the edge to spy out the fate of my guitar. If it had gone, I was prepared to break a few Liverpudlian heads. I was pulled down from my perch by a red-headed copper with a missing tooth. He didn't want to hear any explanations. But before he hauled me down, I had seen my guitar, miraculously still tucked under the shadow of the parapet. Some yards away from it, I saw my sergeant pick up a bundle from the ground. He carried it carefully to the main entrance where some ambulances were drawing up. It was a small limp form. I saw jeans and a mass of dark curls.

I don't think it was Unity, it looked too boyish, but I wasn't sure.

Part Two

Unity

'Sarah?'

Nothingness. Floating on black down. Spacetime a fifth dimension of unreachability. Nothing.

'Oh yes, of course. May I go a bit closer?'

Midgets from nowhere with tiny, squeaky voices, prodding, moving and lifting with their Lilliputian limbs while a great Gulliver of nothing that was once . . . once what?

'Golly, yes. Well, I would know, wouldn't I?'

A shaft of light like bright spears under the eyelid. Another and another.

'Thomas, you're writing up this case. What's your prognosis?'

Prog Nosis. Prognosis. Proboscis. Prog. Noses are prosciform. Prog. Noses. It was very, very funny in the darkness. The silly Lilliputian chatter.

'Stimuli tests . . .'

'Unidentified admission . . . police . . .'

'Intensive care unit . . . lumbar puncture . . .'

'Monitor all responses . . .'

'Pupils are contracted . . .'

Better in the darkness with no bright spears. In the kind and comfortable darkness.

Chemical double speak . . . milligrams per cubic milligram. Intravenous . . .

'Come closer now, if you need to.'

'Sarah?'

Dazzling light in intense concentration, a fierce heat. Crucified on a vertical table while down below, far below, a huddle of white, human ants, robed and busy. Pain. A face looms. One of the ants is swimming upward to the high level. A face . . . a face

42

with no mouth, no head . . . only bright, hard eyes in a white void. Nearer and nearer . . . the white void slit by eyes becoming bigger and bigger filling the world. The table tilts to a new perspective. Not hanging, not crucified . . . lying flat with the light above and busy white ants. Flat under the intense light, the glitter of metal. The ghost with eyes . . . stop it . . . stop it . . . away. White. A scream that doesn't end. No. No. *Nooooo!*

'Sedate her.'

A stab and a slow motion dispersal of the senses. From far, far away.

'Thank you, Miss Williams. Take her away now, if you please.'

'Did I do something wrong? Why did she hit me? Where shall I put this mask?'

Perception dwindles to a small, black point and vanishes.

Little tentacles of sensation return. Awareness of space, warmth, sounds. Hands touching, tending, hurting. Stupid, fussing voices. I shall stay in the safe darkness. I won't come out. I? I? Me? Who is me?

'This patient can be moved to a side ward now. And I want that social worker . . . what is her name?'

'Ruth Williams, sir.'

'I want her to dig out the girl who identified her . . .'

Her? Her? Same as I? Want to stay in the blackness. Stay where it is safe. Patient. Patient? A hospital patient? The operating table and the pale, pleading eyes embedded in white death. No. No.

Who moaned?

Hospital. I kept my eyes shut and began to remember. Time. Time had passed, a long time. A time of pain and terror. Chrome tubes, nausea, lights and whirling, shrieking noises, and afterward, always, the thankful sinking into the darkness.

'Sarah?'

A new voice, a louder, buzzing voice. A wasp underneath the sweetness, making demands.

'Sarah!'

I could make a decision. I could decide not to open my eyes and attend to the wasp. It wasn't for me anyway. Me?

'I know you can hear me, dear. Dr. Reading thinks you might prefer to talk to Laura, but I've promised her that I won't ask her to come and visit till you ask for her. You gave her such a fright, screaming at her like that. But if it wasn't for her, we would never have found out who you were. Sensible of her to go to the police, don't you think? You would have been such a puzzle.'

I had a puzzle. Who was me? Me? Laura? It was too difficult. I gave up. It didn't seem to be my problem, so why did they bother me? Me? There was something else . . .

Thinking stopped. I fell asleep.

When I woke up, the voice was back again. Perhaps it hadn't gone away.

'Sarah?'

I wondered why Sarah didn't answer. It wasn't the sort of voice that one would want to answer. There was an edgy, self-satisfied note to it. I was glad I wasn't Sarah.

'Staff Nurse? Oh, Staff, is there any way of getting this patient to respond? It's all very well for Dr. Reading to say that she's conscious, but I don't have time to wait around all day.'

'Well now, Miss Williams, I couldn't say myself. I'm not one to go against the doctors, but I'd not bother her myself. She'll be asking for help soon enough when she needs it. Now, there's Dr. Reading just come into the ward this very minute. Would you like a word with him yourself?'

Staff Nurse was Irish and sensible. Sarah was far more likely to respond without all that nagging.

'I'll have a word with him then. There really ought to be more cooperation between the various departments in this hospital.'

I heard retreating footsteps on linoleum.

Staff said, 'Those social workers think they run the hospital for themselves, they do so. You talk when you're good and ready. I'll be back to change your drip when the doctor's been around the ward.'

Wards. Hospitals. Doctors. I must have been in an accident. Brilliant, Sherlock Penfold. Penfold. That's my name. Unity Penfold. What accident? When? I couldn't remember an accident. I couldn't remember anything properly, but memory itself was too hard to chase along the dark paths. It would hurt to remember. I'd be told soon, so I needn't bother to work it out for myself. There would be a visiting time. Somebody would come and help me and hold me ... who? ... hold me and take away the pain. Ned. Yes, Ned would come and explain it all to me. An accident? Was Ned hurt too? Ned? I chased after the hurting memory that burned in red hot wires across my mind, a searing, white scorching ... No! Back to the darkness. Back to nothing.

A slow awakening and the stabbing, painful memories came back like needles of despair. A moment, a day, a night of terror and loneliness. Incredulous, impossible memory. The house gone. Phone calls that were manic practical jokes. Nobody I knew. They were gone. Where? Why? Klaus. Pippa. The boys. And Ned. Oh, no no no no.

Walking. Walking. Walking. Waiting for the gauze to dissolve, the transformation scene, the correct pieces of reality to come and take their rightful places in the jigsaw of my life. Walking. Then, in despair, making my way to Euston Station to keep warm, passing Unity House. Then ... Then? Nothing. I must have fallen at the station, or was I knocked down crossing the road? Perhaps I fell, or threw myself, under a train. No ... nothing.

A pulse of longing like the throbbing in my veins, a heartbeat of need and wanting. Ned ... Ned ... Ned ... Ned ... On and on. All useless. He had gone.

The shock of the full impact of my returned memory forced me to open my eyes. I was in a small room, a side ward. Outside the door, visible through the glass panel was the main ward, the normal, floral cubicle curtains, and I caught a glimpse of a starched hat like a meringue whisking past. I must have been very ill for the National Health to treat me to this privacy. A tube was threaded into one arm so that I felt held to the ceiling like a string puppet. My head was facing left toward the glass panel and a slow question, a nasty question formed in my mind. A side ward? Privacy?

Slowly, very slowly, so that I didn't disturb my control string, I turned my head to the right. I saw a bare, white wall with a small, opaque window and on the sill was a wilting hyacinth. That was all.

A buzzer was strapped to my pillow. I raised my free hand and pressed it in panic.

A large, red-faced woman ran in smartly from the main ward.

On her starched bosom she had a name tag. Staff Nurse Mac-Queen. The now familiar Irish lilt said, 'So, you've decided to open your eyes this fine morning, have you? Well, none too soon. You've been taxing the patience of the finest medical staff in the world. Let's get you tidied up, then, to greet the day.' She began ministering with firm but kindly efficiency.

All the while I was trying to ask my question. My mouth was unused to talking, the words wouldn't form. Eventually, I croaked, 'Where's Sarah?'

'What do you mean—"where's Sarah?"—hark at the girl!'

'Who is she?'

'Well, if it isn't yourself, then I'm a Dutchman. On your chart, so it is, Sarah Davies. Back in the land of the living. Be thankful for it.'

'No!' I shook my head in frantic denial. 'No. No. No. I am not Sarah Davies. I am not.'

'Oh no?' She came busting over to stop my thrashing causing any damage. 'Will you stop that now. You'll work yourself into a fever again. Your cheeks are burning already. And, if you are not Sarah Davies, who in wonder are you, if I may ask?'

'I am Unity Penfold.' I tried to haul myself upright clutching at her strong, red arms. 'Please, listen to me. My name is Unity Penfold. My husband and children and home are . . .' My strength gave out and I fell back, through the pillow, down and farther down into oblivion.

'Sarah.' She was back again. More like a fly this time, a busy fly buzzing away and feeding her own sense of importance on the offal of other people's tears. 'Sarah, I brought you some of your own things. I thought you'd be pleased to get out of these hospital nighties. Laura Wilde fetched them for you. Such a nice, kind girl, isn't she? You must ask her to visit you soon, you know, she would love to see you. You're very lucky to have such a pleasant flatmate.'

There was only one way to exclude this obscenity, this idiot charade, and that was to keep my eyes shut. Blank out, with ostrich fervor, the physical presence of this vulgar, buzzing insect. But I betrayed myself. As I turned my head to escape from her voice, she saw that I was only pretending to sleep.

'Sarah? Sarah, I know you can hear me. Laura brought in some pretty nighties for you. And such a smart dressing gown. You must tell me where you bought it. I've been looking for one in such lovely colors for ages . . . Sarah? Oh, really!' The saccharine dissolved in exasperation. 'I'll send for Staff Nurse,' she said in the same tone as a child sneak says, 'I'll tell teacher.'

A surge of temper, so vast that it purged away self-pity and fear, flooded over me. I opened my eyes. She was leaning over my bed and her obtrusive face fitted her voice. She had the wrong sort of perm, winged spectacles and too much lipstick. Her powdered cheeks were about a yard from my face and through the specs I saw watery eyes blinking quickly.

I hurled my hatred at her. 'I am not Sarah, you silly bitch. I am Unity Penfold.'

She had to be erased, discarded; but my instinctive gesture of dismissal was uncoordinated and my flailing hand caught the side of her face in a resounding and satisfactory slap.

Her scream produced MacQueen through the door at a canter. Behind her was a sandy-haired Houseman with the pale, fatigued air of his species, and after him trotted a junior nurse. While Miss Williams explained the outrage in high-pitched indignation quickly modulated to curt professionalism, I closed my eyes again and lay doggo.

'She attacked me. She lashed out and attacked me. It's quite impossible to get through to her at all. It's all very well but I have other and more amenable cases to attend to. She even denies her name.'

The young doctor had a slight Birmingham accent. 'She's only just out of coma. I don't suppose she knew who you were.' All this time I could sense that he and MacQueen were pursuing a complex routine with charts and readings.

The tube in my arm was clumsily jolted and MacQueen snapped, 'Will you be careful there, Pringle,' and the breathy voice of the junior nurse muttered, 'Sorry, Staff.'

The doctor said, 'Her pulse is racing. Haven't you been able to fish out any next of kin or friends that she'd respond to better?'

Williams snorted. 'Respond! She almost blinded the flatmate who identified her. And now *she* won't come near her unless asked for and I don't blame her. In my opinion, Davies would be better in a psychiatric ward under restraint.'

The Houseman sighed. 'I suppose it could be possible that the flatmate is mistaken.' Without opening my eyes, I nodded a frantic agreement. 'Look how agitated she gets. Staff said she had a bad reaction when she was called Sarah.'

'Laura Wilde is extremely sensible and reliable.' Her tone implied my lack of these virtues. 'Davies was found without one single identifying mark, no purse, no papers. How young women can roam about like that, but still ... Wilde was worried, with reason, when Davies went absent for twenty-four hours. She was reported missing and the police checked the unidentified admissions as a matter of routine.'

'Then why does she over-react and deny that she is Sarah Davies?'

They had forgotten me, safe behind closed eyelids. The tendency of the National Health is to assume the total imbecility of their patients when it comes to understanding plain English.

Miss Williams fell into this trap. 'Davies was on the edge of a nervous breakdown. She had just lost her job, her boyfriend and, as you know, her baby ...'

I felt a moment's pity for poor Sarah, but forgot it as I strained my ears to catch as much of this valuable information as I could.

'... her condition serious enough to alarm Wilde when she went missing. In my opinion she is now suffering from this breakdown. I will say so in my report.'

The young man sounded unhappy. 'Head injuries are always difficult. Very tricky. There seems to be nothing organically wrong. She's down for Consultant's round in the morning. I suppose if this irrational behavior and confusion continue, she ought to be transferred to St. Pancras.'

'I endorse that.'

There was a pause as they realized they had reached a temporary truce. I opened my eyes. The doctor shook his sandy head sadly, gave me a wistful look and began to beat the retreat. I gathered that I was his special undertaking, his apprentice case, and I was letting him down.

'Doctor.' My voice wasn't yet under full control but I halted the exodus. 'Doctor, please may I say something?'

They rushed back. 'Yes, of course,' he replied eagerly, clearly delighted that I was normal enough to take notice and converse.

'Please, listen to me. I am not Sarah Davies. My name is really Unity Penfold. I am an actress and I'm married to an actor called Ned Roland. Will you please ask this silly woman to stop forcing the wrong identity on me? She persists in her mistake, and I would be helped to make a full recovery much more quickly if she would only find my husband and inform him of my whereabouts. The address is 4, King Henry's Crescent, N.W.1.'

'Can this be checked?'

'It has been.'

'And?'

Miss Williams pursed her lips. 'This is the wrong place to discuss it.'

'Miss Williams, my patient has asked me a question and I think we both have a right to an answer.' He looked ridiculously young, a schoolboy in a white doctor's coat; but he would fit the role very snugly in a few years' time.

'Oh, very well.' She had the air of one who knows that the bigger guns are on her side. 'Don't blame me if she reacts badly. But since you wish ... She woke briefly in the ambulance and gave the same information to the officer who was riding with her. The name is false and the address nonexistent ...'

'No! No! She's lying! She hates me. No. No!' I began to thrash around and yell. Both nurses ran to hold me still. The doctor looked at me with sad reproach.

'No. No. I want Ned. Please fetch Ned. I need him. Please, oh please.'

'Staff, sedation ...' He issued a series of sharp orders.

Williams sniffed. 'I hope, Doctor, that you will make it clear that I related this information against my better judgment.'

Her satisfaction that my outburst had proved her right and exposed my young champion to her mercy was a strong motive to exercise control. I stopped struggling.

He sighed again. 'It would have been better if your department had kept us more fully informed. In the event we were both wrong.'

They moved out of vision, leaving me passive, but agitated, with a nurse on either side of me, bulwarks against further struggle.

'Indeed,' said MacQueen, 'you've caused a right rumpus. Whatever are you thinking of? Will you stay quiet now, while I go and fetch your injection? Pringle, you stay with her.'

I nodded at Staff and she whisked away. There was a lesson I had to start learning and I had just had my first course of instruction. It was the art of not causing the wrong sort of trouble. Pringle held on to my left forearm as if I were a slippery fish. She looked young, scared and lacking in imagination.

'What's St. Pancras?' I asked.

'It's a psychiatric hospital. They take all the acute admissions in the north London area.'

The second lesson, I thought, is to stay out of St. Pancras. However and whatever. Even if it meant agreeing with the adorable Williams. Even if I had to assume temporarily the immune cloak of pretending to be Sarah Davies. I smiled a pleasant, acquiescent smile at Staff Nurse MacQueen as she stuck a hypodermic in my arm and sent me to sleep.

Days passed and I went on smiling. The tubes and bottles were slowly dispersed. My charts made everybody feel happier. I was no longer the naughty girl on the ward, though I was still kept in my seclusion and I was thankful for it. I sat up. I was allowed to walk to the bathrooms. I went on smiling as I ate proper food, if any food in any hospital deserves the category 'proper'; and I answered if anybody called me Sarah. After a while, Miss Williams came again.

'Good morning, Sarah.'

'Good morning, Miss Williams.'

'Better now?'

'Much better, thank you,' I recited dutifully.

'That's better, then.'

The conversation was going around in a circle. We grimaced at each other in a parody of a smile and waited for the other to speak.

'Miss Williams,' I began bravely.

'Ruth, Sarah, please do call me Ruth. We are going to be seeing a lot of each other until you leave here and I believe in getting on to first name terms. Cosier and less formal, don't you think?'

'Ruth,' I said, swallowing the bitter medicine of hypocrisy. 'I must apologize for all the shouting and yelling. I was very confused, but I think I'm better now. I must have been very rude to you. I'm sorry.' I offered her a deprecating smile tinged with a suspicion of humility. 'I'll have to rely on you a lot, though. You see, the fact is, and I haven't dared mention this to the doctors, the fact is that I can't remember a thing about Sarah's . . . I'm sorry, my life before . . . before getting knocked down. I can't even remember the accident. I understand I was caught up in a football crowd in Euston Station, but I have absolutely no recollection of it at all. As for where Sar . . . where I live, I just don't know. Perhaps you could jog my memory?'

'I think you'll find that the medical staff are very well aware of your amnesia.' There was a surprising hint of humor in her voice. 'The condition is quite normal and generally only temporary after concussion. I'm sure you'll find no problem, once you are physically fit, picking up the threads of your old life.'

My old life. I had spent many hours suppressing such subversive and treacherous thoughts lest they betray me into despair. My old life. A burst of pain isolated me in its terrible strength. When the first rush receded, I heard Ruth still talking. I must have missed a sentence or two, but I caught the name Laura.

'Sorry, Ruth, I was miles away. I have difficulty in concentrating sometimes. You were saying about Laura?'

I was learning skill in the ways of deceit.

'I was saying that you ought to let Laura visit you. She is absolutely dying to, you know. She has been so loyal, fetching you your clothes, sending flowers,' she indicated the sickly hyacinth. 'As soon as the two of you get chatting, you'll find most of the missing pieces will come back to you in a flash. She knows you very well, of course, she's the one you need to do any memory jogging. Shall I get her to come in next visiting time?'

'No!' My vehemence struck the wrong note for her disapproving face returned. I gave her a conspiratorial smile and improvised quickly. 'Oh, Ruth, it would upset poor Laura and I don't want to do that, do I? You told me she was quite distressed when I hit out at her. As you say, she has been kind, but it would be so embarrassing because the awful thing is that I don't remember her at all. Neither her nor the flat. Not even the address. It might upset her dreadfully. I mean, you are a professional and used to this sort of thing, but Laura would find it very hurtful, don't you think, Ruth?'

I must have sounded plausible for the frown vanished. Instead, she assumed a mask of wisdom, which made me think that the word 'professional' had triggered that response, and I filed it away for future use.

'You could be right, Sarah. It wouldn't do to expose Laura to more distress than we can help. It might put a strain on your friendship and you are going to need her valuable support when you are discharged from here.'

'Haven't I any parents?'

She almost giggled. 'My goodness, the blanks do go back a long way, don't they? It's usual to forget only the more recent incidents before an accident. I suppose in your case, all those unfortunate circumstances . . .'

'My parents,' I repeated firmly.

'Well, I do know most of your history from our case notes . . . Your parents . . . Both dead, dear, I'm sorry to say. One of those charter flights to Spain. Worth the extra cost to take a scheduled flight with a proper airline. More reliable. The tragedy happened when you were at University.'

'University.' The question mark was carefully excluded. Any over-reaction might have diverted her from her chattiness.

'York. Economics and politics.'

'Did I do well?'

'Oh yes, very well indeed. You got a First.' A swot, I thought wildly, I'm turning into a bloody swot. 'Then you took a six months course at a very good secretarial college. No problem for you on the job market. You were snapped up. Proves that a girl needs secretarial skills, nowadays. Why, you can go anywhere.'

'Where did I go?'

'A big multinational firm.' She named it but it meant nothing to me, any more than the career structure that she painted so glowingly and Sarah filled so satisfactorily. Secretary to the Head of Personnel. Then Personnel Officer and then finally in line for Head of Department. It was as complex and alien to me as the chemical make-up of a molecule. She rambled on, extolling Sarah's virtues. 'Everything to gain, a tip-top position, such a shame . . . why are you laughing?'

My ability to hold down such a job, much less thrive within its harsh demands seemed to me an absurdity, but I covered my lapse by asking quickly,

'What was a shame?'

'This last year. You let everything slip. The young man with whom you had a relationship . . . To be honest I don't know the details. Laura is very discreet. You should be proud to have such a very loyal friend. But it does seem that he dominated you in a very unhealthy way. You had money saved but he went off with it, left you pregnant. You were ill, off work, though I gather you hid the pregnancy well and it was a premature birth—stillborn. Probably a mercy. Laura wouldn't have told us, but there was physical evidence that you have been pregnant . . .'

Another burst of pain. Chris? Tim?

'. . . so you lost the job. Well, the missing cash was a problem though nobody blamed you. You were too good at your job I expect. People get very jealous of success. Only too ready to step into another's shoes and take all the credit. The more efficient you are, the more likely it is to happen to you. Goodness only knows what would happen in our department if I went sick.' She patted her hair and straightened the skirt of her unsuitable pink frock.

'So I lost the job, the money, the baby and the young man. What was I doing at Euston?'

'We, that is, Laura and I, think that you were so depressed that you just went on walking and walking almost mechanically, going nowhere really. Laura suggests . . .' she pinked delicately, a nasty contrast with her frock, '. . . that you may have picked somebody up, for the clothes you wore didn't belong to you, you must have borrowed them. You were dirty, suffering from exposure, hadn't eaten for hours . . .'

She finished and I knew she was waiting for me to acknowledge the story as my own. In silence, she wandered around the room and came to rest by the wretched hyacinth and concentrated on its spindly growth with a fervor it did not merit.

I thought about it. I had very little choice. I wouldn't be released from hospital unless I had somewhere to go. If I persisted in my rejection of Sarah, the alternatives would appear to be St. Pancras or, if I was lucky, a dramatic escape to walk the streets again, a lost Unity looking for a vanished number 4. But, if I surrendered, if I embraced Sarah, I would risk little more than a blind date with an unknown flat and the unimpeachable Laura. Once free the choices widened. Without authority on my back, I could jump in the river, or follow Klaus up the Amazon or wherever it was he had wandered in this displaced universe.

'Ruth,' I said quietly. The busy fingers around the hyacinth stopped but she didn't turn around. 'I think I'm beginning to remember some of it. There are big gaps still,' I added hurriedly as she bustled over, 'gaps that you will have to help me with. I still can't remember Laura at all.' Nor would I, not until I had no other alternative left. 'What do I do now?'

'Laura kept the flat. It was difficult for her. You owe her two or three months' rent, I'm afraid. Once we get your signature, we can sort out sickness benefits, unemployment payments and so forth. We'll try and help you find another job. Won't be so easy this time,' she wagged an admonitory finger at me. 'We did leave our other job under a cloud. And no references nowadays . . .'

I gave her a retake of my sickly smile and it seemed to suffice for she gathered herself together in a manner that indicated the interview was over.

At the door she said, 'Well, I must have given you plenty to think about. It will all come back soon, I'm sure. I must fly now. I'll be back tomorrow.' Her large pink rump vanished into the main ward, a full stop to a job well done.

Had she known the turmoil she had left me with, her complacence would have slipped. I waited for the usual reaction that swamped me whenever I was left alone, the waves of misery, homesickness and nausea that I had to outride like a rough sea passage. What came instead was the sweating fear that Ruth Williams was right, that her answers came pat and were far too plausible to be ignored. For a while I wavered in my loyalty to Unity.

There was a horrible logic: Sarah, unmarried, perhaps longing for a home and children, undergoing an unwanted and finally tragic pregnancy, trapped in a high pressure job by the financial demands of making a lonely living, afterward having to replace the stolen money of an unloving lover, was more than likely to fantasize about Unity's life, which would embody for her all that she lacked. A loving husband, a cherishing environment, a peaceful domesticity, friends, children, leisure, all these would seem too good to be true. Even Unity's lack of work would seem a thankful blessing to Sarah, work that was both glamorous and undemanding, an outlet for artistic cravings. Sarah might have added the depressive mornings to give a three-dimensional veracity to her daydreams.

Who was dreaming who? Mirrors within mirrors. Was I Unity forced to become Sarah, or was I Sarah who was longing to be Unity? Both of us had wandered without food or rest for twenty-four hours, both of us were under considerable strain, both had suffered major emotional upheavals, both ended at Euston Station . . .

There was one significant difference. Sarah existed in the world around her, had a slot in the mechanism. Unity did not. Unity had vanished without trace. But only Unity had the memory of a life. Was it possible that a knock on the head could furnish such a detailed and distinctive past out of a fantasy?

The sweat poured off me. The Sarah hypothesis was nastily credible. But, I was Unity. Everyone carries within the core of their identity. The sense of standing where one is, and always will be, the center of the world as one sees it. If one is not the center of that world, then one is somebody else in the center of somebody else's concept of the world. I was Unity. Facts were trying to convince me that I was Sarah.

I forced myself to make the imaginative leap of stepping into the center of Sarah's world. The sweat cooled on my body in icy terror as I tried to consign Ned and the boys to the realms of fantasy, diminish them to Sarah's fevered daydreams.

The effort exhausted me. And it failed. Ned and the boys came back from the shades; rescued from disembodiment but still missing. Deep in my innermost certainty, I remained Unity. I was Unity and I would survive. For what, I had as yet no answer. Hope had not entered to give its oblique sunlight. There was much to learn: the tricks of survival, the way through the labyrinth to my lost family. But I was Unity.

They gave me a sleeping pill that night, but I couldn't sleep. There was some crisis in the main ward, and though I was somewhat insulated from the worst of the hushed, nocturnal scurryings, I was disturbed enough to have the bustle reinforce my insomnia. Fact and theories, probabilities and possibilities whirled and jigged and danced in every tempo from a stately gavotte to an eightsome reel. Nothing fitted, nothing made sense. I had no help. I would have to wing it. Wing it. I found it ironic that I thought in such an image. It was from my erstwhile profession. I doubted that Sarah would know the expression for an actor who has not learned his lines and who keeps his script in the wings to read his part hastily between every appearance on the stage.

The crisis died down and the nurses had time on their hands. In the natural rotation of hospital routine, Nurse Pringle was now on night duty. I saw her moon face peering in through my glass panel and I sat up and smiled at her. We had become quite chatty. She was a natural gossip and would provide me with information that better trained mouths denied. She ran off now and came back shortly with a mug of Ovaltine and sat, illegally, on my bed as I drank it.

'Do you watch television a lot?' I asked though I was certain that her mild, vapid nature was a product of such plastic dreams.

'Oh yes, whenever I can. I miss it doing this job, especially when I'm on nights. Still, you can't have everything, can you? I love all the series, 'specially the hospital ones.' She giggled.

It was those series, I suspected, that motivated her to tell her Careers Mistress at school that she would love to be a nurse, please Miss.

'And do you go to the films?' There was no point in asking about the theater, she wasn't the type.

'Used to go to the films a lot at home, me and my boyfriend. But we hardly get a chance now. Not with this job.'

'Do you know all the actors and actresses? By sight, I mean.'

'Oh yes, I'm ever so good at spotting them. I know all their faces and who's married to who. All that sort of thing. It's ever so interesting. I can spot the voices on the commercials, too. Got a good ear. I'm always right. I win ever such a lot of bets.'

'Have you ever heard of Pippa Waters or Ned Roland?'

'Never heard of him. Who is he? But of course I've heard of Pippa Waters. Who hasn't? You must know her. She's ever so thin and she had her nose done when she went to Hollywood. She lives there now. One of the English Colony, the *TV Times* said. You must have heard of her. She's such a big star.'

'Is she?' I wasn't altogether startled by the revelation, it made sense in an odd way. It was a route that Pippa could well have taken. 'Tell me about her.'

'There was ever such a long article about her in the *Sunday Mirror*. About a month ago, it was. Let me see. It said she was in a play that went to New York. She'd done some telly over here, but not much. And then she was picked to be the lead for this comedy series that they have over there. You know, "Don't Think, I'm Talking." They show it over here on Mondays. It's not very good, but she's ever so well known because she appears on all the chat shows and says rude things. Awful really, some of the things she says. My Mum . . .' She stopped, her antennae had picked up on something. She whispered, 'Finished your Ovaltine, have you? It should settle you down. I have to go now, before Night Sister does her rounds.' She patted my bed straight and flitted away to the dim half-life of a night-time hospital.

Pippa existed. I hadn't invented her any more than I had invented Klaus, if my memory of the incident with Dr. Hilliard was correct. I hadn't invented them, only my relationship with them. The perplexing aspect of this new scheme that I had discovered was that it was so very credible. Considering their characters as I knew them, it was more likely that Pippa would assist at Hollywood's rebirth as a television capital and that Klaus would range through strange jungles than that one would still be dragging around the Fringe Circuit and the other meekly commuting between Berkshire and London University. And yet. And yet . . .

If they were accountable, why wasn't Ned? His absence was persistent and insufferable. He would have to be found. As I settled down to sleep, there was much in me of a Unity I didn't remember at all, a determination, a girding of mental loins, a resolution to play the game with my own rules. If I had to became Sarah to achieve freedom, so be it. Amen. Amen. Your turn, Williams.

When she came next morning, I had questions for her.

'Why am I wearing a wedding ring?'

She simpered. 'Oh yes, dear, I queried that, naturally. It seems that it belonged to your grandmother who died just before you met your boyfriend. You wore it as a symbol. I'm afraid you were very besotted with that young man.'

'So it would seem. And another thing, I remember that I had a key in my pocket. Where does that come from?'

'Why dear, it's the key to your flat. Laura wasn't absolutely sure, so she took it home and tried it out. It's a bit sticky, she says, but it's definitely the right key. Don't fret about it, she brought it back. It's in that toilet bag she sent over with all your little personal things.'

Oh, the cunning, pink, permed vixen, she had an answer for everything. A Yale key. It could happen. There are, I read once, only a limited number of variations, which is why it isn't the most secure key to have guarding you and yours. There is a chance, a percentage of possibility that one key might fit another lock. How small a chance, I didn't know. It had stuck a bit, said Laura, giving me a churning, damning ray of hope. I didn't know how to compute a percentage on coincidence.

'Now, about a job,' Ruth was saying brightly. 'Not really my responsibility now we have somewhere to discharge you to, but I would like to help if I could. After our initial disagreement, if you can understand that.' I understood only an empty life that fed off others, a constant need to prove that she made the job, not that the job was her only claim to existence. She went on, 'One of the blessings of your training, dear, is that you can always get a good secretarial job. Not that you can't do better . . .'

I interrupted. 'Listen, that's another thing. I can't type.'

'Nonsense.'

'Or do shorthand.'

'But you were trained . . .'

'No.'

Her mouth which was open, poised to expostulate, snapped

shut. She was teetering on the thin line of temper at my obsti-
nacy, but a happy idea came to her aid.

'Of course you can type, dear. It's just a matter of proving to
you that you can. I'll think of a way, don't you worry.'

She was back the following morning with a gleam in her eye.

'I've found an office in the basement that's about to be reno-
vated. I thought of taking you along to one of the main offices,
but they are so busy and I didn't think you'd want an audience.'
My reaction to her unconscious irony went unnoticed. She had
opened a cupboard to the right of the door, and, after some rummaging, presented me with a green nylon quilted dressing gown
on which writhed mauve and orange serpents.

'What a hideous garment!' I exclaimed in horror. 'Where did
it come from? Can't I wear this old one?'

'But Laura sent it around for you. You were very fond of it. It's
very pretty too, such daring colors.'

Oh God! that I had entered the kingdom, stepped into the soul
of a being with such appalling taste. I wondered where she was
and why she didn't appear and snatch back, safe from my scorn,
this monstrosity of which she seemed to be proud. I consoled
myself, as I followed the indefatigable Ruth through the myriad
corridors around which a hospital is constructed, that the taste
might, after all, belong to the mercifully yet hidden Laura. She
may have chosen it, and sent it to me as a gift, a welcome back to
the land of the not-living.

'Which hospital is this?'

'Euston Hospital, of course. It's nearest to the station, you
know.'

Yes, I know, and I also know that around the corner is/was
Klaus's laboratory, the Rabbit Warren. I wondered if Dr. Hilliard's children, should he have fathered any, called it by the same
disrespectful and affectionate nickname.

We wandered down to the bowels of the hospital. A big
Teaching Hospital can hide a multitude of burrows left over from
successive development schemes, and we found one such. It was
an Impressionist study of an office rather than a working model.
There was a dilapidated desk behind which a typist's swivel chair
lurched crazily to starboard. On the desk, and dwarfing it, stood

a huge, ancient manual typewriter that had the same dignity and stance as a vintage car. One gray filing cabinet, a wall calendar and some dusty paper completed this study in dereliction.

Ruth was delighted. 'Good, now we can get to work. Put some paper in the typewriter.'

I picked up a sheet of paper and blew away the dust. At first, there didn't appear to be any reasonable chance of executing her command; but, by twisting and twiddling in haphazard experiment, I managed to insert the paper, but in the process it had changed shape and was now triangular.

'Straighten it up,' she called out cheerfully.

I pulled at the paper corner that I could reach, but it tore. 'It wouldn't move,' I explained.

'Oh, I do hope that you're not doing this on purpose.' Patiently, she removed the torn sheet and replaced it with another. It was miraculously straight.

'Type your name.'

I searched slowly through the keys. 'U' had escaped. I began a more methodical search and it emerged. I hit the key delicately with my right forefinger.

'Damn it,' I said. 'How do you make a capital? Oh, I see.' With one slow finger, I typed out my name UNITY PENFOLD, all in big letters that stared boldly from the dusty paper.

She came and looked over my shoulder and exclaimed in tones nicely balanced between shock and incredulity, 'Sarah, how could you!'

'I'm sorry, I did it without thinking.' This was true and it was a stupid mistake. I couldn't afford to lose my protective coloring. Hastily, I stabbed out SARAH DAV, then I stopped.

'Is it Davies with an "e," or Davis without?'

'With an "e," ' she replied, very vexed. 'I don't understand what you are trying to prove with this pantomime, but you've certainly convinced me that the head injury has altered your personality sufficiently to make you forget all your secretarial skills. Oh dear! As for this Unity nonsense, I'm very disappointed. I was certain that it had been forgotten. The doctor will have to be told about this relapse. I wish I could be certain that a spell of psychiatric therapy wouldn't be a better course.'

'No,' I begged. 'Please, Ruth, I was being mischievous, I'm sorry. I won't let it happen again, I promise.' I had to placate her somehow and I ad libbed wildly. 'What about one of those courses. You know, Speedwriting or "learn to type in twelve hours." They are always being advertised on the Tube. If I went on one of those, it might all click back into place.'

She examined me like a barrister about to cross question a doubtful witness, a long, steady look. Eventually, she said, 'That's not a bad suggestion. I'll make a few inquiries.' Then she added, 'Good girl,' but I knew it was more to give me encouragement for the future rather than a reward for present virtue.

For all that, she must have told Dr. Reading, for when the drugs trolley came around at bedtime, I was given some additional pills.

'What are these?' I asked MacQueen.

'Happy pills, so I'm told. They take all your troubles away and leave you floating on a cloud. I could do with some myself, and that's the truth.'

'When are they going to let me out?'

'Any day now, you may be sure of that. We need the bed for somebody who is really ill.'

'What are they waiting for, then?'

'You took a bad concussion. The one thing they don't want is to have you walking out of here and collapsing in the street. Somebody would raise an outcry about negligence, you can be sure of that. Right, now are you ready to settle then? All comfy for the night?'

'Yes, thank you, Staff.'

No, I was not comfy, that monstrous palliative word of professional healers and tenders; and I had an insistent and very uncomfortable sensation that Ruth Williams had more credit than I in the account book of feasibility.

I think she regarded me as a refractory bundle of assorted misconceptions that she had to tidy, label and dispatch in a neat parcel. Two days later we marched silently back to the typewriter and I dutifully pecked out SARAH DAVIES without a word being uttered by either party. Suddenly, as if to catch me off guard, she snapped, 'Now, your address.'

It almost worked. My finger was on the 4, before I drew back.

'I still don't remember it,' I said apologetically. 'It's quite extraordinary how bad my memory is, don't you think? I'm very much afraid you'll have to remind me.'

'74c Redcliffe Square Gardens. You do know where that is, don't you?'

'Between Earls Court and the Fulham Road.'

'Good.'

Sarah had walked a long way to Euston and the rendezvous with the pulverizing blow on the head that changed reality for both of us. Yet, by my reckoning, my mind had slipstreamed a day earlier. Where was she then? Where was she now? Would she arrive and denounce me as an impostor? Was it she who walked from the outskirts of Chelsea to a new dimension? Or was it I, following a rational path from Gower Street to North London, that fell and hit my head in the station? She and I? I or she? Her or me? If only my confusion were purely grammatical.

I was released soon after. The consultant neurologist made his rounds, my charts were examined and found not wanting. It was agreed that Ruth Williams of the Welfare Department had done a fine job and there would be no problems of after-care. The young Houseman, under whose medical 'L' plates I had been traveling since off the danger list, bravely gave his opinion that I was fit to be discharged, and all and everybody agreed. Ruth had wangled a grant from a rehabilitation scheme which was going to send me on a six weeks' crash course to re-learn, we never implied learn, secretarial skills, and it seemed a reasonable offer to accept. After years as a kept woman, I was about to face an economic jungle where survival came hard, and typists are in a seller's market.

'Have I any money?' I asked her while she delivered her final briefing.

'You are due for some sickness benefit, about £37. It's being sent over. Now, clothes. Your jeans are here, they've been laundered. Your shirt was torn but I can arrange for you to have one from Welfare. But, why don't you let Laura come in with proper clothes and travel home with you? You ought to have somebody with you. You've no idea how shaky you'll feel.'

'I'm sure you are right, as usual, Ruth. But I'd rather not. Going home under my own steam will seem like an achievement, something positive. I'm not at all worried about the clothes, and I'm honestly sure that Laura will quite understand.'

Oh, but she had better understand, this unknown and unseen Laura, whom I had rejected initially from panic, terrified that she would confront me, ask me questions to which I had no answer. I still had the same reasons but now I was motivated by deceit not fear. Ruth had been fooled. She had convinced herself that I was indeed Sarah, but she had met neither putative Sarah before the bash on the head. It was more than probable that Laura who knew the real Sarah well would smartly expose the substitute. Indeed, I was relying on her with great fervor to do so eventually; but only after I had escaped from these well wishing busy-bodies, after I had established myself, cuckoo Unity in Sarah's nest.

This calculated, cold determination to survive surprised me. Two months ago, I would have dissolved like sugar in tea into sticky self pity and waited feebly for rescue, doing nothing for myself. Now, survival was all. Not for myself alone; but so that I could, like Isis, comb the Four Kingdoms for my lost husband and snatch back from oblivion my vanished children. They waited for me. They would be found.

'When you've finished with the course,' Ruth was saying, 'go and see Liz Wilton of Location Services, Wardour Street. Here's her address and phone number. She's helped me out in the past with some of my lame dogs, if you see what I mean. She sounded as if she might need an assistant during the holiday season. You'll have to get in touch with her yourself. She tends to be off hand, but she's quite kind really. It sounds just the niche for you. You can indulge in all those theatrical fantasies and come to no harm. You might even enjoy mixing in the atmosphere of the real thing . . .'

I might indeed, dear Miss Williams. Oh indeed I might.

The last of my trivial victories over this crusading lady whose zeal on my behalf was relentless was that, through her intervention, Laura had even been persuaded to go to work as usual, to attend to her duties as an assistant in a Music Library, instead of waiting to welcome me home. I wanted, I insisted, a quiet time to get acclimatized without pressures, to get the feel of being 'home' again. I used the word home a lot. It pleased Ruth, but I kept the inverted commas in my mind.

I said the appropriate farewells to MacQueen and Pringle and walked out into the fresh air, physically free yet manacled to the wrong identity. By the time I had struggled through the bustle and bewilderment of sunny streets to reach the bus stop, I was exhausted and, with an odd mixture of both bravado and cowardice, decided to squander money on a taxi to Redcliffe Square Gardens.

The key fitted. There was some resistance, a moment's stubbornness, but I've owned genuine keys that have behaved as badly. Instant depression waited for me in the tiny hallway. It was bed-sitter land. Well heeled bed-sitter land, but lacking the liberating space of a family home. There were three doorways off the hall which held a pay phone and small table, which was thick with circulars, sucker post for Sarah. The first door I opened led to a bathroom. Loo, basin, tub and a cork floor, newly decorated and tidy, Laura wasn't a slut, anyway; but which of the other doors was hers and which was mine, I couldn't even guess.

I stood a long time in the hall playing a guessing game with the doors. If I were Sarah, if the blow on the head had manufactured Unity from the crazy fabric of dreams, then, confronted with this choice, surely instinct, a subconscious recognition, would nudge me toward the correct door.

Actually I made the right choice. I knew that as soon as I opened the door. Not only did the large, and not unpleasing, room have the indefinable air of being uninhabited, but Laura, I supposed, had placed three yellow roses in a vase on the coffee table with a 'Welcome Home' card propped against the base. One quick prowl around the room, a custom built bed-sitter with workable cupboard space and small kitchen alcove, and I went back to the hall. It was too good a chance to miss. I went through the mischievous pantomime of pretending to choose again and opened the wrong door, taking the opportunity to snoop on my unchosen co-inhabitant.

Her room was roughly the same size as mine but differently shaped. It had much the same fittings. In fact the whole wasn't a bad conversion of the third floor of a large Victorian mansion. We had only to share bathroom and phone and most inhabitants of bed-sitter land fare far worse than that. Her room had a better view of the Square, but mine would catch more sunlight. The honors came out about even.

Laura's room was what I expected of a music librarian, a combination of Laura Ashley and the Portobello Road, but on the cheap, the effects awry and uncoordinated. She had more posters than prints on her faded pastel walls and a quantity of musical knick-knacks, a mandolin with no strings, a treble recorder, a book of madrigals, a small wooden plaque, slightly chipped, that portrayed a fiddler, clumsily carved and garishly painted. The kitchen was furnished with jars of pulses and health foods; but the freezer compartment of the small refrigerator held a small, but useful, stock of Bird's Eye's cheaper delicacies.

It was more important to learn about Sarah's life, so I didn't linger. I recognized that anxiety about Sarah's unseen and private self was making me use this excavation of Laura's eating habits as an excuse to procrastinate. I took a deep breath, crossed the hall and began a slow examination of the life I was about to inherit.

In furnishing the room, she had favored a more functional approach. One or two items from Habitat, but most from the basement of John Lewis, white-wood that she had painted herself. The color scheme was porridge and cream with the occasional relief of dark brown. It was bland and unimaginative but not offensive. The walls were bare: one wall had two windows with cream hessian curtains, another was lined with books and ornaments, precariously perched on a homemade artifact of bricks and planks, the third consisted of the kitchen recess and cupboards, but the fourth wall was unadorned, curiously naked. I wondered if she was waiting to find the perfect picture to temper its bleakness. The kitchen was sparse and badly stocked. There were no tins or condiments, no basic stores, only a small jar of instant coffee and a packet of tea bags. The fridge had been freshly stocked with milk, eggs, bread, butter and cheese. With a sinking lurch, I felt I was beginning to remember Laura, but this could have been guesswork, reflecting her room and these trivial gestures of concern.

The first cupboard I opened was the wardrobe and it was a depressing experience. The clothes fitted me, no doubt about it we were the same size, but her taste was as appalling as the dressing gown had led me to fear. She favored synthetic fabrics and garish colors. Most of the clothes were formal, matching sets of dresses and coats, suits with a jacket that could be mated with either skirt or trousers; and all for a woman who would be twice our age. I would never be able to make myself wear them. The job with Liz Wilton became imperative because Oxfam was about to receive a lot of saleable cast-offs and I was going to have to obtain an entirely new wardrobe.

I made a cup of coffee before my next task. I noticed that Laura had not provided sugar so there was one taste I shared with Sarah, anyway. Mug in hand I went over to the bookcase of planks, pleased to notice a radio and cassette player. The shelf at waist level became a desk halfway along, and it was there that I hoped I'd find the essence of the person I had elected to become. Files, folders, a ream of typing paper, a small portable typewriter, a collection of bills held in a bulldog clip, in this jumble I should be able to find the answers to my two paramount problems. I had to prove for my own peace of mind that I was not Sarah, and I had to learn how to convince others that I was.

The bills were meaningless. I saw no reason to keep them, they were for clothing, meals, trivia. I threw them aside. A rent book: rent payable by the month and the last three entries were written in a different hand. The persistent Laura again, heaping coals of obligation on my head, once more. I grabbed a piece of paper and wrote my new signature. I had used it in hospital for my Welfare payments and it had gone unquestioned. Now, I was curious. I compared it with the signature on the cover of the rent book. It was a good match, but then we had the same style of writing, small and spidery and leaning to the left. I threw it all aside. I opened the folders, glanced at letters from unknown friends, souvenirs that reminded me of nothing, newspaper cuttings about a plane crash, an obituary, a wedding invitation . . . I rifled through that woman's life like a burglar in a jewel shop. I threw away precious fragments of an existence I wanted to deny while I searched for the pearl, the prize of the collection, though what it was I couldn't say. I created a snowstorm of paper and, in my impatience, I spilled open a large envelope and was swamped under a cascade of photographs, old, new, snapshots, posed portraits, color, black and white. They fell to the floor and I followed, falling on my knees as I grabbed them in handfuls and scrutinized them with an intensity that stopped my breath.

I was there. In the photos. Dressed in ridiculous clothes, hair too long or too short, with people I had never seen before; but it was I, I who simpered at the unknown and unseen photographer, I who coyly twined hands with a chinless wonder, I dressed up for a school play at the age of ten or blushing at fifteen in my first bikini, I who scowled from a group of lounging students. At York University? I had never been to York in my life.

For some time I sank under the weight of hopelessness and heartsickness. I was stranded, unable to reach my real home, the proper haven in which Ned and the boys waited for me. Here was proof that they might never have existed. Until now it had been Laura's word against mine and I had exploited the mistake under necessity. But here was tangible evidence. The photos blurred through the streaming tears. Where lay the truth?

In a frenzy, I wiped away the tears, seized the photos and examined them again like the Fraud Squad looking for forgeries. It was interesting; physically she looked like me, a superficial glance couldn't tell us apart, but I could see differences. I know my body well enough, an actress had to, and I know the difference between assumed and natural gestures; and, if the gestures and poses in the photos were my own, they were not natural to me. The angle at which the head was set, that habit of raising the right hand to shield the sun from the face, the trick of placing one foot behind the other, these did not belong to me.

The dilemma was becoming clear. A decision had to be made before Laura returned. She had seen me semi-conscious and wounded in hospital, the identification was a very natural error. As soon as we met, the photos convinced me, she must realize her mistake. The moment of truth, the denouncement for which I longed, would be upon us; and tragically, I could not allow it. I could not take the chance of being released from the role of Sarah because Unity had not been written. Unity lacked viability in an environment where bureaucracy denied her. I would have to resume my disguise and soldier on with the plot of this sick farce; and, if I fluffed my lines, missed a cue, I was sure that Laura was malleable and easily to be persuaded that the concussion was at fault, not I.

No argument. I stuffed the photos back in their envelope, shuffled the papers into some pretence of order, and gave up. I had no heart to pry further. I couldn't sit, I couldn't read, I couldn't explore, I could only circle the coffee table like a clockwork toy. The radio on the shelf offered a relief from silence and I switched it on to fill the void as I circled yet again the white-wood coffee table. Sarah owned no television set and I was grateful for it. There would be many lonely evenings ahead and I couldn't face friends and colleagues from my lost domain leaping from the screen to fill the emptiness and drench my face with tears.

Anti-clockwise around the table for a change. Widdershins. Perhaps an earlier, earthier magic could break this space age sorcery that gripped my mind in a vice. Widdershins, around and around and around, pounding a beat of despair over the sensible coconut matting, unable to think, unable to abdicate from thought. The bland music from the radio annoyed me. On the next circuit, I switched stations and disembodied voices, voices belonging to names as familiar to me as my own, floated from the bookcase and generated in me an impotent anger against my fate which, because I had no other outlet for it, was channelled toward Laura whom I now held responsible for my predicament. It was she who had placed me in this room to walk a desperate circle around an ugly coffee table. I hated her, guessing from her room that she would be a vague and incompetent fusspot, overly tactful and solicitous, treading gently over the thin ice of my unpredictable reactions. I could visualize her wet, pleading, don't-hurt-me eyes, her earnest expression, the way she leaned forward when spoken to ... I hated her and I needed a victim. If she but cower once ...

A scene of the verse drama came to an end in a gentle diminuendo of flute. A rich baritone began to speak an epilogue. There was humor, warmth, compassion in the voice and it made me scream in agony.

'Ned!'

I rushed toward the radio, crying and incoherent. Blood rushing to my brain had swamped reason and I screamed at the indifferent plastic from Taiwan.

'Ned, for God's sake, answer me. Say something. Oh, Ned, where are you?'

The play finished and I heard the announcer read the cast list:

'Rufus: Michael Anthony. Elinor: Janet Ash. Geraint: Geoffrey Talman. Constant: Ned Roland . . .'

The rest was a blur as I stood helpless and immobile, staring at the smug contraption that had unaccountably spoken with tongues. Widdershins? My ears cleared in time to hear the announcer continue: '. . . broadcast in place of the advertised program. If you are interested in hearing more drama, tonight at 8:30 we present . . .'

I extinguished him. There had been a Radio Timex in Laura's room. Concerts on Radio 3 had been marked pedantically in red biro and I had wondered whether she really listened to them or left the magazine lying, thus marked, as window dressing. I trembled as I tore through the pages, forcing hands and brain to cooperate and find the right program. 'In place of the advertised program,' but what was the advertised program? The few words of the play meant nothing to me, and Ned had done very little radio work. Where the hell was the published program? I could scarcely work out day, date and time, let alone which wavelength, what channel. A play, so it had to be the B.B.C. The other stations drooled forth nothing but a heady mixture of pop and castrated news.

I was on the floor of her room, scrabbling frenetically at the pages of the *Radio Times* when Laura returned and found me there. She was everything that I suspected and I briefly wondered whether it was knowledge, a half remembered glimpse in my delirium, or guesswork that had made me so accurate. She was a tall, droopy girl on the verge of being bulky with horsy features, lank hair and leather sandals of the perpetually Arty. She wore a long, Indian cotton skirt, a wary smile and she looked as if she'd cry at a harsh word. The type is well known. Art Schools and Drama Schools are full of them. A friend at the Slade called them the Vestal Virgins, but Pippa had christened them Weeping Willows. Laura was archetypal Weeping Willow.

'Golly, Sarah, what are you doing in here? Are you looking for something?'

'No. I like sitting on the floor.'

'Oh.' She blushed. 'I mean, can I help you?'

'Not unless you know the phone number of the B.B.C. and have some twopenny pieces. I must make an urgent phone call.'

'I could look it up,' she said eagerly, 'and I have a bag of coins for phoning just here.'

She went to a shelf and counted some out with a hesitation that was easy to read.

'Do I owe you a lot of money?'

She blushed again. 'You do rather.'

'Tot it up. You'll get paid. I must phone now.'

As I got up from the floor and went to the door, she said hurriedly, 'I've bought some chops. I thought we'd have supper together, is that all right?'

'Fine,' I said absently.

She followed me to the door and I said coldly, 'This call is private.'

She flinched. 'You know I never listen. It wouldn't be fair, would it?'

Two coins later, I had established the number and the extension I needed. I explained that I had heard a program that had been substituted for another and that I was interested etc., etc. Listeners' Inquiries heard me out patiently and said, 'Just a minute,' and went away. I waited. Another coin passed and Listeners' Inquiries returned.

'I'm sorry for the delay but I have made a very careful check. The Afternoon Theater play was broadcast as advertised in the *Radio Times*. *Love on the Dole*. There was no substitution and that was the only play broadcast this afternoon on any of our networks.'

Oh God! The familiar brick wall. I was almost becoming resigned to it. But for the fact that it hurt, stabbing with a searing pain, when joy and fear combined as flashes of hope, the odd twitchings of the veil, which revealed my truth, Unity's truth. Hastily, defying hope, I dialed my home number and my ear was filled with the continuous high buzz of the unobtainable signal. I dialed the Operator.

'There is no subscriber on that number. Shall I connect you to Directory Inquiries?'

No, no no, the effort's not worth the candle. The Operator squawked for a moment while I remained paralyzed by inertia then she cut the connection and the dialing tone buzzed in my ear in parody of Ruth Williams. Tears and despair, a potent cocktail that bred ill will, so that when Laura, who had been waiting for my calls to finish, came cautiously into the hall carrying sherry glasses with a suspiciously dark brown liquid in them, I barked at her.

'Sweet sherry. Jesus Christ! Do I drink that?'

'I'm sorry, it's all I've got at the moment. You don't mind it sometimes.'

'What do I prefer?'

She gave me a startled look. She'd been prepared for a bad memory but the totality of it shook her.

'Vodka and tonic is your favorite. And white wine.'

'Well done, Ada,' I said bitterly. 'How extremely accurate. If I had any spare cash, I'd go and buy a bottle right now and drink it all.'

'I could, well, I could just lend you enough for a half bottle. I'm ... actually, I'm a bit short myself, paying your share of the rent ...' The flushed cheeks went a deeper shade of magenta as she suffered an agony of self-reproach for having reminded me of my obligation to her. She said the rest of the sentence almost inaudibly, as if she could redeem her sin by diminishing herself, 'So, though I am rather short, I could perhaps just squeeze enough for a half bottle if you think you should ...'

Poor Laura. Gauche, earnest, without malice or backbone, a lolloping doormat who could have been played by a young Joyce Grenfell, she was all that stood between me and an even grimmer reality; a choice between a therapeutic institution or a grimy, one gas-ringed back room on Social Security with only the clothes I stood up in to call my own.

As if reading my thoughts, she broke the silence by saying in a bemused tone, 'I've never seen you wearing jeans before.'

'Didn't I wear them?' Unity wore them all the time.

'No. If you wore slacks at all you preferred something tailored.'

Her tentative smile would have stampeded a guru, but I accepted the sherry and her co-operation. I had no alternative.

'Cheers!' I managed not to make a face as I swallowed. 'Sorry, Laura, if I snapped at you. I've not been having an easy time. Not really feeling myself.' I was childishly pleased with the ambiguity of this platitude. 'It must have been a hell of a knock on the head. I'm going to have to rely on you for a lot, really. My memory is bad, absolutely terrible. Please, do understand and bear with my bad moods.'

She brightened, eager and girl guidish. 'Oh, of course, I mustn't let myself get upset, must I? After all, you're the one who's been ill. But you can rely on me. Honestly, for anything.'

'Bless you,' I said, and wondered what bushels of boredom I would have to endure for her protection.

There was a hiatus, a hesitation in the tiny hallway. She looked as if she thought our pact should be sealed with a gesture, and she shifted her weight from leg to leg before making a lunge at me for the sickly, sentimental kiss that she would have thought fitting. The buzzing of the phone that I was still holding gave me an excuse to turn away and the moment fled beyond retrieval.

'Supper will soon be ready. I must go and see to the chops.' She waved her glass in my face and sipped like a bird drinking. 'Cheers! Well, I must dash. Come in when you're ready. About twenty minutes.'

She had tried very hard. On her table was a paperback Elizabeth David, but the pork was underdone and the sage decidedly overdone. The rice was mushy, but the salad was fresh and the dressing well balanced. Perhaps because it was the first salad after weeks of hospital food, I asked for more and she almost cooed with delight.

During the meal, she chattered on about her work, names, incidents and places with which I was supposed to be familiar. Her social life was sparse, but there was Roy, met at a concert, whose utterances were to be regarded as oracular.

At the end of the meal, she produced coffee. It was freshly ground and badly made, but she presented it as a special treat, a birthday present, which perhaps it was, for her.

As she stirred sugar into her cup, she took a deep breath and broached the subject that I had sensed her edging toward for the last half hour.

'While you were in hospital, John Lang phoned. Twice. But I didn't tell him where you were. I didn't think you'd want me to.'

'Who's John Lang?'

The spoon dropped in astonishment, slopping coffee into the saucer.

'Who's John Lang?' she repeated in amazement.

'Oh, is he the unsatisfactory boyfriend?'

'Golly!' she said, at a loss for words. 'Golly, you have changed a lot.'

The secretarial course started a few days afterward. I became suspended in limbo. By day, a mechanical doll learning mechanical skills at which I would never excel. At night, shutting myself up in my room and anaesthetising the pain in any way I could, numbing my mind with cheap thrillers and filling the aching emptiness with noise. I kept the radio blaring also with the hope that Ned's voice might return in the same inexplicable way and I could have some contact with him for a brief moment. I drank vodka instead of eating properly and I waited for the waiting to be over.

I avoided Laura as best I could. Her sympathy became unbearable. Her pale eyes would drip with concern and then fill with genuine tears when her concern was brushed aside. We talked occasionally, we had to, and once I asked her over to have supper with me. I made a dish that seemed elaborate and showy but was a cover-up job on packets and tins.

'Golly, Sarah, where did you get this recipe? It's absolutely super.'

I shrugged, not interested in the conversation. 'Not bad for a cheat, is it? It's the sort of thing you have to learn when you've got a young family to cater for.'

I had been caught off guard. I realized my mistake when the cow eyes watered and she caught her breath in her effort not to exclaim out loud.

We exchanged what news there was. I told her about the course as there was little else to talk to her about. I kept apart from the other students, preferring to be unpopular than join in the pathetic gossip. I did the required tasks and came home, that was all.

'Don't you mind the others thinking you standoffish and talk-ing about you behind your back?'

'No, why should I? That's their problem. It's rather charitable of me I think, to provide them with an object to dislike. Think how boring their lives would be without me to bitch about in the "Ladies." '

She sighed, 'You're so tough. I wish I could be. I'd mind terribly if I heard people saying things about me that you've heard about you. You've always been strong-minded, but since your accident you've become much, much tougher. Almost hard, if you don't mind my saying so.' She watched to see if I was going to react to her audacity, but I was following my own train of thought.

Tough. Hard. Odd words to describe Unity. As Unity I had been surrounded by love and protected by tenderness. I had no necessity to fight, no need for a fighting spirit. Any hurt, slight, problem would be smoothed away for me by Ned or Klaus. Even Pippa had contributed by offering me a share of her protective cloak so that I could, from a safe corner, enjoy a vicarious thrill as I watched her battle with the world. Now these supports had gone, perhaps for ever, I couldn't afford luxuries like gentleness, sensitivity and good manners. Hope and love would cripple me. It was why, I realized, I had postponed the search for my lost ones. It had distressed me, this seeming callousness, but now I understood. Hope was the luxury I could least afford. Hope fol-lowed by a disappointment and I would crumble. I would return to illness and despair. I had built, and must maintain, the iron determination to survive. One day at a time. Today I will survive was a healthier waking thought than the old morning sickness of depression. Today, I will survive. Love and hope were weak allies. Yes, I was tough now; and, surprisingly, I was proud of it.

The six weeks of the course passed. Before that, six weeks in hospital. Three months since I lost my identity. Mid April then, mid July now. It was hot and I would have loved to be able to escape the fumes and the swarming tourists. In August, Laura was going away. She had saved up leave to be able to take a whole month and she was going to Devon where her parents had retired. Roy was hitchhiking around Wales and Scotland and I think she was unhappy not to have been asked to join him, but such a holiday would clearly be unsuitable for her, and I think she knew it. She had broached the subject obliquely, apologizing so much that it was impossible to unravel for what. She felt guilty, she said, for leaving me all alone, but she couldn't see how to put off her holiday, her parents would be horribly disappointed. And so on.

It was hard to hide my relief at her departure and yet, if I had overdone my regrets, she was capable of making the quixotic gesture of refusing to go. However, as we both wanted the same thing, we made the correct ritual noises and agreed she would go in two weeks. Time, she said, to see me settled into the job with Liz Wilton.

'If I get it.'

'But you are bound to. Miss Williams thought it was quite a strong possibility. And you said that Miss Wilton sounded nice on the phone when you made the appointment.'

She had sounded abrupt and busy, a no-nonsense voice that had asked some searching questions. I was glad. Another wispy do-gooder would be the penultimate straw. The final back breaking straw was one I refused to consider. That would be not getting the job with Location Services at all.

'When's the interview?'

'Thursday. I think I'll spend tomorrow sleeping in the Park.'

But it rained. Steamy, drenching, summer rain that soaked the brave cottons of coach parties from Milwaukee and Osaka that came in droves to watch the Guards change and the Yeoman guard. So the day was spent in my room walking widdershins around the coffee table or rummaging through Sarah's clothes and despoiling them with scissors and needle until I had carved myself some more or less wearable costumes. For costumes they were, not mine, but something a wardrobe mistress had given me for a part I was to play. Some of my grant had been squandered at the cheaper end of Oxford Street so that I could now alternate jeans and shirts. Laura had donated one of her Indian skirts, having watched with wonder my rejection of all I had once held dear, and I had taken it in and shortened it; so I coped, in a limited way. During all these unrewarding occupations I kept the radio blaring. Sound will deafen thought, if it is loud enough.

No doubt that is the reason that every public place is bombarded with noise; it doesn't do to think in a sick society.

That night I did all the conventional chores expected of me before an interview. I wasn't going to lose the job by default. I pressed my clothes, dowsed my hair with conditioner, slapped a face pack on my skin and dozed in hot water full of Laura's bath oil. It was the accustomed ritual, the sacrificial cleansing undertaken to placate the Gods.

I lay in the bath with the transistor radio on the loo seat. For once, I was listening to a program for its own sake. 'The Forbidden Voice' was a weekly exploration of Protest songs, and the strong rhythms, the catchy tunes and militant, stance suited my mood admirably.

One particular song alerted me.

> *We're low, we're low, we're very, very low,*
> *Yet at our plastic power*
> *The dirt at the Rich Man's hall will grow*
> *Into palace and church and tower.*

The meter of the first line struck a deep chord in my mind. The meter and a vague familiarity about the singer. I leaned a dripping hand out of the bath and turned up the volume.

> *We're low, we're low, mere rabble we know,*
> *We stand at the Rich Man's door.*
> *We're not too low to build the wall*
> *But too low to tread the floor.*

The meter revolved in my mind, elusive and tantalizing. From nowhere came a similar rhythm with different words.

> *We were young, we were merry, we were very, very wise.*

I chased after, trying to grasp the slippery memory, and by so doing missed the beginning of the next verse. I heard the last two lines.

We're not too low to grow the grain,
But too low the bread to eat.

The guitar chords resolved to an ending. After some enthusiastic applause, an announcer said, 'That new adaptation of an old Chartist song was composed by Face Mallet, a young Australian new to the folk scene in this country of whom I hope we hear a great deal more in the future.'

Euston Station. A song. A brown man who had listened. A silence and then a tumult. Fear and emptiness . . . But first, Face. Lean cheeks, scarred with smiling, the full lower lip of the sexually successful male. Late twenties, early thirties. Dark brown eyes and untidy, wavy hair. It all came back to me with the clarity of film. Buried details, hidden for months, came back into focus, the green and blue tassel on his guitar case, the flattened 'a's of his Australian accent, eyebrows that began late after a wide gap, and thickened at the other end with a tuft. Kindness and curiosity. I wondered what he remembered from that evening. To him I must have been just another railway station encounter, a ship that passed in the night sending out Mayday signals, to whom he was prepared to launch a lifeboat if the signals proved genuine.

Good on you, Face, wherever you are.

Wardour Street was sunny and smelled slightly Parisian after the rain. Location Services was on the fifth floor. There was a lift, a wrought iron 1930s affair that had been casually added during one of the many upheavals the building must have suffered since birth. Even if I got the job, I decided, the lift and I would not get closely acquainted. I walked up the cramped, dark stairs taking care not to trip over the cracked lino. At each landing, an assortment of name plaques proclaimed that behind the shabby paint was a fairyland of delights: 'So and So's Miracle Films,' 'Such and Such Intercontinental Distributors,' 'Wonder Productions,' and 'Incredible Editors,' and among these was a smattering of Rag Trade names. It was hard to see where all this glory could be housed within such narrow confines.

Location Services had a dark blue door that wasn't chipped and a minute reception area. A girl sat at a desk which held a switchboard, a typewriter and the morning's post through which she was sorting.

'Good morning,' she said cheerfully. 'Can I help you in any way? I'm nice now. I get much nastier as the day wears on.'

I laughed, the first proper laugh for weeks. 'I have an appointment with Miss Walton.'

She checked a list. 'Sarah Davies?'

'That's right.'

I never used the name myself unless I was forced to. It was all right if others used it, I could just nod and agree. But for me to announce it was a defeat.

The girl said, 'I'll tell her you're here. There's nowhere to sit as you can see, but you're welcome to a corner of the desk.'

She flipped a switch and pressed a button. 'Engaged. I'll try again in a minute. My name is Trej. Short for Treasure. That's because they can't run this madhouse without me. Real name's Teresa, but who cares?'

I looked through some casting books while Trej juggled with lines of communication. Three phone calls, some angry buzzing and a crossed line later, I was sent in to see Liz Walton.

'Through the first office. Mike and Mark in there. They're interchangeable so don't worry about which is which. Their secretary is Pat. Beyond her is another door. That's Liz. Good hunting.'

In my nervous and hurried progress through the outer office, I caught a glimpse of two young men in suede jackets who did indeed look remarkably similar. Their office was full of noise and chatter and under a litter of papers, cans of film and assorted props. Pat was on the phone but she gestured at the door behind her and mouthed, 'go through.' For all her involvement with the work in hand, she spared time for a quick, inquisitive once-over. I wondered how much of Sarah's history was known.

Liz's office was equally small but, by contrast, it was tidy and carpeted. The walls were covered with a jumble of schedules, time charts, posters and signed stills from many films. She sat in the hollow of an L-shaped desk and waved me to a seat opposite her. On one side, on the short arm of the L, sat a typist who tapped at her machine with a speed that dismayed me. To her right was a high window with a cushioned window seat, a fragmentary reminder of when the house was a fashionable dwelling over a century and a half ago. On the seat was a plump, untidy woman who was reading a script and sipping coffee.

Liz was about to speak to me when a red telephone rang on her desk.

'Damn it!' she exploded. 'I told Trej to hold all calls.'

The woman in the window seat said, 'It's the direct line,' and rose rather lethargically to answer it. She managed to stand in the way of our eye line, so Liz fumed while the call lasted and either couldn't or wouldn't look around her at me.

'It's Vic,' the untidy woman said while she covered the mouthpiece with an ink stained hand. 'He's going bananas. He wants to talk to you.'

'Deal with him, Maggie, can't you for heaven's sake. Tell him I'm out.'

'He won't believe me.' But she removed her hand and made soothing sounds into the phone. While this little scene was being enacted, I had a lucky chance to examine Liz, the arbiter of my fate.

She was short and would become plump with age. She had the healthy complexion and clear voice of one who had been nurtured in the countryside, but there was nothing rustic about her. A good boarding school and some Hunt Balls were tucked away behind her wide, snub nose and pretty mouth. Her hair was mouse and unusually thick and wiry, so that though it was tied back in a bun, it framed her face like a hat. Her age was unguessable; she would look the same for ten years either side of thirty-five, not by artifice but through lack of it. When she smiled, she looked attractive, but while Maggie was making heavy going of placating Vic, she frowned ferociously which made her look truculent.

'Right,' she said, when the phone call had dwindled to a close. 'Let's get on with it. You two clear out. I'd better explain. That's Maggie who is my assistant but can't type, and that's Shirl who can type like a demon but knows nothing about any aspect of the Media whatsoever. I want somebody to replace both at once. If you're a good secretary, you'll have no problem with Shirl's side of things, but you must remember that Maggie knows the business backward, though now she wants to go off and write scripts of her own, silly lady.'

During this explanation, Shirl had sidled out of the room while Maggie plonked cups of coffee in front of us.

'Sugar?' she asked me.

I shook my head.

'Well, I'll go and lurk. See you later, maybe.'

Liz and I looked at each other for the summing up, the silence before the talking that asks whether the interview needs to dig deep, or whether there is an instinctive antipathy which would make the proceedings a formality only. An almost imperceptible little nod told me that she was prepared to dig.

She said, 'Ruth Williams told me about you.'

'How much?' I asked boldly.

'That you were mown down by a football mob. Concussion and some confusion, but that you were intelligent and highly educated.'

'Did she tell you why she thought I might fit into your office?'

She grinned. 'Who's interviewing who? No, that was all she said. I don't suppose she knows enough about this office to know who would fit and who wouldn't. I'll tell you what we're all about. We're geared to provide a complete location service for films or TV. Whole or part, whatever the company which hires us requires. In general, we find the location, get the right permissions, provide staff, phones, lights, catering, vehicles, extra scenery if needed . . .'

'Cast?' I queried.

'If asked. Not for the big film companies, if we're lucky enough to land one. Then we just organize the extras. Sadly, we only get work from them or the major TV companies occasionally. We're not big enough. Most jobs are commercials, small TV films usually for export like educational video cassettes. It all sounds very complicated but it's usually a case of balancing a small budget against the good ideas. Any idea of how to cast a commercial? You've got to find an actor who looks exactly like the advertiser's idea of, say, Falstaff. Not over exposed and in the right price bracket. Who would you choose?'

The question was rhetorical, but I thought of a friend of Ned's, an actor he admired and who had the wrong sort of luck. He was fat and bluff and had a woebegone expression. I named him.

She reacted strongly. 'That's good. Quite remarkable. He's exactly right. That sort of instinct can't be easily taught.' She stared at me steadily and muttered, 'York University and Personnel,' as if these attributes were evidence of a misspent youth. She was all frown, her prettiness drowned in concentration.

I changed the subject. It was too soon to deny the wrong past. 'What do Mark and Mike do?'

'All the technical leg work. They're very experienced production managers and I'm lucky to have them. They know the job so well they could do it in their sleep. We'd collapse without them.'

'Don't they want to work on big first features, then?'

Another questioning look from her. I knew more than inexperience should.

'And have a long spell out of work afterward? Not worth the prestige. They like to be in work and they like the constant demands of so many diverse projects. They take all that side of things off my hands and leave me to do all the budgeting, casting, hustling for new projects, invoicing the customers, pouring oil on troubled waters . . .'

On cue the red phone rang. She snatched it up and said, 'Yes, Vic,' at once, and then settled down to listen with single minded intent, forgetting all about me.

I wanted the job. Very much. It would be hard work and I would tax Liz's patience with my inadequate shorthand and typing, but it was work that I could learn easily. Work I sensed I would grow to enjoy. I liked the office, the close yet casual comradeship, the pleasing lack of a boring routine, the constant pressure, the excitement, the proximity to a profession I had failed in. It was another side of the business that I had never considered in the past. Now, this aspect of it stimulated me, offered a challenge that made me feel more alive than I had for years. I could thrive where a hectic timetable gave me little time to brood.

But I could not, would not meet this new challenge propped up by a lie. The job must be offered to and accepted by Unity, a failed actress who was starting again. I could not allow Sarah to pinch the job under false pretences.

The phone call finished and she looked vaguely in my direction.

'Miss Wilton,' I said hurriedly, 'I must tell you something. I want this job very much indeed, so much that I want to do it honestly. Before we go any further I must tell you something, even at the risk of losing the job. If you employ Sarah Davies, you are getting Unity Penfold.' I told her the story as briefly as I could.

She was silent for a long time. She sat twiddling with her pen and staring at a folder. Even upside down I recognized Ruth Williams' handwriting. Eventually, she said, 'It's completely crazy. That must have been quite a crack on the head.' She lit a cigarette and coughed.

I said nothing. If she found that interpretation of the facts more acceptable, I wasn't going to argue. I had told my truth.

She said, 'Who is Unity Penfold?'

'An actress.'

She looked startled.

'And married to an actor called Ned Roland.'

She said carefully, 'I've been in casting a long time and there are still actors whose names I don't know. I've never heard of either of those, but I'm not infallible. Are they in *Spotlight*?'

'No. I looked while Trej was getting through to you.'

'But the fact that you looked them up means that you were pretty sure that they might be there.'

'They used to be. Ned's photo was terrible.'

She picked up the beige phone. 'Trej,' she said, 'get me *Spotlight* on the line. The Record Department.' She stubbed out her cigarette and lit another. 'It's the same organization that puts out *Contacts*. Do you know that publication?'

'Of course. We always had one at home.'

She nodded. Sarah would not have known of its existence. She blew smoke in the air, then impatiently brushed it aside. 'Not all actors can afford the fees to put their picture in *Spotlight*, but it keeps track of all working members and some who have . . .'

The phone interrupted her. 'Yes,' she said, 'Liz Wilton here, Location Services. Oh, it's you. Good morning, dear. Can you tell me the whereabouts of Unity Penfold and Ned Roland. Last job and last known address, if you have it.'

She waited for them to search their files, but I knew the answer that would be given. She heard them out and repeated it to me. 'Nobody with those names.'

I shrugged. 'Now you see the problem. It's not easy.'

She stared at the folder again. 'It says you were in Personnel.'

'Sarah was.'

She sighed. 'This is all bloody difficult.'

'I know, but I had to tell you the truth.'

'But you can type?'

'Yes, I've just learned. I'm not very proficient as yet, but I daresay I'll get much better with practice. I hope so. I want to hold down this job.'

'You owe money to your flatmate?'

'Miss Williams seems to be very thorough. Yes, about three months' rent. While I was on the secretarial course, Social Security paid for most essentials, but my debts go back a long way and I owe Laura for electricity and phone calls and countless other little things. I must pay her back and she won't ask.'

She lit another cigarette. The room was already thick with smoke. 'If I take you on, I'll pay well. But I'll advance you a sum to pay her back whatever you owe her and deduct it monthly from your salary check. What do you think of that?'

'I think it sounds too good to be true.'

'O.K.,' she said crossly, as if making a kindly decision upset her. 'Here's what we'll do. Maggie and Shirl are leaving at the end of next week. I've taken my annual dose of liberty, but the rest of the staff are off in rotation till September. I'll take you on initially to cover the holiday period. If it works out, I hope you'll stay on. We're going to be busy this winter. If it doesn't work . . . well, you've covered the holiday period for me, and you've paid off your debts. And we will both have learned a lesson. If you do stay we'll negotiate a permanent contract. But as far as I'm concerned, you are Sarah Davies. Fair enough?'

My gamble had paid off. 'More than fair. Thank you.'

'Right!' By now, her acceptance of the situation had put her into a temper. 'Start today. I'll get Maggie to brief you.'

Her finger remained on the buzzer until Maggie and Shirl came running.

'Sarah starts at once. Maggie, deal with her. Shirl, take these letters,' and she started dictating at breakneck speed without looking at me again.

Maggie jerked her head at the door and I followed her. We went to a coffee house in Dean Street. 'It's the only place to talk in peace. Besides I'm a coffee addict.'

'Are you a lame duck?' she asked, when we were served.

'By whose standards?' I asked warily.

'I know Liz when she reacts like that. Under that granite look there beats a heart of mush. You have to dig and find it.'

'Do you know her well?'

'We were students together before the Flood. She keeps me around because she thinks it's good for me and I need the money. Actually, I'm useless to her and I've become no more than a licensed jester.'

'So she likes lame ducks.'

'She took you on so fast that she must see you as a cause. No, don't tell me. I don't want to know. Listen, I'll tell you a cautionary tale. Once, I was conned by a starving, or so he said, writer to pay a large advance for a script. That night I was phoned by the police because he'd ended in jail and wanted me to stand bail for him. I then discovered that he'd sold the script I'd bought to three other TV companies. Liz is hotter than hell on budgets. Overspend or lose money and she goes into a cast-iron sulk. When I went to her all atremble to confess my error of judgment, which had cost us plenty, all she did was to give me one of her icier stares and say, Have you checked that the wife and children are all right?" I just told you all that so that you will know the right things to worry about.'

I went back to the flat exhilarated, my head swimming with Maggie's facts and figures. But once within Sarah's room there was the expected reaction. The old, dead feeling of shipwreck returned. All day, my disloyalty, if such it was, to Ned and the boys had gone unquestioned. I had had no time to think. I had found a function at last. Here, the room stifled me with echoes from a past not my own, smothered me in somebody else's alien history. Misery and hopelessness swept away the morning's hope. I was locked out from what was rightfully mine and I could not get the gates to open.

This seesaw of emotion made me curious about Sarah's birthday. I asked Laura.

'Golly, I don't know. Fancy forgetting your own birthday. It must be on some of the papers in your room. Can't you work it out from a driving license?'

We found it. She was Gemini as well, but the digits of her birth date were a mirror image of mine. I was born on 13th June, she on 31st May. I worried at the coincidence, trying to force it to make a shape; but, as nothing emerged, I memorized my new birthday and forgot the rest.

By the following Thursday, I was ready to get Maggie and Shirl out of my hair. I wanted to prove myself. I had already, to my surprise, thought of some innovations in the day-to-day running of the office that I wanted to put into practice. So far, I had had little to do with the production managers and would have lost a bet to who was Mike and who Mark, but I had begun to know and respect Pat. She worked at great speed and never wasted a word, but she packed up on the dot to rush home and cook supper for a husband and daughter.

Trej said, 'They must be the best-fed family in London. She never stops cutting out and collecting recipes. I don't bother myself. I'm anybody's for a steak.'

Lunchtime on Friday, all eight of us trooped off in an office crocodile to the nearest pub to say farewell to Maggie and Shirl and an official hello to me; neither ritual being completed in canon law without benefit of alcohol.

While Mike and Mark collected orders and battled with the lunch-time press at the bar, Pat looked anxious and constantly checked her Timex.

'I hope they won't have to wait too long,' she fretted. 'It wouldn't do to be late, really.'

Mike returned with the first half of the order. He handed vodka and tonic to me and Liz, and placed a sweet Cinzano in front of Pat.

She looked at it and giggled. 'I shouldn't really. What would the teachers think if they smelled my breath.'

'Suck a peppermint,' Mark suggested, as he balanced beer for the men and red wine for the other girls.

Shirl asked, 'Whatever are you going to do?'

'Sports Day at her daughter's school,' Mark said. 'An obscene orgy.' He turned to Mike. They had a habit of reciting jokes antiphonally, which was amusing or irritating according to one's mood.

'A feast of flashing legs.'

'The bare thighs of pubescent girls.'

'Jouncing young boobs.'

'Lustful thoughts in middle-aged fathers' breasts.'

'What about the mothers?'

'Those strong young men.'

'At their sexual peak, they say.'

'After sixteen we are past it.'

Pat giggled again. 'Oh, you are awful.'

The chat became general, mostly shop. Liz produced a ten pound note and sent Mark for refills and a selection of sandwiches, sausages and pork pies.

'On the house. We've got something to celebrate, I think. Sarah is going to be a real asset to the company. I'm sorry to see Maggie and Shirl depart, but they go on their own volition. So, here's to Sarah. Welcome.'

They toasted me and the lads demanded a speech.

'Strictly a silent asset,' I told them. 'At least on official occasions.'

Pat gathered her belongings. 'I must fly, else I'll be late. 'Bye, all. Thanks for the drinks. See you on Monday. Drop by sometimes, Maggie, Shirl. 'Bye!'

Liz said, 'School sports are an abomination. I used to suffer agonies. My legs are too short to run very fast, but it didn't stop them trying to make me. It was the most humiliating day of the school year.'

'I used to be quite good,' Trej said. 'I used to win the Obstacle Race.'

'Which accounts,' Maggie said, dismembering a sausage roll to extract the pitiful gobbet of meat therein, 'for how you manage to get around your desk with such alacrity. I agree with Liz. They are a horror and an imposition and have probably warped the mind of many a sensitive child.'

'Not only for children,' I said. 'Parents can have a pretty thin time. I remember once at my boys' school, I was bullied to join in the Mothers' Race. I didn't mind at first. I thought it would be a gentle canter over the course exchanging such pleasantries as, "can little Johnny come to tea on Tuesday?" Not a bit of it. The mums took off like a stampede of buffalo. I didn't understand it at first. I mean, none of us cared. It was a token, a gesture. I caught on eventually. You see, no mother gave a hoot for being first, but each and every one of us was determined not to have the awful humiliation of being last. So, off we went. It was a ghastly experience . . .'

The atmosphere had congealed like frozen syrup. While I had been speaking, I now noticed, they had gradually stopped eating or drinking, rigid in mid-gesture. All six of them were staring at me as if I'd levitated or sprouted wings. They were caught in the social embarrassment that besets a gathering when somebody makes anti-Semitic remarks unaware that the host is Jewish.

For some seconds I confronted their horrified gaze before I understood the solecism I'd committed. It was my first encounter with the efficacy of the office grapevine. Sarah's history would be known, relayed around the desks and charted from birth to breakdown. And on that journey the stillbirth was surely recorded.

For my part, the telling of the story had crossed the barrier between my private grief and my public face, the elaborate structure of normality that I'd carefully constructed for the office. The structure was now in ruins, and the pain of my exile had not diminished. It was bitter to think that I'd been happy on that ridiculous Sports Day.

Trej broke the silence by launching a ferocious attack on Maggie for her defense of an ill-made television SF serial. The others joined in the conflict with an energy born of relief.

Liz didn't join in. She frowned, chain smoked and watched me, while I sat staring at my hands in my lap.

'Right!' she said loudly. 'Party over. All of you, get back to the office. Do some bloody work for a change. Sarah and I were going to look over those wine vaults at Charing Cross Station to see if they'll do for that chase sequence. Drink up. Off you go!'

They went gratefully, giving me the little, furtive look that school kids give the one singled out for punishment. When they had gone Liz fetched us more drinks and lit yet another cigarette. She wanted the situation clarified. She hated ambiguities.

'That was a true story, wasn't it?'

'Yes.'

'If it wasn't, you're the best actress I've ever met.'

'It happened.'

'But not to Sarah?'

'No.'

She sighed. 'Why the hell do they think you are Sarah?'

'I look, talk, sound exactly like her. She went missing the same time that I was found.'

'Then what makes you sure that you're Unity Penfold?'

'What makes you sure that you're Liz Walton?'

We remained silent as the pub slowly emptied. The lunchtime rush of office workers went back to snooze or skylark the last few hours before the weekend. She smoked another cigarette and said, 'We'd better get going then.'

'You're not giving me the sack?'

'Why should I? You're right for the job I want you to do. I don't pretend to understand and I suggest you censor stories of your past life. Causes confusion and upset. Talk to me if you need to get something off your chest. Oh, I'm not being kind.' She waved aside a speech I was about to make. 'I'm selfish and I'm extremely nosy. I think it's all fascinating, so if you need an ear, you can have mine with pleasure. Better me than somebody who might not understand at all.'

We walked down Old Compton Street to Cambridge Circus.

'Are there really wine vaults to see?' I asked.

'Certainly. There's no hurry to make any decision about them, but today's as good a day as any. Look at that!' She pointed to the placards outside the Palace Theater. 'Seventh Glorious Year! Tattsville! There was a musical in that theater that I was involved with before I went into films. It was a sell out success everywhere in the world except London. That theater! I'll never forgive it.'

Her chatter was designed to make me feel better and it did

so. It was a lingua franca with which I was happily at home, and therefore I was relaxed enough as we passed Wyndham's Theater to say, 'Ned was in a long run there. I used to sit in his dressing room during matinees and hear the show on the tannoy. I was seven months pregnant with Chris and it seemed important to be together as much as we could. We'd have a meal together between shows. Dressing Room 5 on the second landing.' Without warning I burst into tears.

'Jesus Christ!' Liz was badly shaken. 'God Almighty, forget what I said about talking to me. It's too much for both of us. I certainly can't take it. It's beyond me how you appear as sane as you do with all that churning inside. Go home! Now! Get some rest. I'll do the vaults myself.' She walked off abruptly, her fury a deterrent against argument. 'Go home!' she shouted back to me.

I stood irresolute. Perhaps I was meant to run after her, demonstrate that I could submerge my inner conflicts to satisfy the demands of a working situation. But I couldn't move. I knew what these tears were: I was mourning as if for the dead.

In the hospital where illness and recovery had been paramount, time had been suspended. In the outside world, the harsh battle for survival had used up all my energies. Any tears then had been tears of rage, exile, loneliness and despair. I had never mourned for my dead and it was time to mourn now. Now, I had won some early rounds in the fight, I had achieved a job, shelter. Now I had time, space, need to mourn. Had the loss of my husband and children occurred through a normal disaster, an accountable cataclysm, the world's sympathy would have been heaped on my head like confetti. I had to mourn alone and in silence.

Valedictory tears streamed from my eyes, a forecast of further storms. I was the center of giggling and embarrassed curiosity. I ran into Leicester Square Station. I held on to my grief for the few stops to Earls Court and the short distance to the flat; but, once inside, the deluge came, a wrenching, tearing, cathartic tempest that ached and drowned the sodden victim. I wept for hours, finally falling asleep from sheer debilitation in the early hours of Saturday morning, then I woke again and wept. Laura pounded on my locked door and I heard her wheedling voice begging me to stop and offering soup or cocoa or other unsuitable beverages.

Pippa would have offered gin; and then I wept again for loss of her and Klaus.

By lunch-time on Saturday, I was forced to go to the bathroom and Laura was on hand to nab me. She frog-marched me into her room and made me swallow tea and toast. The initial violence of the storm had passed, its intensity proving its cure. It had been a purge, a true healing and I felt better, almost light-headed. I told Laura that if she'd like to make the soup, I'd happily drink it. My blotched and swollen face would heal with sleep and a bath. But my widowhood was just beginning. A year and a day. The traditional time for widows' weeds. One year and one day.

The soup was tinned but she had the imagination to sprinkle grated cheese on it, and I gulped it greedily.

'I say, Sarah.' She was wide-eyed like a child, a pose that her bulk rendered ludicrous. 'I say, whatever brought all that on?'

'I started to remember.'

'Golly, of course, I suppose one would. The baby and all. But he really was a most unpleasant man, a pig . . . horrible.' She went pink while I slowly caught on that she meant John Lang. 'He even made a pass at me.'

'Did he?' I asked with interest. What, I wondered, constituted a pass in Laura's world?

'I was on the phone. He came by on his way to the bathroom. He . . . put his hand—well, you know where—and he made some crude, suggestive comments . . . about . . .' Her cheeks flared.

'About what?'

She shook her head. 'I couldn't repeat it.'

By evening I was melancholy rather than mad. My mental muscles ached, a deep layer of hurt remained and I wanted to be alone for the process of recuperation. And I wanted to go on a pilgrimage.

On Sunday, I slipped out of the flat muttering some vague words about going for a walk. Laura's attention was diverted by a phone call from Roy so I evaded her habitual cross-examination.

I had planned the journey carefully so there would be no hesitation, no chance to let indecision divert me. A series of buses that left me by the Roundhouse. Gentle and easy, an outing through Sunday London that would end with a stroll toward Primrose

Hill, an oblique approach so that the emotional jolt would be less hurtful.

King Henry's Crescent was the same as when I saw it last. Our house was still gone, but a less hysterical inspection revealed that there was an extension to Number 3 which was new to my eyes though it had clearly been there for some years. Space that was once occupied by a demolished building looks ridiculously small, the area insufficient ever to have held the vanished structure; but it was still doubtful whether the extension and the intervening garage, which had, I now noticed, a lean-to greenhouse to one side, could have contained the missing home. A careful drawing, an architect's measured plan might prove the point, but it was not worth it. Whether it had been flattened by the Blitz and the subsequent rebuilding, or whether it had been snuffed out like a candle that April afternoon made no matter. The house and all its inhabitants were consigned to nowhere and only I escaped.

A chill thought, an ugly supposition struck me. I, too, was consigned to nowhere. There was no Unity Penfold. Suppose what had happened to me had also happened to Ned and the boys? Suppose Ned was locked in some hospital ward for bravely affirming his lost right to be himself? Suppose the boys were in some local authority care, a home for disturbed children?

'Then how can I find them?' I muttered to myself. 'Just tell me how?'

A Sunday car cleaner peered over his gleaming paintwork at me, a polishing rag in his hand. I hurried away. I knew the man, of course, he had cleaned his wretched car every fine Sunday since we moved there; but his questioning glance lacked recognition, and I was old enough in disaster not to challenge him and precipitate a scene.

Lost in a maze of fretting thoughts, I found myself on Primrose Hill. There was no way I could think of to instigate a search for lost people whose names and backgrounds were literally untraceable. I could waste time and check laboriously through every home and orphanage while all the time the boys were tucked away with foster parents. Or while I combed the mental wards, Ned might have found another identity imposed on him, so that he was a cuckoo, a parasite like myself.

It was sunny, so that I sat on a bench while I thought over the implications of this supposition. There must be a statistical chance, if my hypothesis were correct, that we might meet by accident, but I supposed that the odds against that would flummox a computer. At that moment, as if in answer to my unasked question, a go-cart came to a crumpled halt at my feet spilling out two small boys.

For a while I was blinded by tears so that I saw only the similarities through a film of moisture. They were the right age, build and coloring. They were even wearing the right sort of clothes: the dilapidated and grubby high-priced clothes that proclaim the offspring of the professional classes in London. But then my sight cleared and the differences lacerated me even more.

My tears intrigued them.

'What are you crying for?' asked the younger boy, climbing on to the bench beside me.

'Spect she's sad,' said the elder.

'She's been naughty. She's been naughty and now she's sorry.'

'What are your names?' I asked.

'Alan and Timmy,' the elder said nicely enough, but he was losing interest and wanted to return to the go-cart.

'Timmy?' I repeated, certain that I felt my heart bruise. 'Which one of you is Timmy?'

The little one snuggled up to me. 'I'm Alan. He's Timmy. He took my sweeties. Have you got any sweeties?'

'You are not to ask for sweeties. I didn't take his sweeties. He wasn't allowed any 'cos he didn't eat up his pudding.'

'I did.'

'You didn't.'

'It tasted all yukky.'

'I haven't any sweeties,' I admitted.

Alan abandoned me. 'I bet we can go all the way to the bottom of the hill without stopping. You watch us.'

'I'll watch,' I promised.

'Goodbye,' said Timmy, then he added politely, 'I hope you don't feel sad any more.'

'Not any more. Thank you.'

'You watch us,' Alan insisted.

'Yes.'

'We won't fall off.'

'No.'

They did fall off. Alan grazed his knees and his squalling produced a harassed father who scolded them out of sight. I sat on for some time until the ache subsided and then walked to the bus stop to make the slow journey back across town.

Work on Monday was a relief. Much as I enjoyed Maggie's company, and had envied Shirl's expedition in dispatching office chores, I was pleased to be on my own, to know for certain which little victories and failures were on my own head. Liz and I soon established working territories. I learned when to ask before acting, and when to leave her alone. When I made the wrong assessment, which happened frequently for she was not consistent and I very inexperienced, then she either glowered or giggled and I learned not to mind either. My peculiarities were not referred to by anyone, for which I was grateful, and the work routine left no time for fretting. The fatigue at the end of the day was from time and talent being well used and not from the sense of waste that sterile work induces.

We had several projects on hand. We were providing all the locations for the second unit director of a big feature film about the Civil War. This meant period houses and battlegrounds to keep Mark 'n Mike extremely busy. We had a handful of TV commercials. And 'Raindew.' 'Raindew' came from an advertising agency where the account executive had built up for his product a reputation and a valuable increase in sales by conceiving a series of witty and topical television commercials. Because they were topical, 'Raindew' cropped up all the time as no single advert was allowed to get staler than the news it parodied.

'Many and often. Raindew Detergent pays the rent,' Liz would say when its priorities became a nuisance. 'We'd go broke without it.'

We were also involved in rounding up rival gangs of children aged about eight, black and white respectively, for an American SF film being shot in the Cotswolds, and this was proving difficult, costly and a logistic nightmare. And, in our spare moments, we were casting but not servicing a series of educational films for TV to be shown in the States only.

Liz was firm. 'But, if anybody phones and you answer and they offer us more work, accept. It's better for us to take on more staff than get the reputation for saying no. But, and I mean this, find out first whether they pay well and promptly.'

There was no time to brood and the bustle was therapeutic. I stayed late many evenings to browse through the files and learn what I could from them about technicalities and budgeting. I was, for all my blundering, on the road to becoming a model employee.

' "Raindew" occasionally slip in a quickie with a visiting celebrity, especially if they're homecoming Brits. Burton, Bisset. We once got Chaplin when he was alive. I think he thought it was a news interview. That type of person.' Liz brought this up one morning as she opened her post. 'I hear that Pippa Waters is coming over for the Royal Command. She'll be nabbed for all the chat shows, of course, but I think we should get on the bandwagon too. I'll talk to the advertising agency but, if you've got a minute, have a word with her agent, Jamie Marriot. I think he deals with her in the U.K.'

'Pippa Waters.' Liz was too shrewd to miss my slight inflection. She was alerted, even though her back was turned. 'Pippa Waters. Yes, she is one lady I would very much like to meet.'

'Part of that other thing, I suppose,' Liz snapped.

'Part of part of it.'

The daily deluge of ringing telephones began and we were both thankful that there was no chance for the discussion to continue.

The beginning of August passed. Laura went to Devon and Trej went to Majorca. Pat was preparing in a welter of lists and worries for her family holiday, an annual pilgrimage in a caravan. A temp manned the switchboard and distributed messages muddled enough to convince us that Trej was, indeed, a treasure. We buzzed busily along and enjoyed our complaining.

Most evenings I would make my way home along the same route that Liz and I had taken after that unfortunate pub lunch. It would have been quicker to walk to Piccadilly, but the walk through Soho relaxed me and avoided the theaters in Shaftesbury Avenue where lurked too many memories. Often, on my way, I would buy my evening meal at a delicatessen or takeaway. One night I dawdled longer than usual and, when I got home, I was tired and made a weary task of the three flights of stairs to the flat. As I reached the last flight, my way was barred by a man who deliberately prevented me passing. His arms, well tailored and expensive, stretched from wall to banister, his face was in shadow and he smelled liberally of cosmetics, which failed to mask an ugly body odor.

'Excuse me,' I said, as normally as I could for his stance frightened me.

He didn't reply. He was a duelist waiting for me to draw first. We faced each other on the steps, locked in a battle I didn't understand.

'Look, can I get past?' I said when his silence and his smell made it imperative that I move away.

'Where have you been, ducky? Doing your good deed for the day?' He giggled, a high-pitched, epicene sound that made my flesh creep.

'I can't see that it's any business of yours where I've been,' I said.

He giggled again. 'Can't even do that properly, can you? I can't see . . .' he mimicked my accent, accentuating its tendency to tweedy vowels. 'Business of mine. Ducky, anything you do is always my business, you know that.' He grabbed my handbag. It was the only one of Sarah's belongings that I liked. I used it all the time.

'The bag I gave you.' He was searching for the key. 'Miss me, do you ducky? Not getting any without me? A sentimental gift. I found it in a junk shop for 50p. I didn't think you liked it, but here you are toting it around. Touching.'

He found the key and forced me up the remaining steps. He shoved the door open with his shoulders and pulled me in after him into the tiny hallway. He shut the door and pocketed my key.

I could see his face at last. He was a thin man with languid elegance, but his face and his hands were puffy, plump and pasty white. His fingers as he took my key made me think of maggots. His eyes were gray and well shaped, but his facial hair was so sandy that his brows and lashes were almost invisible, which gave his whole face a bald, reptilian look. His mouth flanked by his jowly cheeks was wide and thin. An amiable man would have lent charm to these contradictions, an innocent joke against himself; but there was in my unwelcome visitor a warped energy, a malign sexuality that denied charm.

I came out of the stupor of shock and realized who he was.

'John Lang,' I said idiotically.

'Ten out of ten, ducky.' He pushed me against a door, backing me hard against the wood so there was no escape. He licked my mouth and rubbed his body greedily against mine. One hand stroked my breast with intent to hurt.

'No bra,' he said into my lips. 'Improving aren't you, my pet.'

'Laura . . .' was all I had breath to say.

'Is on holiday. We're all alone, ducky. The night is young, but you are not.' His voice was as contradictory as the rest of him, a pleasant tenor overlaid with spiteful, camp overtones. He pushed himself from me and went into my room.

'I need a drink,' he said petulantly. 'You must have some money. I know you are doing a new job. Anything in it for me?'

I followed him too stupefied to think intelligently. There seemed no escape. Screaming rape, phoning the police, any normal reaction would be futile. He had, in theory, been my lover for years; 'a lover's tiff' or 'she likes him to knock her about' would be the kindest comments I would be likely to endure.

He sat back in the easy chair, crossing his legs with calculated grace. A few inches of leg showed above his sock, his flesh was white and hairless. He saw where I was looking and smiled, sinking his thin lips into the puffed-up pastry of his cheeks. He was quick, a sharp one, it was not surprising that the end of a relationship with him sent Sarah wandering through the night-time streets. His smell lingered on my flesh. I watched him with his foul odor on my body. The violation of my space, my bodily privacy, had stunned me.

'Go away,' I managed to whisper. 'Go away at once. I don't want you here.'

'Not moral indignation this evening, please. Sarah, ducky, I go a long way to pander to your kinky sexual daydreams, but moral indignation and I'm-not-like-this-really are your most boring. Not tonight, please, ducky. I'm still waiting for my drink.'

'There is nothing in the flat.'

I kept my pitiful little supply of liquor behind some books on the shelf. I think it was to protect Laura from the realization that her roommate felt better for a stiff vodka before supper. I was certain that she would think that I was nearly an alcoholic. I lied, safe in my hiding place.

He giggled and leaned toward the books. He dislodged the correct ones, revealing my secret.

'Same place as always, ducky. You mustn't lie, if you can't do it better than that.' It was the duel, silent and still.

'I want a drink,' he commanded at last.

'Help yourself.'

'I want you to give it to me, ducky. You know I don't do anything for myself. Anything,' he repeated with an innuendo that was unmistakable. He had the vulgar air of a man who thought it witty to find risqué double meanings in the New Testament. His smirk disappeared behind a mask of anger and he hissed, 'Get me that drink.'

I mixed a vodka and tonic. He ordered ice and I could scarcely fetch the ice from the freezing compartment because of my trembling. I was as slow as I dared in order to give myself a chance to think, but my brain was numb and could manage little except wild and impractical nonsense such as locking him in the bathroom, or trying to bolt for safety down the stairs, though I realized that either of those schemes would only produce a temporary respite.

'What are you doing in there?' he called. 'Putting the arsenic in?'

'If you think that,' I said shakily, 'you must realize that I don't want you here.'

'Of course, you want me. Mad for me, can't get enough.' He giggled. 'Little joke, ducky, that's all.'

I came back with his glass and held it out for him to take.

'I can't reach.' He lounged back, forcing me to go nearer to him, but as I approached him, he sank back.

'Nearer, ducky, I still can't reach.' His lounging forced me into a ridiculous posture so that I had to come into contact with his knees to prevent myself from falling.

'Nearer.'

My legs were pressing against his when he sat up with a dancer's skill and his arm, like a striking snake, went up under my skirt and his maggot fingers entered my body. I went rigid with shock and rage, a sick, seething anger that he mistook.

'Oh, ducky, you love it, don't you. The pleasure is all yours and you must pay for it.' His voice took on a soft crooning note. 'Yes, ducky, how much have you got in your purse tonight?'

I threw the contents of the glass into his fringeless gray eyes. The second before the stinging liquid blinded them, I caught a flicker of fear, the cowardice of a bully whose bluff has been called. His hand went to the aid of his eyes and I was released.

While he screamed curses and obscenities at me, I went to the kitchen again and fetched a carving knife, but the gesture seemed over melodramatic and I sensibly exchanged the knife for a carton of ground pepper. As I passed his chair, I threw a tea towel to him and sat on the divan.

We sat opposite each other in suspended wordless conflict. I, on the divan, was a pillar, unmoving and unforgiving, made from the steel of anger and the iron of disgust. He, on his chair, writhed and shouted, a pathetic bundle of broken and discarded pretensions and accumulated mannerisms. When finally he was quiet and his reddened eyes able to see again, though they watered continually, his elegance, his modulated, camp voice and his sexual swagger had melted and had been mopped up with the tea towel. He was a con man whose cover has been blown, an actor who has forgotten his lines, a trickster who has found the wrong victim. His body odor drenched the room, a trickle ran along his nose to drip unnoticed from nostril to shirt front, and when he spoke he had the whining, indignant twang of one of London's poorer suburbs.

'Here, what you want to do that for? You always went a bundle for that sort of chat.'

I said nothing, locked in my anger.

'That sort of garbage always pulls your sort of bird. Don't get it myself, but I do what pleases the paying customers. Specially old bags like you what don't even know they're fucking paying for it.'

I still said nothing. No discussion, no form of explanation would be possible with this creature. Sarah had been hooked to the sick sexuality of the man, entangled by the needs of her loneliness. She must have known she was being exploited, but had been unable to break away from the excitement, the play acting, the pleasure and the danger.

'Listen, give us a fiver and I'll buzz off. Here, don't just sit there like a fucking dummy. Give us a fiver and I'll give you a quick roll in the hay for old times.'

Anger finally spoke. 'You are repulsive. Offensive. I can't imagine any sexual encounter with you that could be other than totally degrading.'

'Here, watch it!' His indignation lifted him from his chair and he made a threatening lunge at me. Then halted by my lack of fear, he stopped and giggled.

'The old bitch has remembered she's got teeth, then.'

He prowled around the room, cleaning his nails with my tweezers, using my comb to restore his hair to the effortless wave that required hard effort to maintain. He threw back his shoulders, then hunched them again, tensing like a gunfighter while undulating his hips. He spun around, relaxed and straightened his cuffs and the hang of his trousers. Wherever he moved, he left a trail of his stale scent behind him, and occasionally he giggled again. Piece by piece, stroke by stroke, he was reconstructing his scattered image, rebuilding and repainting layer upon layer until his masterpiece, his life's work, stood before me as at first, with only a damp stain on his shirt front as evidence of his defeat.

'Well, ducky, it's your choice. Never thought you had it in you to say no. I'll leave you to yourself then and your no doubt pleasant memories. I must admit I'm sorry it's over. You're quite a gamy little thing. Not a bad body for over thirty. I prefer them younger for my own pleasure, but you weren't too bad. You want to watch that left nipple though. I've heard that inverted nipples lead to breast cancer. Nasty way to go. Oh, and I should get a plastic surgeon to fix your appendix scar. Worth the cost. When your belly sags, it'll become a deformity, that scar and the mole underneath just above your hair line. Like an exclamation mark. No, ducky, I'm wrong. More like that road sign they put on roadworks meaning "hazard ahead." Yes, I like that. You and your sagging belly and a sign over it saying "hazard ahead." ' The giggling rose hysterically. 'I'll be off then, but I need a contribution.'

He opened my handbag and emptied the contents of my purse, settling the notes and coins about his person with practiced speed. 'Not enough, ducky.' He looked around the room and went to the closet. Sarah had kept a leather case in a drawer in which was a good Victorian ring and an ugly, but expensive, wrist watch. The case seemed large to hold so pitiful a store, but now I understood where all the treasures that had once filled the case had vanished.

The ring and the watch followed the same route. As they were slipped into his pocket, I could see that he was trying to arrange an exit, a parting line or gesture to restore his faith in himself. Against my pillar of silence and anger he had no weapons. He giggled once more and walked over to me, looming over me with his stink and his sickness. Suddenly he seized my chin with his hand and tilted my head up to face the fury in his eyes. He filled his mouth and spat into my face, then he turned and slammed out of the flat.

I ran to the bathroom and vomited violently.

He knew my body. The scar, the mole, the nipple. He knew and had touched, had invaded my body. A maggotty man whose touch would corrupt, whose breath was tainted.

The scar, the mole, the nipple belonged to me, to a body that had known only tenderness and adoration from Ned . . .

The night was spent in scrubbing the flat with disinfectant, pounding at the surfaces he had soiled, making a laundry bundle of chair covers and clothes. Myself I could not clean. Contamination like a filthy canker had invaded and raped me. That a man whose very nature was the type to curdle my blood, from whom I would shrink under any circumstances, knew my body, its private marks, its personal blemishes, knew it because he had possessed it, was an undeniable fact: that much could not be Sarah's domain alone, the coincidence was untenable. Had I, as Sarah, fawned on his rancid carcase, co-operated in the sadistic fulfillment he demanded? Had I needed to be used and abused? I was degraded. Dirtied by fantasies that were full of corruption and malice, made to wound because his existence depended on his awareness of pain and fear.

As I scrubbed and bathed, then bathed again, a dawning and terrible idea formed that could not be avoided though I fought hard to deny it. But it could not be denied. I could not avoid the supposition that Ned and the sharing love he had with Unity was an invention, a desperate mirage invented by a fragile mind that needed an antidote for the ugly, black side of sex.

Horror and shame overwhelmed me. I tried to assimilate the concept that Ned was no more than a dream remedy, a psychic fairy tale for an unhappy, neurotic woman who was looking for a refuge. I tried to decide whether, if this was so, Sarah was a victim, or whether, as John Lang maintained, she was a willing participant, getting pathetic kicks from his sickness and holding on to an uneasy equilibrium by believing in Ned, a mythical Ned, a nonexistent and chimerical figment.

I rebelled. My body, my soul, my heart rejected this utterly. Ned was no figment. His love could not have been fabricated with the countless, warm details that I could remember with aching clarity. I would prefer him to be dead, lost to me forever, if his wholesome reality could be proved. I would rather face the pain of his irrevocable loss than the obscenity that he existed solely as an unreal escape from a perversion of love.

In the morning, weary and desperate, I phoned Liz.

'I could say that I had a headache, that I ate something that made me ill, but I haven't. I have had an unspeakable experience based on my problem and I'd be no use to you today. If you think I'm being irresponsible, I'm sorry. It will probably go against me when you come to decide about keeping me on in the autumn, but I can't lie to you about this. I'd like to stay. You know that.'

'Get well. We need you,' was her only comment.

The long day passed. I took my bundles to the Laundrette and I found a locksmith who was willing to change my lock and keys. John Lang had pocketed my key and it was not worth the risk that his courage, or greed, might drive him back to try again. I also had a chain fitted to the door. I put a spare key in an envelope and sent it to Laura with a short note. Nobody said a word about my absence at the office the following day. With Trej away and the pressure of overwork, I doubt if anyone even noticed, except Liz, and she scrupulously hid her concern under the brusque manner that always seemed to disguise her response to an emotional appeal.

Exhaustion waits to catch the unwary when the nervous energy that sustains the victims of insomnia has been dissipated the following day by a meager ration of sleep. I fumbled through work, making foolish errors of judgment, muddling simple instructions and feeding a growing sense of inadequacy with gobbets of paranoia and hysteria. I made a ridiculous scene over a phone call that I mismanaged. Liz bore it all in comparative silence, but I was mortified. I left the office dead on time, for once, and thus found myself trapped by the worst of the rush hour.

Leicester Square Station was a whirlpool, a spinning Catherine wheel, that spun great streams of people on and off the escalators and in and out of its dozen entrances. A speeded up film or an aerial view of the process would confirm the theory that mankind was a single organic entity, a conglomeration of cells each unaware of its place in a wider pattern like corpuscles in a bloodstream, or bacteria in a culture. In Leicester Square, the streams of hurrying commuters were more like the tentacles of a giant squid. Once assigned to a stream there was no more choice. Any deviation would be chopped down and excised, the healthy cells expelling a malignancy.

I fed myself into the down stream to the Piccadilly Line. There is a mathematical law used in statistics: the law of queueing. It deals with appalling problems such as how many more exits than entrances are needed to keep incoming customers processed to move smoothly through car park or supermarket. Our escalator had broken that law. The concept of a moving lane on the left had no meaning, both streams were static, two abreast. I was fixed into my slot on the slowly descending stairway when I heard a shout.

'Unity!'

On the upward escalator, a familiar figure waved and gesticulated.

'Unity, where the hell have you been hiding? Get in touch with me at the usual number. I must talk to you.'

He sailed upward in the steady, stately flow of the escalator's pace. Neither of us could move.

'Your number is out of order. Love to Ned.' He used his actor's voice to carry across the expanding gap between me and sanity. 'Hey, get in touch. It's about a job. See you.'

I was off-loaded at the bottom and rushed across to the up escalator. I tried to run up, barging past the unyielding lines, but I was forced to submit. The theater-goers, the night-outers were swapping space with the daytime workers and were packed as tightly. A fuming mixture of elation and anxiety, I was yet another breakdown of the law of queueing. I glided upward at a snail's speed, past underwear advertisements and theater bills, blocked and barricaded from the one human soul in London who had known my name.

He wasn't there, of course. He had yelled my name across the void of space and time. He had known me and I had recognized him. But who was he? An actor, clearly, an acquaintance; theater life breeds these casual and intrusive intimacies. My memory, so steadfast with regard to Ned, had reneged, abdicated. He was familiar, but who? Who was the man?

Unity. Love to Ned. I phoned myself that night again. Asked the operator. No subscriber on that number. 'Hey, get in touch. See you.'

In the office I combed through *Spotlight* to unearth the face that had nodded to me from a happier world. But it escaped. Long after the office closed, I went through both volumes for the third time. He wasn't there, and the harder I cudgelled my recalcitrant memory, the harder it stuck. Finally, I abandoned the task as hopeless. With luck the name would be dredged up from my subconscious when the pressure to remember it was removed.

I concentrated harder than ever on my job. I made many mistakes which, though Liz was charitable and dismissed them as beginner's hazard, I knew well enough came from my lack of necessary skills. I was unused to office routine. The formality of the financial dealings, the legal and contractual side of a business that I had only known from a limited, personal standpoint, surprised and confused me, the etiquette of bluff and counterbluff eluded me. Had my mistakes been purely secretarial, I wouldn't have minded as these I would overcome with time; but some of my errors had been of judgment and tact and these I should have avoided. With each fault, however tiny, I sensed Liz's disapproval and the ensuing lack of confidence naturally gave birth to a greater crop of errors. I wasn't wholly incompetent. There were rewarding days when the effort stimulated me, leaving me wilted but triumphant, and it was for these days that I worked, so that they might multiply in time.

'Did you talk to Jamie Marriot about Waters?' Liz asked me, a few days after my phantom on the escalator.

'Oh yes, I'm sorry, I forgot to tell you. She'll probably do it, if the fee's high enough. Would you phone him and talk money.'

Liz grunted. 'The fee will be high enough. She lives high, that lady, so her earnings have to be equally high to keep pace. She always does a deal with any management that she must wear couture clothes. Then she does another deal and gets them off the management for a quarter of the price and she's only worn them once for a TV show. Mind you, she looks fantastic in them.'

Seedy harem pants topped with a Shetland sweater. My Pippa would have relished the outrageous wheeling and dealing over couture clothes.

One night, when I was alone as Laura was still in Devon, I was preparing to go to bed when the door bell rang, an interruption so unexpected that the note of the chime stabbed like a wound and released the adrenalin of fright. There was no way of pretending to be out. The hall light was burning, anybody would see it from the landing through the fanlight, and my radio was playing.

I waited, trembling, to hear the fumble of key and lock as white, puffy fingers tried to force the stubborn door, angry at being thwarted. I was secure behind the chain and the altered locks; but I was frightened that he might retaliate with spite for my precautions, or provoked by my resistance, he might lurk in ambush, now or later, and the sickness rose again at the thought of John Lang's hidden proximity.

The ring was repeated; this time in the cheeky street rhythm, the five beats of 'we are the greatest.' It was so uncharacteristic of Lang, as I read him, that I doubted that he'd use it even to mislead me. Then the cold thought followed that he might have brought along an ally, a decoy, and I knew that I was no match for two.

I went into the hall to check that the chain was firm. On the other side of the door, I could hear the tuneless whistling and jiggling footsteps of impatience. He must have heard me, though I moved as quickly as I could, for the whistling stopped, and we stood either side of the wooden door, two invisible beings, sensing, listening, guessing at each other's presence. The music on the radio had been transmuted into the dull monotone of the News. I could begin to see the thin lips, to prepare my nostrils for the assault of rank skin.

'Laura?'

It was a male voice and not, I was almost certain, Lang's, though the partition between us muffled the sounds.

'Hey, Laura, is that you?'

'Laura is not here.'

'Flaming Moses! Where is she then? Is she coming back soon?'

'She's on holiday.'

He whistled again, this time in exasperation, and I could hear some heavy bundles being dumped on the threadbare carpet of the landing.

'I was counting on her. Hey, can I come in?'

'No.'

'Why not? I haven't got two heads.'

'No.'

'Why?'

'Reasons.'

This ridiculous conversation, conducted in harsh whispers through the door, ceased while he sighed and grumbled; and, though I listened for signals of consultation with the hidden John Lang, I could detect none.

'Are you her roommate, Sarah?'

Others could mis-name me. I still hated to have to do it myself.

'Yes.'

'Sarah who? Sarah Bernhardt?'

I kept my silence. He could be a drifter, bribed with a pint of beer, who had fallen for a plausible yarn.

'Well, can you hear me, Sarah Who? A friend of your buddy

Laura, one Roy by name, said she'd give me a corner of her floor to sleep on if I was ever stuck. And am I ever stuck!'

Roy could well pledge Laura's floor and Laura honor it, but these were facts that Lang knew as well as I. They were no passport.

I still said nothing and he sighed again. He shuffled and bumped and then he too was still, a manoeuvre which, I guessed, had left him sitting on the floor with his back to the door. My guess was confirmed when he next spoke; his whisper was at waist level.

'Listen, Sarah Who, I've got a treat for you.'

A guitar chord, gentle and subtle, wafted surprisingly from the landing.

> I am a beggar at your gate,
> Lady, wise and fair,
> And though I know the hour is late,
> I'm far too bushed to care.

I smothered a laugh, but he heard it and added another verse,

> I am a singer at your door,
> Lady, kind and sweet,
> Is there space upon your floor
> For me to rest my feet?

The guitar chords faded softly away, a pure beauty wasted on such doggerel.

'Actually, I'm not much bothered about my feet. They can rest anywhere. It's my head and my eyes. The flaming things just won't stay open. Let me in and I'll guarantee to sleep like the dead for ten hours. Sarah, on the word of a troubadour, I am not, repeat not, a mad rapist. If you want to know the truth, I wouldn't have the strength if you paid me for it.'

I caught it then, the accent that had been tantalizing me, filtered by the door and lost in the whispering.

'What's your name?' I asked, but I knew the answer, word for word.

'Phil Mallet, known to my friends as Face.'

I withdrew the chain and opened the door. He sprang to his feet with a juggler's agility and offered me an exaggerated and courtly bow. As he straightened up, he saw me and his brown face froze in the comic mask of astonishment.

'Well, I'll be a monkey's . . . Unity Penfold. Sarah Who? Here's an extremely pretty turn up in the book of my life. Well, Unity Sarah Who Penfold, we meet again. May I cross your threshold?'

Part Three

Face

I have, I repeat, an insatiable curiosity. One of my ancestors must have been the tribal genius who went around tasting every living thing, grunting to the rest of the tribe 'nice' or 'nasty' or 'wait and see if I drop dead.' With me this curiosity amounts to a genetic malformation. In a village community, I could set up shop as the local gossip but for the fact that I rarely tell what I hear, the knowing is all.

However, that night we took a rain check on our tale-telling. She had an early start in the morning and, besides, she was drained from the fright I had given her, details to follow later. On my part, I had reached the end of my ration of stamina, three hours of sleep in as many days is over my endurance level.

'Tomorrow, after I get back from work. We'll talk then,' she said as she rummaged for a cover for Laura's downie.

'Tomorrow,' I agreed through a yawn that hurt my mouth muscles. She nodded and turned to go.

'Hey!' The yawn had settled itself. 'How come you're Sarah Davies?'

'When I got out of hospital they told me who I am.'

She was good at one liners, my mysterious waif. When I got home, it wasn't there. When I got out of hospital, they told me who I am. Good, cliff-hanging technique to hook the irredeemably nosy. I drifted down to a thick, full sleep, my guesswork trying to outrun the narration of the Perils of Pauline, or Unity in Danger.

I didn't wake until after midday. There was a note on the bedside table.

'Use my kitchen. Not Laura's. Help yourself to anything.

Instant coffee on shelf. Real coffee in red tin. Back at 6.' It was unsigned.

I lay relaxed and lazy for a long time, doped by an overindulgence in sleep. I thought of her and was attracted, intrigued: round eyes, the mop of dark curls, the delicate nose, good figure if you like 'em skinny and I do. A puzzle woman composed from contradictions, a tough fragility, a frightened strength; she was a tender survivor. It had taken me several seconds to wipe away the grime of Euston in my mind's eye and see her again in the woman who had opened the door. She had been laughing at my nonsense, relieved to see a familiar face; but she was poised like a cat, tension in her stance, a fresh wariness in her eyes and a few, poignant strands of gray at her temples. No longer to be mistaken for a girl; a woman, an honest person who had been battered by contrary winds.

I wondered how long I should stay in the flat. Roy had hinted at a more or less permanent welcome, but maybe he was trying to off-load Laura. I would like to stick around, but for all my curiosity and compassion, I was chary of an involvement with a very mixed-up lady; and, whoever she was, she should not be asked to take further punishment. Perhaps I should have to try and find a new hat. Sir Galahad Mallet for a change, not Face the Philanderer, terror of the doxies. A halo instead of a hat . . . Well, a change could be a spur to a sluggish imagination; but, if I stayed for more than a couple of days, I would have to shoulder a share of responsibility, and responsibility toward anything except my guitar is a very short commodity in my storehouse.

Yet I was becoming very weary of folk club groupies: the wispy Ophelias, the strident protesters, the grubby, hip gypsies. An adult woman, a real person with whom I could exchange trust, nurture a process of growth . . . Hold hard, mate. Nobody asked you, sir, she said.

I took my laziness out of bed and into the bathroom. I washed, shaved and pondered over my choices, or whether I had the choosing anyway. I was tempted to skip away, leave a note of thanks and opt out; but I recalled the relief in her voice, the smile, the eager hands that welcomed me in, and an ache began in my gut, a twist of sadness that I couldn't account for. I tore up the note and thought of breakfast, though eggs and bacon cured nothing except hunger.

After I cleared away my meal, wandered around the flat and made a few phone calls, I took to my guitar. It's the way I think. It is also the way I work, relax, waste time and even make love. One doxy said that my guitar was my third limb and she wasn't making a dirty crack. I am bereft, crippled, castrated without it.

I took it out of its case and tuned it, letting the task allow the slow, sure merging of ears and fingers into a sympathetic tripartite marriage. I doodled a while, loosening up like an athlete, then I found a theme, worked with it, played with it, chased after it, hoping to use it in the project that I had come to London to pursue. The project was important, a challenge; but I kept losing the theme in thoughts of her. She intervened, interfered with the music. I couldn't escape the memory of her distress, her oblique beauty and the weird, crazy tale that she had told me in the police-ridden station. I remembered the song I had been playing as she approached. My fingers plucked again at the memory.

> *O, still grew the hearts that were beating so fast,*
> *The loudest voice was still.*
> *The jest died away on our lips as they passed,*
> *And the rays of July struck chill.*

I hadn't heard the key turn or the door open, but I sensed her in the room. Her room, for I felt an intruder in the unknown Laura's. She stood behind me so I couldn't see her. 'Go on singing, please go on,' she said.

> *The cups of red wine turned pale on the board,*
> *The white bread black as soot.*
> *The hound forgot the hand of her lord,*
> *She fell down at his foot.*

'Face, oh Face it hurts.' She came around and knelt in front of me, her eyes filled with tears. 'I've shut away anything that's beautiful because it hurts too much. You've made a marvelous, painful melody for those sad, sad words.'

Low let me lie where the dead dog lies,
Ere I sit me down again at a feast,
When there passes a woman with the West in her eyes,
And a man with his back to the East.

The evening sunshine slanted across our silence long after the music had become floating dust motes. The conversation we were having didn't need words, we both knew what was being said.

Finally she spoke. 'Which old sheila?'

'Mary Coleridge.'

'I can't, you see. Not at the moment. Ned ... it's still Ned for me. I've not yet had enough time to learn how to come to terms with the fact that he's as good as dead. And I haven't, not yet. I'm sorry, Face, I think I'm asking too much.'

I leaned over my guitar and ran a finger along the tear line. Fresh, clean tears this time, not the grubby riverbed of before.

'I'll stay, love,' I said. 'For as long as I can.'

There was gratitude in her face, followed by embarrassment. We had said a great deal in two sentences; but we were unsure of ourselves, unable to shed the normal, human habit of spelling it out, exchanging a vulgar, verbal certainty for a deeper, unexpressed understanding. It is hard for marred mortals to be secure in their interpretation of such moments.

And now was not the right moment for explanations, not of that kind. I broke the quietness with a strident chord and complained in my broadest Aussie, 'Can't a man get a can of lager around here? I've got a bellyful of nothing and I'm more than ready to eat.'

Another grateful look. Watch out, Mallet, you're becoming a mind reader. She jumped up, all eagerness and expectation, circling the coffee table with a dexterity that told me it was an old habit.

'What shall we eat? Shall I open tins? Or shall we go out? It's odd, I know so little about you. What do you like to eat? Curry? Chinese? Spaghetti?'

'Hey, calm down. I'm not fussy, me.'

'Where then?'

'Somewhere quiet where we can talk. I want to hear the whole story, not a detail missed out. And I've some news for you. So, we go forth and find a dull, quiet place. It's on me tonight, my treat. I've found the lollipop at the end of the rainbow.'

During a long, relaxed meal in a restaurant with no gimmicks, silent waiters and tasteless food, she told me of her gallant stand against the inexplicable. The contest, ladies and gentlemen, which is the authentic lady? On my left, Unity—the evidence for her is slim and purely subjective. On my right, Sarah—her case is based on objective, though circumstantial, evidence. The veracity of all witnesses doubtful and confused. On the face of it, Sarah's case was the stronger, but Unity took the oath with greater conviction. I couldn't tell her this; her dedication to Unity's cause was absolute and to disbelieve in her was treachery and heresy. I wasn't prepared to cast a vote at the present, so I stayed up on my fence.

'What do I call you?' I asked. 'If I go against the main stream and call you Unity, it will cause confusion in public.'

'I hate being called Sarah. It still upsets me.'

'What then?'

She looked troubled and made no answer.

I said, 'We put loving endearments out of fashion back there in your flat. Usually I count on them to fill in the gaps. A sound gambit when I forget the doxies' names.'

She wisely didn't make an issue of it; but either her conscience or her sensibility was touched for she had the stricken air of one in the right but with no rights.

'O.K. I'll think of something. A name will emerge, it always does. Like kids bickering over a name for a new puppy. It always names itself in the end. I'm good at improvisation. You'll get another christening yet, lady.'

The waiter came to the table with the bill discreetly folded on a plate. My wallet was in the inner pocket of my old, denim jacket, my life support system as it was dubbed by a whimsical groupie. As I reached for my wallet, my fingers found instead a scrap of paper carelessly thrust behind other, more vital documents. It was a cutting from a newspaper. I fished it out and gave it to her.

'Can you reckon that? See how I was thinking of you. Came across it while waiting in a Chinese takeaway on Merseyside.

Lead a colorful life, me. Hit the highspots in any town. I remembered the name and kept it. Don't ask me why.'

It was a News in Brief item from a posh daily.

'Following border incidents in Sudan, the Agricultural Agency of the United Nations in Khartoum is concerned about the safety of an experimental settlement on the upper reaches of the White Nile. The leader of the experimental team, Professor Klaus Narraway and his wife, Dr. Suriya Narraway, failed to make their usual report last week. Since then, all radio and telephone links to the settlement have been severed.'

She turned the cutting over in a futile gesture as if the back of it might possibly provide more information.

'When did you see this?'

'Three, four weeks ago.'

'They must be safe then. There would be more of an issue about it if they were in danger. It's the sort of thing the papers go overboard about.'

'I expect so.'

'You haven't seen more about it anywhere?'

'No, but I don't go in for reading papers or watching television. Whole wars and disasters pass me by.'

'I don't watch television either.' She shivered though the night was warm. 'But for a different reason.'

I paid and we left the restaurant. She regarded the banknotes with some anxiety as they disappeared on the white plate. 'The lollipop?' she asked. 'I think I'd better stand you a drink in a very cosy pub so that you can tell me all about it. Before I let you pay out for my meals again, I need to be convinced that the lollipop isn't a very tiny boiled sweet.'

The lollipop had been discovered not at the end of a rainbow, but at the end of a telephone. And it was I that had been discovered. In Liverpool, the home of mob rule when it came to the Kop, those soccer supporters to whom I felt I owed an unspecified debt. Discovered, I might add, not by the fleshpots of tin pan alley, but by culture with a capital K. BBC 2, would you credit it? A type called Roger, but I'm not particular, I won't hold that against him, left a note and would I call him at his hotel that very night as he was going back to Town by the early train.

'I admire Londoners of that class, I really do. Town with a capital T. As if no other town in the kingdom is entitled to the name.'

'Did you call him in spite of his lapse?'

'But, natch, what else? He'd heard me play, had been at the gig that night. Said he'd particularly liked the settings that I'd given old poems and rhymes. Then he came out with the usual garbage about the continuity of a cultural heritage. All this in a plummy voice with strangled vowels. I listened to him and said yes, yes and yes.'

'Nothing more?'

'I added a bit about mixed marriage of old and new, miscegenation. Verse meters and rock rhythms lending a new dimension to each other, and he came down a little cautious way from his high horse. He had me cast as an untutored native, a noble savage. It's the Aussie accent. It makes all Pommies think we're uneducated and inarticulate.'

'Which of course, you are not.' She was teasing me gently and I was glad to heat it.

'We are mainly, but don't start me on the Australian problem, I'd keep going all night. I finally got Rog down to brass tacks. He shudders when I call him Rog so it's irresistible. It appears that he is getting together a series of concerts for the Beeb. Late night, low budget and experimental . . .'

'How fantastic for you.'

'Cool your enthusiasm, lady. They are each to be quite short and nobody will watch them. They are to be based on visual themes. He is asking musicians of all types and complexions to compose new works around a series of pictures that he will shoot but will be chosen by the musicians themselves. He wondered, in his plummy voice, whether the idea appealed to me and if I might have some ideas for a song or two.'

'Stop laughing and tell me what happened.'

'Ideas, I told Rog, were coming out of every orifice. I just wanted a market stall on which to display my wares. "Oh, in that case," says he, "do you think you could possibly manage a whole program based on the sort of material I heard tonight?" Yes, dear Rog, you bet your life I could. He said goodie, and I said how about an advance. He said that they didn't work like that, but eventually he scraped through the budget and found a trifling sum. Let me tell you that the same trifling sum is about what I'd been living on for months. So, I've come to London to seek my fortune like in all the best fairy tales and I've even found me a lady in distress.'

'No fairy godmother?'

'But definitely. That's Rog. But I also have a bundle of hard work, hard thinking and hard playing ahead. I must work out some themes.'

She didn't gush, hoot or pry. She expressed delight and encouragement with shining eyes and quiet words. Altogether a very superior lady; and, I have to admit, that I hoped that Laura's return in about ten days—for that was the length of time that I could hold on to my tenancy of Laura's bed—would cause, by force majeure, the obvious and simple solution to the accommodation problem. On the shallow level where I have always operated when it comes to my love life, it did seem to me that Ned was taking his time to step forth and claim her. She was resigned to wait, but I knew that I'd soon find chivalry was more than a trifle irksome.

We established a domestic routine as quickly as holiday tourists who, after eight days on the Costa Brava, come back home and say, we used to do this, or normally we did that, as if they'd been inhabitants of their synthetic, sun-drenched paradise for months. But it was surprising how quickly we found a workable pattern that included both our lives. We would travel to the center of London together each morning, she to go to her office and I to ramble through precious bits of the city rescued from reconstituted London. Rog and I had agreed on a London motif, a visual exploration highlighting a single building, a monument, a painting, a cornice, a carved doorway or the long sweep of windows in a crescent. He saw it as a voyage of rediscovery by the Wild Colonial Boy. I didn't care very much how he saw it. I was leading him by his thin, elegant nose to where I wanted to go.

Rambling is a weak word to describe the highly charged inner life that motivated my explorations. I probed into myself as carefully as into the hidden splendors of Apothecary's Hall, the church of St. Bartholomew the Great at Smithfield, Kenwood and the Middle Temple. I listened with my internal ear to the sound that sunlight makes on polished wood, or the chords in ancient stones. Pictures sang with their own luminosity, the ceiling of the Painted Hall in Greenwich thundered in march time. I skipped as many of the tourist-ridden places as I was able, but tourists go where these glories are preserved. Away from the crowd it is still possible to see surviving fragments shining in an ugly world: a cobbled yard, a tombstone, a wrought iron lamp standard, ivy on old stone walls; but never unscarred, never whole, only a pathetic leftover from a past with an unselfconscious aesthetic sense, rare enough to my hungry eyes, the blight had destroyed too much.

London is not a summer city. She is an old lady and can't show her face in the noonday sun, dirt and dust are bad for her complexion. Nor is she a winter city, she is eclipsed by the cold and grays in the bitter, harsh nights, though she cheers up at Christmas, taking an old tart's delight in cheap finery. But in spring and autumn she can recapture her good looks, become for a short season sprightly and handsome. Though not for much longer, she won't be able to manage the optical illusion for many more years. Architects and vandals have pillaged her. Neon, concrete, high-rises and hooligans have warped the great sweep of her river and diminished the soft twilight, dimmed the gray and the pink. The Wren skyline is hidden under a film of rubbish. I wanted to sing her elegy, a lament for a great, lost city.

With my head full of the sights and sounds of a quieter past, I would end my walkabout at Wardour Street and watch and wait for the moment when my other lady would run down the tatty stairs to meet me. Her face would lighten when she saw me, and I would see her brush away the fatigue and anxieties of the working day. I think she was always frightened that I wouldn't be there. Not because I'm feckless and footloose, she'd have understood that and she trusted me to tell her goodbye, a wave, a phone call, a postcard. She was terrified that I'd follow Ned into the vacuum and leave her dangerously close to madness.

Then we'd go to a pub, the one on the corner, which had a smoky wooden interior that hadn't been decorated for years where they serve a beer shandy with mint and cucumber. At the tag end of the August day, we'd drink our shandies and she would slowly unwind, chatting about Liz and the work until she would dwindle to a halt and afterward I'd tell her of my day as we went in search of a meal.

One evening, she said, 'Do you remember me telling you about the Raindew commercial? Well, I've been left on my own with it.' She was highly keyed, more tense than usual. 'It's up to me, now. Liz says she hasn't the time, but I'm not geared to that sort of responsibility yet. I'm not used to the pressure of handling large sums of money. And, besides, it involves Pippa.'

'Will you have to come in contact with her?'

'I want to.' Her hands were fists. She rubbed them against the bar table, old wood mellowed with generations of spilled ale. 'I want to. I must. That way there's still a chance that it might turn out all right. I might find the right turning. I have got to meet Pippa again and find out.'

'What do you think will happen?'

'I don't know. Perhaps she will recognize me. Or have some news of Ned. Up to now I've come up against comparative strangers, Marion Hill, the secretary at the school, Jamie . . . But Pippa . . . I can't believe that she can look at me and not know me. I won't believe it.'

My gut ached for her. 'Lady,' I said gently, 'prepare yourself. I think she won't know you. Prepare yourself by believing instead that she won't . . .'

'No!'

'Yes. It's the only road to any salvation or sanity.'

'Oh God!' She hammered the beer-soaked wood. 'Why, Face, tell me why?'

'You must have thought about it, sifted through some ideas. I know we've never discussed it. I was waiting for you to be ready to talk about it. Haven't you hit upon a theory? What do you think happened?'

Again the grateful look, the quiet smile of acknowledgement. She had been alone, unable to talk to anybody for there was nobody she could trust. She had resorted to censoring her thoughts as much as she could out of fear, lest they trap her into weakness and despair.

'Go on,' I urged, 'tell me what you think.'

She hunched forward, holding her half-pint glass between her denimed knees, eager and tense.

'I think that somehow, I don't know how it works, but somehow Ned and I were never born. Everybody else, all the other people in our lives, they were born and are doing all the things they might well have done whether Ned and I were around or not. It would make no difference whether we existed, not for them. We just . . . didn't get born. Naturally, then neither did my boys . . .'

Her voice cracked, so I said quickly, 'Who are you, then?'

She shrugged helplessly. 'I don't know.' She paused and then whispered, 'The sick answer is that I am Sarah.'

'You're not keen on that?'

'Would you be after what I've learned about her?'

'O.K. So what about the guy who recognized you as Unity? And the time you heard Ned on the radio?'

She shrugged again. 'It's still only my word for it. I can't prove either incident happened. I don't know and I expect that I never shall.'

She petered out into despondency. I took her glass and went for refills. I watched as I waited at the bar, the intensity of her concentration etched lines over her forehead. As I settled back with the drinks she leaned toward me and spoke very fast.

'Listen, if it were a proper haunting, like in a ghost story, the sort of now-you-see-me-now-you-don't conjuring tricks, I'd understand it better. I think I might even accept it almost. But when these occurrences, for want of a better word, happen, there is no alteration of the reality about me, no change in perception. I suppose that there is only one available answer, and you pay your money and you take your pick. Either Sarah is a very sick lady, or I am right. I am Unity, held back in exile by a gossamer wall, a veil that occasionally lifts . . . haunted by my own life on the other side of an invisible, intangible screen. Why, Face, why me?'

'Where is Sarah, I wonder? With Ned?'

I shouldn't have said that, for her face fell apart and I could see the shock waves travel through her body.

'I never thought of that,' she whispered.

I had to make it easier, joke her out of the self pity that was always lurking behind her courage. 'Oh, come on! Where would they be hiding then? Gone to Brighton for a dirty weekend? From what you've told me of the pair of them, I don't reckon the relationship would last very long. They wouldn't like each other very much.'

'No, they wouldn't. Poor Ned.'

She made a wintry attempt at a smile, but I had to change the subject. She had spent the day preparing to confront Pippa in this alien world, and now I had tactlessly bedded Sarah with Ned. She was unable to take a dose of such heavy medicine.

I said, 'Well, I spent the day fleeing from my fellow countrymen.'

'Oh?'

'I went into a pub at lunch-time for a beer and a sandwich and found that it sold Foster's.'

'Is that bad?' Brave lady, she tried to raise a very flat interest.

'Aussies come in two types. Type A flog around Europe in dormobiles. They despise Frogs and Poms, want everything to be like home, are homesick all the time and have a large Waltzing Matilda bubble coming out of their backsides. They live in Kangaroo Valley and go home after a few months thankfully having, they tell the folks back home, seen the world.'

'And type B?' More interested now. 'You?'

'We're the invisible ones . . .'

'Oh . . .'

'Well, almost. Do you know that the English National Opera is fed from Sydney? A proper type B doesn't want to escape from home, he will even go back there occasionally, but he can thrive and bloom better in an older culture. One day he finds that he's become resident and forgets his origins till the press rake them up. Shall I give you a list of closet Aussies?'

'No, most decidedly not.' But she was smiling now. 'Where do you fit in?'

'I'm halfway, me. I'll go home when I'm not hungry any more. When I don't need the snow, a stained glass window soft with age, Le Palais des Papes, or Glastonbury wallowing in far too many legends. When, and if, I have no more appetite for these, I'll go home and contemplate the hot, wide, dry emptiness of home with its skirt of surf nibbling at the edges . . .'

'And me? Where will I be?'

Laugh, lady, laugh. Don't drown in regret. So I clowned, I exaggerated my accent. I embroidered the account of my lunch-time adventure. I launched into a ridiculous anecdote. 'This hefty blonde complained that all Brits smelled. "Don't they ever take a shower? I can't breathe on the Tube trains." Her buddy said, "Hold your nose, Diane, this pub is full of Brits." Diane gaped, "No kidding? How did they get in here?" '

It was a nice smile, polite, the cocktail party smile of one whose attention is elsewhere. Two gay boys, slim faggots mincing up the ladder to queen bee, had sat at our neighboring table and were gossiping, theatrical gossip, intimate, knowing and unavoidable.

'My friend, you know who I mean, the one who works in wardrobe at the studios. He's quite definite. Padded, he says, no doubt at all.'

'Padded or not, Louis, she's like Dietrich, indestructible.'

'Not Dietrich, Martin, definitely not Dietrich. Streisand per-haps. Not quite Wasp, if you see what I mean.'

'But she's ever so Wasp. Not a touch of the tar brush any-where. Not like some. Not that it matters in this day and age. Do you know Stuart? Yes, you do, dear, you met him in that bar the other evening. He was at Drama School with her. Ever so close they were, he says he always knew she'd go far. She had that little extra. What we all need, don't we? Stuart told her, "Pippa, you'll go far, dear, if you can develop a bust." '

She was listening transfixed, tuned into the tittle tattle. Pippa had become, it would seem, one of the Grandes Dames of the gay circuit, one of the line from Piaf to Garland who exude a larger than life ebullience, a grotesque femininity that lacks any tinge of a cosy domesticity. I was concentrating on her, watching her suffer this travesty of her Pippa, so that I can only recall in retrospect the next ration of twittering.

'I've no time for him at all. Well really, Louis, I ask you. Such a dreary little man.'

'He must have something if Waters is so keen on him. I've heard that she likes to use him in all her sketches if he's available.'

'Let's just hope he's not available.'

'I'm sorry, Martin, but I do think he has a little something. He's not *au dessus de sa gare* like some I could mention. You must admit that whatever else Ned Roland is, he is not big-headed . . .'

She leaped up, a bar stool spinning from her like an overgrown top.

'Who?' she demanded through the clatter. She confronted them, trembling and wild. 'Who are you talking about? You must tell me.'

They looked at her agape, then they turned to each other in a little pantomime of exasperated surprise, though not much would surprise them ever. What knowledge they might have had she had driven back behind sallow and shallow features.

'Who were you talking about? Please tell me, please. You must.'

'What do you mean . . . must. Cheek!'

'You shouldn't listen to other people's private conversations.'

'Who do you think you are, anyway?'

She sat by their table on a spare stool and forced herself to speak reasonably. They recoiled from her in exaggerated horror.

'I didn't mean to overhear, I'm sorry, but I couldn't help it. You were talking about Pippa Waters and I am . . . interested. Then you said something about Ned Roland. You were talking about Ned Roland,' she insisted into their blank faces.

'Never heard of him.'

'No, who's he?'

'You were talking about him just now. You said he worked with Pippa Waters when he was available . . .'

'No I didn't. You must be hearing things. I never said anything like that, did I, Martin? You didn't say anything, did you, dear?'

'No, not a thing. If you've finished your vino, Louis, I think we'd best be getting along. It's getting a bit crowded in here. Funny types, you know.'

She grabbed one, Louis I think, and held him by the arm. She appealed to me. 'Please, Face, you heard him, didn't you? You heard him mention Ned. Please, don't let him go. I must know about Ned.'

The other drinkers began to enjoy the little scene and Louis played up to it. He squealed and beat feebly at her offending hands as if they had been snakes.

I had no choice. I said, 'I'm sorry. I don't know for certain what he said. I wasn't listening to him. I just don't know.'

She released him, betrayed. To underline his victory, Louis smiled at me winningly and said, 'One of those sort, is she? Poor you. Honestly, love, I'd tell you anything if I knew what she wanted. As it is, I haven't a glimmer.'

He and Martin then made an ostentatious job of leaving the pub. They turned in the doorway, deliberately provocative, and favored us with a withering stare.

'Funny lady.'

'But he's so butch.'

Exeunt with flourishes. Afterward, I took her away quickly and we went home and cooked up some eggs. She was withdrawn and bitter, and though she knew that her anger against me was unjust, I was the only object in sight. I accepted it in silence and soon it melted leaving exhaustion in its wake. I longed to hold her, give her comfort, joy, physical release, kiss clean the fright and the pain; but she wasn't ready for me yet. She was bound to her hidden world, remote from me. Sir Galahad was uncomfortable that night. The halo kept slipping.

Another day passed. Another day of rambling, full of reward and interest. I never planned my routes. I'd take a starting point, a gallery, a museum, a library and I'd meander from there. Toward evening, I found myself wandering from Fleet Street to the Strand when I passed by Somerset House. A fleeting idea that had been skipping about my mind came back to me and I walked under the narrow archway until stopped by a uniformed commissionaire, a retired soldier with a row of long service medal ribbons.

'Can I help you, sir?'

'You most certainly can, sport.' I became all Tourist with a capital T. 'What goes on in this building?'

'Quite a lot of things, sir. A great deal. Just here, for instance, we have the Registry, Family Division, Probate and Divorce. But that's not for you, is it, sir? I reckon I know what you're looking for. Yes, we used to have Births, Deaths and Marriages but they've gone to Kingsway.'

'Oh, they have, have they. Where in Kingsway?'

'St. Catherine's House. Number 10. Corner of Kingsway and

Aldwych. Are you looking for an ancestor, sir?' He smiled benevolently. He must have seen us in our dozens looking for a genuine convict to take back home in triumph.

'Yes, you could say that I was, in a way.' I turned to go, but he put out a fatherly hand and pulled me back.

'No good now, sir. No point in hurrying. Five-thirty, you see. It'll be closed. Government departments aren't like the big stores, sir. You'll have to find great granddad tomorrow.'

'Thank you, sport. One thing, though. Isn't Probate all about a bloke's Last Will and Testament?'

'Yes, sir.'

'Can I take a look at any Will I want?'

'Any that have been proved, sir.'

'Now?'

'No, sir. Like I said. Government department. Wouldn't do to keep it open to the public all day, now would it, sir?'

Next morning, I went straight to Kingsway. The Will could wait until I had proof of Doctor Samuel's birth. In the Search Room, I laboriously filed slips for the birth certificates of Samuel and Unity Penfold. Susan had to be left as I didn't know her maiden name.

The birth of Samuel Adam Hope Penfold was recorded in Chichester in 1907, but of Unity's birth there was no trace.

'It's as if I had never been born.'

A longer search and I found Dr. Samuel's marriage certificate. I had to make an approximate guess at the date and work back and forth until I hit the correct year. He and Susan Hilary were married early in 1937, a year before Klaus was pulled from the gas ovens that were waiting for him. Where was Unity?

I checked Samuel's death and went back to my friend in Probate and Divorce. The Will was simple: half to his wife, Susan; and half to his godson, Klaus Narraway. Facts, more and more facts to substantiate Unity's conviction that all were present and correct, all accountable, the characters of her little opera singing sweetly in the right key; all, that is, except herself and Ned. I didn't even attempt to check on him. There were a thousand Edward Taylors born every month. I needed more information and I wasn't keen to waste time on a search for which I expected a negative result.

Samuel had left a substantial sum. They had lived frugally; he had lectured, published, perhaps inherited money. I wondered where it had gone on Susan's death, so with a wild notion of bringing home the family fortune to lay at my lady's feet, I looked up Susan's Will.

No Will.

Back to Kingsway. Susan was not dead. You can learn a surprising amount about a person's life from scraps of paper, especially if you have my overdeveloped inquisitive streak. I had had the sense to note the defunct Samuel's address from the Will. I dialed Directory Inquiries and asked for Mrs. Susan Penfold of the above address. An impersonal voice delivered to me a set of digits as if it were a normal occurrence to give you the phone number of the dead. I am a rational being and I baulked at that, and dug deep into my memory of the garbled life history at Euston Station. My memory failed; but either way, I now had Unity's mother at the end of a long rein and I could haul her in whenever I wanted to.

On an impulse, I dialed her number, my brain concocting wild cover stories. The long lost Australian cousin was too much, even for me.

'Hello?' The distant voice quavered an uncertain question, an old voice intolerant of interruption.

'May I speak to Mrs. Penfold?'

'Speaking.'

'My name is Phil ... lips, Jeremy Phillips. May I have your daughter's address or phone number, please?'

'Whom do you want?'

'Your daughter. I'm an old friend of her husband, Ned Roland.'

'I'm sorry. You have the wrong number.'

'Mrs. Penfold, I'm looking for your daughter, Unity.' I stopped there because I thought I heard her gasp, a hurried intake of breath, the body's reaction to threat. 'Your daughter, Unity Penfold.'

'I've just told you. You have made a mistake. You must have been given the wrong number. I've ... I've ... I haven't any children.'

'But, Mrs. Penfold ...'

'I don't want to talk to you. Please, don't bother me any more. I am not at all well.'

She rang off. I nursed the receiver, trying to catch, hold and analyse her final inflection, that gasp that could easily be no more than an asthmatic cough. But there had been a subtext, I was sure of that. I had detected a note of panic and distress, a skeleton rattling in the cupboard. Stop that overactive imagination, Mallet, most likely it was nothing more than the normal reaction of the elderly and infirm to a disturbing and intrusive phone call.

It was, none the less, a pretty catch for a morning's fishing. An old trout at the end of a line and, as far as I could judge, no red herrings. Shall I leave this haul to stink and rot in the August sun, or must you, lady, weak as you are, gut it for yourself?

I went on walking down the Strand to the quiet of the National Portrait Gallery where I sat in the oldest room and thought of a poem that needed a melody. I had my own and very private poetry that was asking to be sung; but I had to store the insistent images away to root more deeply in the darkness and borrow from my betters. Roger did not yet trust a barbarian's tongue, but he would. Yes, by God, he would.

Two days to Laura's return and I had a gig in Chelsea. Thursday night is Folk Night at this pub and it had a good reputation among aficionados. I asked her to come with me.

'I'm going to try out one of the pieces I've been brewing up for Rog. He'd spew pink kittens if he knew, but I've never worked without a direct contact with an audience before. I want you to tell me what you think of it and, more important, what you think that they think of it.'

'Is that English?'

'None, but It's Show Biz.'

The night was hot and packs of the young spilled over the pavement, but even so, the back bar which housed the Folk Club was crowded like rush hour, hot and heady, full of the bravado that comes with being young, healthy and wealthy, and standing up bravely to clobber all the things that Daddy stands for that allow them to be healthy and wealthy and privileged. My taste runs more to real people, kids with guts because they had no silver spoons, less beautiful, less clever, but also less petulant and demanding. But this was Chelsea not Newcastle.

The kids were young, some extravagantly so. I saw many an

under-aged drinker of bitter beer. The landlord must be turning the blind eye of one who knows better than to challenge this category of young to back up his middle-aged judgment. A bold stare and a blatant lie would be the most courteous answer he'd be likely to receive. Besides it was a club and, for all I knew, different rules might apply.

A young doxy who must have been all of fourteen, lithe and tall in straight jeans and her grandfather's shirt, pushed herself eagerly in my direction, but pulled back with a pout when she saw that I was not alone.

'It's no use, Em,' I heard her shout above the babble. 'He's booked. And he is a real dish. Why do all the dishy ones get booked?'

We struggled through to the table reserved for us. Her smile was thin and strained. 'You are free, you know. There are no ties. As you know, I'm not offering you very much.'

'That one? You're joking. Statutory rape. She's a morsel of jail bait. And I prefer women, not children.'

'Yes, I'm sorry. I'm feeling a bit exposed here, over sensitive. I am, after all, old enough to be her mother.'

The reference to motherhood, which I had expected to conjure up a storm of tears, slipped by without a comment. Her concentration was focused on her imagined rivals, so I took a chance and nudged the conversation further along, a dangerous course.

'You'd have to have been a child bride. All the same. I imagine it's a tricky moment for a woman when her daughter starts to poach on her territory and the predatory male glance passes her over and lights on the girl.'

The organizer of the evening bustled over at that point and fussed over drinks and arrangements. I cursed him, the interruption had lost the logical train I was pursuing, but she didn't seem to notice the ridiculous non sequitur when three minutes later I topped the loud chatter and shouted, 'How did you get on with your mother?'

'We were very distant. She was a reserved person, almost cold. I don't think she received from life what she wanted. She was always unable to reach out to us, either to me or my father.'

'You talk in the past. Is she dead then?'

'She died about two years before father. She was still quite young. I think she wanted more children. A son. I suppose I wasn't enough, not the child she really wanted. She should have had a hysterectomy, but she refused, still hoping for the son. Ironic because that is what killed her.'

'Cancer?'

'Of the womb. There's a moral there somewhere. The wrong growth inside her, killing her instead of producing new life.'

Whether I was going to tell her or not, I don't know because we were stopped by a burst of clapping and a dimming of lights. At the adjacent table, the first singer perched her backside on the table, placed her foot on a chair to balance her guitar and strummed some preliminary chords to let the chatter die down and the room settle into a living expectancy. They were going to be a responsive audience, if we could hold them. They wanted to listen, become involved with the patterns of words and sounds, the simplistic and basic ritual that creates folk music.

The girl was a poor guitarist but she had a good voice. A rich chest voice with no tricks. She was an honest craftswoman and the audience loved her. She would be hard to follow.

When it was my turn, I did some fancy finger work to show them that I could, and then I let the guitar speak alone for a while to give them a lull and lower the emotional temperature. Then I pounded out a rip-roaring favorite at full speed and strength that had them clapping in the choruses and chanting a comic refrain. They were with me then.

Two more songs, letting my voice mellow and my fingers flow with a life of their own devising, and I was ready to try my new one. I thought about the painting that had led me to the poem. A Cavalier in lace and velvet sending a *billet-doux* to his lady via a serving wench. The lady in the background simpered behind her fan and the Cavalier waited, his hat in his right hand, a feathered plume about to be flourished in a courtly bow, while his lecherous left hand, hidden from the lady, crept around the back of the serving wench and caressed her breast.

I gave them a word or two about the painting, and then I began. A good, strong, lyrical melody for the first three lines of the stanza, an elegant modulation for the short middle lines and finally, a heavy rolling beat for the punch line.

> *Let us drink and be merry, dance, joke and rejoice,*
> *With claret and sherry, theorbo and voice!*
> *The changeable world to our joy is unjust.*
> > *All treasure's uncertain*
> > *Then down with your dust!*
> *In frolics dispose your pounds, shillings and pence,*
> *For we shall be nothing a hundred years hence.*

A ripple of laughter, but no more than a commitment to listen further.

> *We'll sport and be free with Moll, Betty and Dolly,*
> *Have oysters and lobsters to cure melancholy:*
> *Fish dinners will make a man spring like a flea,*
> > *Dame Venus, love's lady,*
> > *Was born of the sea:*
> *With her and with Bacchus we'll tickle the sense,*
> *For we shall be past it a hundred years hence.*

Loud, firm laughter that time. I thought of the centuries spanned by the idiomatic final line of the stanza, contemporary slang that needed no translation. I laughed with them.

> *Your most beautiful bride who with garlands is crowned*
> *And kills with each glance as she treads on the ground,*
> *Whose lightness and brightness doth shine in such splendor*
> > *That none but the stars*
> > *Are thought fit to attend her,*
> *Though now she be pleasant and sweet to the sense*
> *Will be damnably moldy a hundred years hence.*

A roar of laughter, then the buzz of an excited awareness of a new experience, an innovation that they could accept, no easy matter for such rabid traditionalists as folk fanatics.

> *Then why should we turmoil in cares and in fears,*
> *Turn all our tranquill'ty to sighs and to tears?*
> *Let's eat, drink and play till the worms do corrupt us,*

> 'Tis certain, Post Mortem
> Nulla voluptas,
> For health, wealth and beauty, wit, learning and sense
> Must all come to nothing a hundred years hence.

Through the applause, a solid wall of sound that had held back for the exactly right few seconds of assessment and appreciation before it burst, she spoke to me, her features lovely with the fullness of her enjoyment.

'Wonderful, Face, truly. Auntie Beeb and Roger almost don't deserve it. But he'll be delighted, he'll have to be. And you must show me the painting. It seems to fit almost miraculously. Oh, Face, are you not pleased?'

'Not all that much,' I said, though I nearly was. 'It needs a lot more work yet. It needs to be more sophisticated, less rollicking for the program. It ought to be more subtle. I played it for laughs tonight, for fun. I must dig out the underlying streak of sadness.'

'No, please, no. There's enough sadness. It was so lovely. I wish I had a recording of it.'

'So do I. If I had, I'd be rich, rich, rich, I tell you. Beyond the dreams of a penniless minstrel. Then I could take you away from all this.' I gestured manically, high on the music and the applause.

'I'll give you a copy for Christmas,' she promised without thought. She saw neither the irony nor the commitment implicit to that promise.

I took her hand and kissed the soft skin on the inside of her wrist.

'I'll hold you to that.'

'No problem. Rog is going to make you a star.'

'A drink before they close?'

'Then we can walk home singing.'

'Can you sing, lady? I've never heard you.'

'No, I'm not that stupid. I've got a weedy voice, a pathetic little warble that can't keep in pitch. But I want to sing tonight for the first time in years.'

'Why tonight?'

'I want to sing. To serenade Roger.'

'Hold on, you're skipping to my tune.'

'I'm hot. It's so hot in here. Oh, it's such fun. I didn't realize that there was still fun in the world. I haven't been able to believe anything as lovely and crazy as fun.'

After the heat of the bar the air seemed cool, but it was a rare summer's night. Doors and windows of every house and restaurant were open wide, the secret lives of Londoners were spilling out into the streets.

'It's like Paris,' she said, flinging out her arms. 'I can't remember when it was that I went to Paris, but I do know I've been there. It was a long, long time ago. A lifetime ago. Paris in the spring.'

'Lady, you are a trifle pissed.'

'I am. I most certainly am. But I am having fun. And, my fine Aussie friend, I am also hungry.'

'We'll eat in the streets.'

'A kebab, or spring roll, or fish and chips, or . . .'

'No fish and chips. The shops have all been sold.'

'I see one. Chips ahoy! Look, Face, there's a fish and chip shop.'

'The last fish and chip shop in the West.'

'South West ten, to be accurate.'

'Limp cod and two pennorth?'

'No, I want flaccid haddock and six pennorth.'

'Vinegar and salt?'

'Of course.'

We strolled through streets alive with summer, eating messily from paper packages with greasy fingers and laughter.

She flicked away a bone. 'Fish dinners.'

'Definitely make a man spring like a flea.'

'I love that poem. I don't suppose our Cavalier meant this plebeian stuff.'

'No, only the best. Lobsters, oysters. Shellfish is meant to be an aphrodisiac.'

'A pint of whelks?'

'Cockles and mussels, alive, alive O.'

We sang ourselves back to our secret house. In the privacy of the hallway, I drew her toward me as she searched for her door key. She hesitated, but then came to me and nestled into the shape of my body. Slowly and gently, I raised her head and saw her eyes were soft with consent. I bent to kiss her and I felt her lips accept mine, an enchantment, willing to give and take, a beginning and a growth.

Then she screamed and I lost her. Her body stiffened and the magic collapsed like soggy toast. Before I could ask questions, I saw her eyes staring in terror at somebody behind me.

I didn't let time pass for thought, I couldn't afford it. I pushed her to one side and turned in a spin, crouching, so that when I came up, my shoulders caught him in the chest. He was unbalanced and I whipped him around and held him in an arm lock before he could blink; but he wasn't a fighter anyway, so the effort was wasted.

She was kneeling on the carpet, sobbing, the fun knocked out of her like wind. I might have to rebuild my tarnished image for her later, but meanwhile this creature was going to get a kick in the balls. I was going to confirm my guess when I smelled him. She was right, he stank; and now fear had released another layer of rank sweat.

'Hefty, isn't he?' he sniggered. 'Paying for brawn now, ducky. You must have a good job for you to be able to afford him.'

'Watch it, you bastard!' Then I hesitated. I wanted to finish him off and throw his body to the vultures, but I was reluctant to leave her, a crumpled, pitiful heap. He sensed my hesitation and it gave him a chance for a final sick act of revenge.

'Shall I tell you what she likes? All the details? One professional to another. You want to do the job properly . . .'

He said enough by the time I broke his front teeth, a few snippets of obscene advice that wouldn't shame a sailor's brothel. Her heart was breaking on the floor but I had to leave her.

'Go on in,' I told her gently. 'I'll be back when I've broken a few bones.'

I took him into the mews opposite and roughed him up some more, but it seemed an unprofitable exercise. It wasn't a warning; he wouldn't come by again if he thought I was there, and his damage had been done. There was no remedy for that, no easy healing. He had extinguished a glowing spark that might well have blazed into a flame that he would never know, even in dreams. His dirt had tarnished more than his imagination could encompass. The blight would take a long time to cure.

He was down on his knees and snivelling. I was contaminated by handling such vermin, so I walked away from him and back up to the flat to see what I could salvage from the wreckage.

'I'm sorry, Face, I'm sorry. It's unkind to you. To us both, but more to you and what might have been. I can't now. Not any more. I can't. I feel it was a punishment for betraying Ned ...'

'Lady ...'

'I'm not ready yet. I'm sorry. Maybe not ever. I shouldn't have let you think ... I can't touch anybody. Anyone who has truth and love and honesty. Not until I can be certain, until I know for certain that I was never touched by him. He taints love. He makes it as ugly as death.'

I know, and what comfort can I offer? I had known the same revulsion as I punched his swollen cheeks. I could walk away, but he had claimed her, stated his one-time ownership. Against that she could offer no proof to refute him, nothing except her fierce loathing and the memory of another love that she must cherish though none believe her. And I was the loser. Now she had to cling to Ned, to the precious memory more closely than ever. He was the bolster against insanity.

'And, Face, I can't stay in this flat. Not here, not any more. He might come back. I'll always be terrified. Never feel easy coming up the stairs or staying in alone. Do you remember the night when you knocked on the door? I thought it was ... was ... that animal. But where will I go? What will I do? And oh God, Face, what right have I to ask you for anything?'

'You'll see, we'll think of something. Tomorrow, not now. Tomorrow.'

But Friday was a lost day. Laura's imminent return and yesterday's shock hung over us. She was exhausted and incompetent at work; and I, the housing situation a brooding issue, made an abortive attempt to be constructive. I inserted myself into the grapevine of Kangaroo Valley, hoping to snare some departing youth whose about-to-be-vacated bed would solve the problem temporarily for myself. But all I encountered were enthusiastic newcomers with cash enough in their pockets to pay for expensive and seedy rooms, and green enough to see the discomfort as part of the experience of 'doing Europe.' Thus the effort I made was unproductive and debilitating and wasted a day's good work, a day when musical patterns were running clear and I could still reach for the excitement of the gig before it evaporated. By the time I met her in Wardour Street, I was as jangled as she. We went back to the flat and she cooked an unappetizing fry-up that she forgot to eat. Her face was closed to me, withdrawn and sore.

We didn't speak. There was little to say and neither of us could give the other the comfort and ease we wanted. I couldn't give her Ned, or remove the crawling, spider fear of John Lang's claim. And neither could she come back to me again with softened eyes, willing lips and a warm and ready promise. As for the practical problems, we knew them well enough. There was little point in a discussion that could yield no solution and only aggravate the fret and the desperation.

We kept the radio on to hide our inability to communicate. LBC, all news and comment. My mood would not have taken kindly to bad music. The news churned on predictably, the usual ration of chaos and stupidity. Then a familiar name sprang from the gabble and we were on the alert at once.

'The whereabouts of Professor Klaus Narraway is giving rise to some concern. The situation on the Sudanese border continues to be very confused and reports from the area speak of sporadic fighting. The experimental ecological settlement, led by Professor Narraway, has been completely wiped out. It had been carrying out long-term research which would have been of great benefit to the area's future. Troops entered the settlement yesterday and found the bodies of the research team and their families as well as some of the local population who were working on the project. Although the body of Dr. Suriya Narraway, the wife of the settlement's leader, was found among those slain, that of her husband was not found and it is rumored that he is being held by the terrorists as a hostage, though this is not confirmed by the Sudanese Government who deny that the destruction of the settlement was a political act. They said, in a statement issued this morning, that the strength of the terrorists, who are in strong opposition to the current leadership, is much exaggerated and that the tragedy at the settlement was the result of criminal not political action.'

I switched off the radio.

'I don't know what to say other than I'm sorry. Things are piling up for you more than somewhat at the moment.'

'I'm sorry too.'

Her face was without expression, nothing of her distress showed through, but when she spoke after a pause it was with a subdued intensity. 'Not for myself. Understand that. I'm not sorry for myself at all. He wouldn't have recognized me. Seeing him again wouldn't have changed anything. He wouldn't have known me any more than Pippa will. I've been deleted, excised. The only person who recognizes me for certain is John Lang.' Her laughter brushed the edge of hysteria. 'John Lang knows who I am. Klaus wouldn't have. But I am sorry for him. He would hate more than anything to see his work destroyed, his people murdered, his wife dead. He would be lost among the greed and the violence. Poor Klaus. Poor, darling Klaus.'

She cried quietly and I let her, for her tears were gentle and could bring her relief and a small measure of healing. We went to our respective beds early for there was little more to be said that evening and tomorrow would need a decision and, maybe, a parting. I went to Laura's room but not to sleep. I had done nothing all day, had made no music, was unused and wasted. I needed work like a junkie needs a fix. I picked up my guitar and played, softly so I wouldn't disturb her, but it didn't still my restlessness or provide the right tone to satisfy my mood. I wanted a note, a mode, a tune, I didn't know what, but something to calm me, to spur me, to pin the scattered emotions and direct them to a channel, a creativity.

I paced about Laura's room and picked at her belongings like a dispirited sparrow. Not at her music, for I didn't want to hear any, I wanted to make it. Her prints and her books promised more. But the books soon became no more than hunks of print, too heavy or too light, both metaphorically and actually as she appeared to have no taste for poetry; and her pictures were trite through overwork, they were reproduced well and widely.

At the far end of her bookcase was a wedge of small books parked sideways in a neat pile to save space. One was a school Bible and I fished it out, an idea stirring, an excited quickening.

Mourning and bereavement and the calm, eternal ritual to comfort and assuage. A picture came to fill the image: the great circle of round, solid Norman pillars in St. Bartholomew the Great, the majestic sweep of the Ambulatories, the calm reassurance of old stone. Then a shaft of sunlight through a mullioned window and the austere beauty of Plainsong. An affirmation and a confidence trick.

After a clumsy search, for I am not renowned for Biblical studies, I found what I was looking for. I reached for my guitar and struck some harsh Dylan-esque chords, borrowed his nasal tones, his stern rectitude.

> *Or ever the sun and the light*
> *And the moon and the stars*
> *Be darkened and the clouds return*
> *After the rain:*
> *In the day, when the keepers of the house*
> *Shall tremble,*
> *And the strong men shall bow themselves*
> *And the grinders cease*
> *Because they are few . . .*

It worked. Just and only just. It would shock, I hoped, make the imagery come alive again, the Jacobean prose of the Authorized Version bouncing off the Blues, Old Testament poetry given the rhythms of a Work Song.

> *And the almond tree shall blossom,*
> *And the grasshopper shall be a burden*
> *And desire shall fail . . .*

Less Bob Dylan now, much less. More Mallet. Dylan had given me the booster shot, shown me that it could be done. I discarded him. Reached for my own illumination.

> *Or ever the silver chord be loosed,*
> *Or the golden bowl be broken*
> *Or the pitcher*

> *Broken at the fountain,*
> *Or the wheel broken at the cistern,*
> *And the dust return to the earth . . .*

It was after three o'clock before I fell asleep, my head whirling. I was hopeful that I'd found two jumbo-sized goodies for Dodgy Roger. *One shall rise with the voice of a bird . . .*

I slept late. So late that Laura walked into her room and yelped. A naked man! I've never owned pajamas and the night was too hot for covers, but reason was beyond her. She backed out nervously and I heard her twitter and witter as if she'd been confronted by a flasher.

'Sarah, oh golly Sarah, are you in? I've just come home and there's a man in my bed. Without clothes. Whatever is he doing there? I had such a fright, I didn't know what to do.'

As I dressed, I heard the soothing voice calming Laura's nerves with coffee and explanations. Roy's name apparently made me kosher in her eyes, so by the time I joined the coffee party, I was welcome.

Laura had come back early in the morning to get things sorted out before starting work on Monday, she had shopping to do and needed to restock her larder and so on. She liked to get back into the swing gently. She'd had a super time, a trifle dull, Mummy and Daddy were getting on, you know, but really, an absolutely super time. She was very glad that Roy had spoken about her. Matter of fact she had received a postcard from him. She had it in her handbag. She was so very glad that I forgot to mention that Roy had a doxy on each knee at the very moment he was being so liberal with her address.

Here it was: the future was upon us. We both made the noises expected of us about moving out and leaving the room for the other. She wanted to escape from the threat of John Lang and I had no claim to the room anyway. But we wanted to remain together for our own complicated reasons; and if Laura was bewildered that we didn't simply shack up together, she had to stay that way. Neither of us was prepared to spell out for her sake a relationship which we had failed to sort out for ourselves.

The question of the two girls doubling up and leaving the other room for me was discussed but was not popular, though it was, clearly, the only solution for the weekend. It was decided that they would fiddle the rooms, arrange it how best they may and, meanwhile, it was my job to find other accommodation for us while Laura advertised for a replacement for the vacated room.

Decisions are notoriously easier to make than to execute, but progress of a sort had been made and, I was certain, I was due a large ration of luck to provide the solution. I had been more than usually clean-living, hard-working, forbearing and even, a new one, chivalrous. If all that virtue hadn't stored up enough good will for the Fates to manipulate me into a flat, then I'd take to a life of crime. In the event I was proved right. Somebody up there loved me.

On Monday, I had tried my ideas out on Rog who had gone overboard with enthusiasm. He had run like a sprinter around the ambulatory of St. Bart's, making a little square of his fingers and uttering delighted moans as camera shot after camera shot occurred to him. My two-timing Cavalier had him muttering about dissolves and actors, an idea I found appalling. We were arguing hard by lunchtime so he took me to an Italian restaurant in Soho where the cognoscenti know that you go to the unadvertised first floor to eat. It was crammed with Beeb types and one came and sat at our table and gossiped to Rog. He wondered— would you credit it?—he wondered whether Rog knew of a reliable person, somebody that he, Rog, could vouch for, some reliable person to look after his flat for six months while he was away in Washington. I mean, it was a marvelous opportunity to be sent to the States, promotion too, but he couldn't give up his flat, he'd never find another nearly as nice. He couldn't leave it empty, not with vandals and burglars and there simply hadn't been the time to vet a reputable agency ... I let him ramble on and looked at him with a seraphic smile, my dark, brown smile reserved for doxies, landlords and BBC types. I told him that his troubles were over; and with Rog on my side—after all I was genius of the month—the deed was done. We could move in on Sunday week. The Fates had even thrown in a suitable address.

Far from the hunting grounds of John Lang, but not, as I feared, back into the Ned-ridden haunts of N.W.1 or N.W.3. The flat in Chiswick was a reward for more virtue than I deserved.

We moved. A busy time for us all. Roger and I became obsessed with our program, provisional title, 'The Singing Eye.' His, not mine, I didn't care for it. Location Services was making her hop and kept her too busy to fret. The logistics of moving are always a bore, but she simplified it by deciding to leave Sarah's furniture behind. It cheered her to shed as much of Sarah as she could, and the junior from Laura's library, who was coming to fill her place, was overwhelmed by what seemed to her astounding generosity.

All through the week, when we were almost swamped by the pressure of work and domestic riddles, we were bombarded with news from the Sudan. The situation had worsened and, because of the complexity of the political picture, the Media, looking for a 'human interest' story, had homed in on Klaus. He was now officially known to be held by the terrorists, or guerrillas depending on where lay your allegiance, and a ransom of vast sums of money and the freeing of political prisoners were being demanded for his life. These demands were geared to a deadline that moved, held firm, wavered then moved again. Klaus became an instant hero, a captured jungle savior, a Dr. Albert Schweitzer held to sordid ransom. Indignant commentators argued that no cost would be too much to pay for such a valuable life, others said with equal fervor that a firm stand must be taken etc. etc. etc. All garbage. Klaus was captured. Badly wounded, one source said. He was probably dead.

The newsmen went to town. The cliffhanging deadlines made every broadcast and news sheet. 'Captured scientist. Deadline at dawn.' 'Jungle siege, no moves yet.' Truth being stronger and rawer than fiction, the Media kept this story on the boil to extract the last ounce of flavor. The next thrilling installment: read on . . .

Biographies, old photos, his home, his past, his background were all displayed, each reporter, each program delving deeper and yet deeper in the hope of scooping its rivals. Dr. Samuel Penfold's gallant rescue of the lad, his dead foster parents, his brilliant but brief academic career were blazoned across the globe. I was terrified that, in their zeal, Susan would be unearthed and interviewed. I hadn't yet confessed my knowledge of her existence. The pressures of the moment and the emotional distance, still a wedge between us, made me chary of attempting it unless I was forced to. But my luck held again. My credit up above was better than I thought possible and Susan was undisturbed; and my lady could live through the hammering of the news on her nerves, safe from additional burden. All the same, I wondered what the owner of that withered voice and asthmatic cough would think as she watched the apotheosis of Professor Klaus Narraway into Saint and Martyr. Perhaps she had shrivelled too much to care any more.

Our new quarters were but chic. Care, taste, love and money had been spent in the conversion of an Edwardian artisan's cottage. There was a huge studio living room, light and white, with a divan tucked neatly in a recess on which I slept. A bedroom for the lady, a luxurious bathroom and a sunny kitchen that opened onto a small, paved courtyard. We ate in the kitchen, but the weather was unseasonably warm for September and we occasionally carried our meals to a wobbly iron table in the courtyard and balanced on the unsteady garden chairs that our enterprising host must have reclaimed from a stage set of a Victorian folly. This small opening, this pinprick to the great outdoors, was a panacea. We both felt less pent in, less closed up, imprisoned by our own complexities. We both began to relax again and to discover the easiness with each other that we had known before John Lang's traumatic intervention.

We had been there only a few nights when a thunderstorm broke. It started after midnight though it had been building all day. The sunshine had slowly gone livid and the air grew as solid as cotton wool. With evening, the darkness pressed the heat heavily down on concrete and metal. The tension broke with a liberating burst of rain, the lashing tongues of water making a drummer's intro to the big number. Climactic rolls of thunder rumbled nearer and nearer until they roared overhead in time to the forked spears of lightning. I could see through the skylight of the studio from my bed without moving my head. The local church spire either flared dazzling white against a jet sky, or became a black needle silhouetted against a momentarily brilliant skyline. The fierce music, orchestrated and illuminated by the light-show, compelled my whole attention, focused my concentration to concert pitch. Because of this, I didn't hear her till she stood by my bed, shivering in a thin nightdress, though she had picked up a flimsy shawl that half covered her shoulders and at which she clutched as if she were in a high wind.

'Face,' she whispered. 'Oh, Face.'

'Hello.' I sat up. 'All this Beethoven keeping you awake? I'm not surprised. It's a real beaut.'

She swayed, her teeth chattering.

'Face, Face, Face . . .'

'Frightened of the thunder, lady?'

'I saw them. Kissed them. They needed me . . .'

In the flare of a lightning stroke, I saw her. Her eyes were glassy and she swayed as if in a trance. She looked stricken and she repeated my name again and again interspersed with odd, disjointed sentences. I waited for the next flash and then flapped my hand in front of her face, but she didn't even blink.

'Here,' I said, 'get into bed and I'll make some cocoa.' I pulled her into bed and drew the covers over her. For a moment, I nearly persuaded myself that she would need my body heat to warm her; but I remembered her shocked, glazed eyes, and had an attack of the Galahads, God damn it! I moved away from her intending to fetch the cocoa, but she held on to me with fierce need until I lay back. Then she nestled into the crook of my shoulder and talked very fast into my neck. Hey, you up there, I hope you are taking due note of all this. You're in my debt again, getting into the red. I'm in credit for a bundle of favors for this.

'The thunder woke me, Face. I didn't know where I was, not at first. Then the lightning showed me the room and I remembered. But I was confused for I heard a pattering of footsteps and, for a moment, I thought I was back home. Proper home. If there was a storm, the boys would always come in. They hated thunder. They'd scuttle across from their bedroom to ours and get into bed with us. All four of us would curl up under the duvet and the boys would begin to giggle and Ned would try and scare them with silly stories. Just now . . . tonight, Face, just before I came down . . . I heard Timmy say, "Mummy, can I come into bed?"

and I felt his hand looking for mine. He was there, really there, wide eyes and so frightened. Face, I touched him, smelled him, kissed him. He was there, a breathing, living thing. Then Chris said, "Mummy, why are we in this place?" And I hugged him and said, "I don't know, darling, not exactly. But it's all right now as we are together again." Then Tim cried and whimpered that he wanted Daddy. So I kissed him and said that I did too, but at least the three of us had found each other again. Chris asked why we couldn't go home, and I said that we would, oh we would. The thunder and lightning hurled above us and we settled down. Tim lay and shivered on my shoulder and Chris lay on my other side and pretended to be brave though he flinched at each clap of thunder. We must have dozed—we were so cosy together, for I suddenly realized that they were gone. My boys had gone. The precious moment . . . the veil lifted and I saw behind the screen. They've gone back again and they need me. Where are they, Face, where are they? They were frightened and they need me and I can't get to them. Why? Why? I want them so much. They need me, I want to get to them.'

I let her babble on, telling it again and again, around and around to re-live the tender moment when her kids came back to her. A dream? I don't know. Perhaps she was separated from her real world by an intangible wall, divided from her family by a curtain we couldn't understand. I had the unworthy thought that I wished the bloody curtain would never lift again. She was becoming used to her new life, the exile she was condemned to in her dreams or in truth. She was finding an equilibrium; she laughed occasionally and yearned less. Then she was given these glimpses of her loss to tease and torture her. My lovely, haunted, hunted lady.

She quietened eventually and I worked myself free from her grasp. We both needed the cocoa by now, cocoa laced with a large dose of alcohol. We'd made a bargain to replace what stores we used and it was time to invest in a bottle of brandy. The stock of liquor had been found and shoved away out of temptation. But I searched it out now, pouncing on it with quick dabs as I waited in the dark pauses for the flickering light to show me my quarry.

The result was tea laced with Drambuie. It's hard to decide which mixture was the more barbaric.

I shook her back to the present. 'Here, drink this.'

'What is it? Where are they? Tim and Chris, where are they? Why don't they come back? Face, was I dreaming?'

'I don't know. Drink it, you're shivering and it will warm you.'

She crouched on my bed, her ridiculous shawl awry; and, though she warmed her hands on the mug, she wouldn't drink until I bullied her.

'I can't go back to that room. Please, Face, can I stay here with you?'

'I'll swap beds then. Goodnight. Try and get some sleep.'

'I'll get cold again. Please, stay here.'

'Lady, you ask too much.'

A long and miserable silence. 'I know,' she said, 'I always ask too much. I'll go on asking and you'll go on giving until you can't give any more and then you'll run away. I can't stand being alone.'

'Not many people can, if they're honest enough to admit it. Those who say they can are usually liars or warped. They take it out on the wrong objectives. Of them fanatics are made.'

'I'm useless, Face. A parasite. I give nothing.'

'No. Your fight has lasted a long time.'

'They were here. I held them in my arms.'

'Yes, lady.'

The thunder rolled on down the Thames and out to sea. The lightning lost heart and the rain lashed the skylight in a last tattoo and then died.

She said, 'The storm's over. I'll go back to my room now.'

'Be brave and of good courage.'

'What's that, Face?'

'I heard it somewhere. I'm a litter bin.'

'Epitaph for a Dustbin.'

'You're crying again.'

'Yes. Thanks for the tea. And everything else.'

She stood up, fragile and tousled, and walked to the door of her room.

'They were, they really were here. I wasn't dreaming.'

'Sure. Try and sleep. Goodnight.'

'Goodnight.'

Hey, you, go easy on her. Let her rest.

Location Services were to throw a party, pre-dinner cocktails for a client.

'Get 'em in, twist their arm, and chuck 'em out,' was what Liz said when she told me. I was in on it because, instead of the usual bland Musak, it was hoped that I'd condescend to make a few soothing passes across the strings. I'd get a fee, of course. 'Whose idea was that?' I asked.

'Liz,' she said, lying. 'She knows about you and thought that you wouldn't mind.'

I didn't, it was a good fee.

They had a routine for parties at the office. Coats and bags stowed away in the small reception area, drinks and chatter in the Production office, and any private or urgent negotiations adjourned to Liz's office. It was cramped and, to my great surprise, fun. I sat cross-legged on a desk, a glass of vino at my elbow, and I experimented with the theory that the faster I played, the faster they drank, and vice versa. After an hour of playing God and controlling the alcoholic intake—it is I who pull the strings, ha ha—Liz thought them sufficiently mellow for she signaled me to stop.

I liked her, a no-nonsense type who knew her job and would punch from the shoulder with no nasty business. When I stopped playing, she nodded me into her office with the ferocious frown which I'd been warned meant she was about to do or say something favorable.

She lit a cigarette. 'Sarah has told me a lot about you.'

'Same here.'

'I also know most of the details of her—er—so-called life story. I gather that you do too.'

'Yep.'

'Any ideas?'

'Nope.'

'Well, listen to me.' She leaned toward me, blowing away her smoke with intense concentration. 'I called you in here because I'm in a grave dilemma. As you know, I promised her that I would let her know soon whether I intended to keep her on a permanent basis. My problem is that I don't know whether I can afford to.'

'Isn't she any good at the job?' I asked, startled.

'Not as a secretary, no. A step above useless. But I'm not

bothered about that. I can buy secretarial skills. But I do need an assistant, a back-up for myself, and as that she'd shape up very well indeed. But . . .' She stubbed out her cigarette with a great deal of energy.

'But what?'

'I can't afford a blunder on a major contract, and I can't trust her nerve. She's erratic. Ruled by her crazy emotional problems.'

'So?'

'So, I could tell her just that. I could stand up and say, "Stop being bad news. Stop being neurotic, or else . . ." But then she'd go to pieces, blow it at once. I can't even hint that she might be letting me down, it would sound like a threat. I need cooperation.'

'From me?'

'She has told me that she trusts you absolutely.'

'Yeah? Thanks a bundle.'

The bitterness didn't escape her. 'Trust is better than fear,' she said sharply. 'I'd like to give her a chance to prove to herself that she is capable of dealing with any situation we throw at her. But you have got to help.'

I was sorry that I'd let that one slip out. It was my own doing that I'd assumed the mug's role, the trusted buddy, the brotherly dogsbody, and I was stuck with it beyond the point of bellyaching about it. 'O.K.' I said, 'lead me to it.'

Liz started another cigarette. 'Pippa Waters,' she began and coughed.

'You smoke too much,' I said as I handed her the drink that she had planted on the blotter of her desk. 'Pippa is dangerous territory.'

'Precisely. I want to exorcise her and, at the same time, convince Sarah that she is more than able to handle an assignment like this. On her own. I can't afford to lose the Raindew contract, but the thing practically runs itself after all these years, and I'm prepared to gamble, if it will give her the confidence she needs. Which she will get, if . . . For one thing, she knows how important that contract is to the economic survival of this company. I'll chance that she won't make a balls up of it, but you will have to play your part . . .' The smoker's cough cut her off again.

'How?'

A burst of laughter from the other room reached us. Liz cocked her head sideways like a sparrow to judge the character of the laugh, then with a small cough of satisfaction, she turned back to me. 'You can undertake not to leave her, abandon her, double-cross her, walk away from her, or two-time her until after the meeting with Pippa Waters.'

'Now, hey, hey, hey, Ms. Wilton. That lady is asking a lot from me and I've been happy to give what I could. Now you are adding your two ha'p'orth and wanting me to sign a contract on a monk's life with no guarantee of a hereafter.'

'That's it, is it?' She slammed her hand on the desk. 'That's the problem for you, is it? A stud. By God, a stud. The sort that doesn't know he exists unless he proves it to himself ten times a week. I thought better of you . . .'

'Watch your tongue.' We glared at each other.

'I read you differently, Face. I made a mistake. Somebody or something is destroying that woman. Now, I'm not that certain that it isn't you.'

'Listen, you daft bitch.' I seized her wrist. 'Did she ever tell you about John Lang?'

'No. An easy alibi for you?'

'Will you listen before you pass glib judgments?' I told her the John Lang saga quickly and graphically, not omitting a single sordid detail.

She was shaken. 'O.K. I was wrong. I seem to have jumped to a very wrong conclusion. I'm sorry, you've had a basinful as well.'

I offered her in return an apologetic smile. 'You're right, of course. It is a problem for me. I'm not accustomed to sublimate my libido, as Papa Freud would say. I usually get who and what I want. But I'm a big, strong man and I do know better, I can promise you that. Fact is that I'm . . . I'm somewhat keen on the lady and I hate to see her want to bed only with a ghost.'

'That's fine, then.'

We were caught in a ludicrous position. I released her wrist and she lit a cigarette as if it were an oxygen stick.

'So,' she coughed, 'where did we get to?'

'I'll hang around. But I'm not aiming at canonization. I could well hit bad trouble.'

'Phone me.'

'Would that help?'

'It might. If she can win through, she can go with me as far as I get. She'll be as good as cured. If not . . .' she shrugged. 'Social Security. The half life of the half sane. I can't do that to anyone without trying first. We have a stake in cooperation. Let's make a compact. A capable assistant for me and a healthy human being for you. Are you with me?'

'Yes, I am.'

'Right. We won't make it harder for any of us than is absolutely necessary. First step is that I won't sack her without first consulting you, and you won't ditch her ditto. Agreed?'

'It's a fair offer.'

'And we talk on the phone. Keep each other in touch.'

'O.K.'

'Good.' She put out her hand and we shook on the agreement. Then she scowled as if I'd rejected her proposal. 'What are you doing here?' she snapped, 'I'm paying you to entertain my guests. Go and play.' She slammed out of her office in a fury and I followed meekly to my tabletop and went back to manipulating the communal thirst.

A doxy came sauntering past. Mid-twenties, blonde and neat, clinging on to the residue of a holiday tan. 'Hello,' I said.

'Hello indeed. Where did Sarah find you?'

'The bargain basement.'

'Cheap for the price?'

'No price tag. We're just good friends.'

'Interesting.'

She juggled possibilities. She wasn't a poacher, but she liked what she saw and was making it clear that she fancied it. She was my type, small bum and saucy eyes. Liz was watching me across the room and I rebelled, wanting at least the illusion of choice.

A gleaming pink fingernail flicked at the back of my hand.

'If I gave you my phone number, would you keep it or lose it? And I'm not interested in the polite answer.'

I grinned. There was a thread between us, the acknowledgment that we were mutually attracted, an awareness that neither of us was asking or wanting anything deeper than the pleasure we were prepared to give. 'I wouldn't frame it, but I wouldn't lose it.'

'Cautious.' She opened a drawer in the desk on which I was perched and scribbled on a sheet of paper.

'The name is Trej, short for Treasure. I'm nice now, but later in the evening I get real mean.' She nipped me with her pink nails and pouted in a send-up of the heavy-lidded, sulky screen siren. Then she winked and stuffed the scrap of paper in the pocket of my life support system.

'Tra ra. Mustn't flirt with the help. It makes Liz scream.' She wafted off after miming a kiss, while I noticed Liz was pretending not to see.

On the way back to Chiswick, she asked me what Liz had wanted.

'She thought I might be able to play for a commercial. I can't remember which. She's going to send me the music.'

'Did she say anything about me?'

'Not really.'

'I wondered. She's due to make up her mind about retaining me. But she hasn't said a word.'

'Do you want to stay on?'

'I need to.'

'Given a free choice? That's a different ball game.'

'Yes, given a free choice. I'd like to stay very much, if she wants me.'

'Well, she didn't say anything. I'd forget it till she decides. These things take time.'

'You seemed to get on well with Trej.'

'Yes.'

'She's nice isn't she?' Absently said, absorbed in herself, with no perception of where I might be straying or why. I threw away the scrap of paper, but I glanced at it before I consigned it to the gutter and the numbers formed a pattern in my head like a tune and I knew that I wouldn't forget them.

They found Klaus by accident. The Sudanese army were chasing marauders over the border when they were hampered by a stalled jeep blocking the road. In the back of the jeep was Klaus, bound hand and foot, unconscious, his body racked by bouts of fever. The young officer was more concerned with catching invaders than in the welfare of a white man alone in a jeep and so handed him over to a Catholic Mission House. To be fair to the young officer, Klaus was meant to be five hundred miles away and heavily guarded.

The priest at the Mission House recognized him; but, by the time the government received word of Klaus's whereabouts, they were themselves in the process of a backstairs deal with one faction of the rebels. Thus, after much bumbling and misman-agement, Klaus was flown to London, still unconscious, without the proper clearance from the now chaotic Sudanese authorities. He was incarcerated in a hospital for tropical diseases and from there bulletins were issued daily about the probable diagnosis and his response, if any, to treatment. The Media, driven to peaks of ecstasy by his illegal rescue by the RAF, filled in the gaps in the scanty facts with debate and speculation, progress and prognosis, both medical and political.

'If Professor Narraway has contracted this rare tropical fever, it would seem that his chances of recovery are extremely slight . . .'

'The Sudanese government are in a serious dilemma. If they acknowledge that they allowed an important political prisoner to escape, they are underwriting the validity of the rebels' claim. On the other hand, if they welcome Professor Narraway's escape as a happy outcome, they will have to admit the inadequacy of the search . . .'

The night that they announced that Klaus was not suffering from any rare or exotic complaint but only from concussion, severe debilitation and malarial complications, we were watching the news on the absent Beeb type's magnificent flying television machine.

'Would you like to see him?' I asked.

She brightened. 'But how?'

'Go and visit. There's been enough about your father to give you a valid passport, I should think. Tell them who you are. They might even ask Klaus, if he's conscious. Try it. You have nothing to lose.'

'They might check up on me.'

'Who with?'

Susan, I thought. I'd forgotten Susan. But why, come to think of it, would they bother?

After work, we went to the hospital and were met by an unmoveable wall of red tape.

No. Impossible. Not to be considered.

We explained very carefully who Doctor Penfold was, who Unity was, and her relationship with Professor Narraway. We were very patient and very reasonable. We refused to be intimidated and we didn't ruffle any feathers by assuming a hectoring stance. We made it clear that we were prepared to wait calmly until they came to the right, proper and only decision available to them.

She carried herself with a dry dignity that I had never seen in her before, an after-image of the mother she had described to me and of whom I'd heard a faint echo on the phone.

If you outface officials, sooner or later you instill in them an uneasy doubt, the fear that they are about to make a massive and public blunder. I used the threat of an avid Press, ready to pounce, on the senior nurse who refused to let us further than her suzerainty. Scarcely subtle, but it worked.

We were passed up the nursing ladder of command, then the doctors', then the administrators'. My lady was magnificent, neat and trim, the gray streak in her hair adding weight to her argument. She was an actress, playing to the hilt the part of the cool, courageous intimate of the Great Man, a member of the charmed circle of initiates. She talked of her father, of Suriya, of Klaus's work, though she knew nothing of either work or wife in their present form. Oh she was good.

Later, I realized that she was not assuming a role. She was in her own territory, giving a true portrait of herself before her exile. In similar circumstances in that other world, with Ned at her side with undisputed rights, she would have behaved just so.

Eventually we won. We waited in the Matron's sitting room with tea and biscuits on hand. A delegation had gone forth to discover whether Professor Narraway was a) in one of his brief moments of consciousness, and b) was prepared to see Miss Penfold.

We waited like prisoners in the dock waiting for the verdict. As the scuttling footsteps came down the corridor, I found myself using the traditional phrase to announce the jury's return, 'They are coming back in.'

'Miss Penfold,' the doctor had a quick, shy grin, 'can you come now? I mentioned your name to Professor Narraway and he is most anxious to see you. I'm sorry to hurry you, but his periods of consciousness can be quite short.'

He and his side-kick set out at a brisk trot. We followed after, a nurse at our heels.

I'm allergic to hospitals, the machinery and apparatus of healing looks to me much like a cleaned-up torture chamber, the rack, the thumbscrew, the knives and needles are polished and sterile, germ-free and guaranteed to cure. When I'm due to go, I won't submit to the indignity of their mercy, strapped to automatic organs and kept half alive by their painful skill. I shall find a hilltop overlooking the sea and I'll watch the sun die in the dusky ocean and follow down after it.

'*Timor mortis conturbat me.*' The fear of death perturbs me. William Dunbar. The poem and the tune. Would Rog buy these neon-lit lino corridors, the Edwardian building, the last outpost of the Raj dragged reluctantly into a century that was bringing about the decline of the West?

'Here we are.'

A bare room, a bed, some screens and the littered paraphernalia of medicine. On the bed a shrunken man ravaged by disease and eaten by suffering, white hair and yellow skin. His eyes were shut and he looked deader than a mummy.

'Please sit here, Miss Penfold.'

They placed a chair by the bed and the junior doctor, with an apologetic smile, offered me another by the wall. The doctors moved discreetly to the corridor, but the nurse remained to monitor our vigil.

'Klaus, darling Klaus. It's Unity. Can you hear me? I'm sorry, dear Klaus, that you've been hurt so badly.'

His lids flickered, a gentle quivering that told of the immense effort that he was making. He managed to prise his lids open and look at her, a sudden flash from prune dark eyes. Then his face heaved in a massive convulsion, his mouth opened and his lips peeled back, sending his other features askew. The whole upheaval was a telling strain, but then I understood that he was attempting to smile at her; and, to me, it seemed that the smile, torn and battered as it was, was radiant as dawn.

Speaking was another struggle for him. 'Unity,' he gasped. 'Dear girl. It is good of you to come all this way to visit me ... a long way ...' he lost the thread of his thought and his voice faltered into silence.

He had recognized her, the other lady from another world, the unborn Unity. It was the first time that I'd had a direct confrontation with the lifting of the veil and the flesh crawled over the base of my skull. She shot a probing and victorious glance at me, for all her grief, before she gave all her concentration to the dying man.

'Dear, darling Klaus.'

His wandering wits gathered together in a momentary burst of strength. He gave her another of his distorted, warm smiles. 'I'm a fool, Unity. At my age to go riding for the first time. I deserve this.'

'Get better, Klaus, please get better.'

'Of course,' he sounded surprised. 'I only fell from a horse.'

'How's Barbara and the girls?'

'They'll be here shortly. You will see them if you wait. Barbara wants ... was asking ...' He was distracted by the light that shone by the bedside and his strength was fading.

'Unity? Unity, are you there? I can't see you.'

'Yes, Klaus, I'm still here.'

'I must tell you, Unity, it is important for you to ... to understand ...' He lapsed back into silence. I could see him sink down into the inner quiet.

The nurse said, 'He's unconscious now, Miss Penfold. There is no point in you waiting here and I'm sure that Dr. Brill would like a word with you.'

'He talked about Barbara, his wife, coming to visit him and about an accident with a horse. Does he speak about them a lot?'

'His wife died in the Sudan, as you know. I'm afraid, Miss Penfold, that his mind rambles. He is often delirious.'

The nurse bustled us away. She had seen nothing amiss, but I knew that reality had skidded, turned a sharp corner to nowhere.

We went back to the hospital twice more. He had never regained consciousness and now the doctors thought it was unlikely that he would. He was sinking into a coma. We stopped visiting then; there seemed little point and the Press had begun to hint about a mysterious visitor, though we had done our best to evade them, but they seem to cull information from the air. So we left our phone number with Dr. Brill who promised he would call if Klaus ever asked for her again.

Brill didn't call and the Press abandoned their constant coverage and departed to the next excitement. It was acknowledged that he was gradually sinking into a peaceful death.

I don't think she was particularly distressed. She had mourned him once, when she had said her goodbyes to all the others that time at Leicester Square. His sickbed recognition of her had been a bonus, an unexpected extra that did no more than prove to her, and to me, the validity of her predicament. There was no reassurance in this. She was only too well aware of the contradictions. The Klaus who recognized her had been found in Africa where his wife, Suriya, had been killed. Yet he spoke of Barbara and of a horse that threw him. It was a contradiction of reality as inexplicable as her own brief and painful glimpses into another dimension. Klaus thought he had been in Berkshire, but the facts placed him in Sudan. She thought she was married to Ned, but facts put John Lang in her bed.

'Forget about John Lang,' I said when we talked of this one night in our shandy pub. The weather had broken and we were no longer on anything as innocent or summery as shandy. 'Just forget about him. The case is non-proven. Take a Gallup poll of passing females and a fair percentage will be found to have inverted nipples, appendix scars and moles.'

'How to compute a coincidence? I've asked that before. The proper question to ask is what can I offer any more. What can I be to any other man when I've been touched by such filth?'

'It makes no difference to me. I'm not that dainty.'

'But I am. I find it hard to live with. And yet I am an exploiter on my own account. I exploit you. I've made of you an emotional safety line. A handy sharer of space, a male Laura.'

'A built-in plumber, handyman and chucker-out. Living on the premises and always on call.'

'No!' Her distress was palpable. 'Dear God, I despise myself. Face, I know the danger. I see myself age like a speeded-up film and I know, I'm not that self-absorbed, I know that I'm using blackmail to keep you around.'

'Lady, guilt is a mug's trip.'

'For you, or for me?'

'I've not welshed yet.'

'But you will. Yes, you will.'

I became angry. 'Don't push me beyond choice into a preconceived attitude. Credit me with enough self-knowledge to know why I do what I do. I am not frozen into a stereotype. Sex is an overrated commodity in a consumer society. Only a fool buys it with the wrong currency.'

She went pale. 'I don't mean that.'

'I know what you mean and it degrades us both. Stay cool, lady, and don't force any issues. I'll stay cool and take my chance. What's the song? "I'm a rambler, I'm a gambler, I'm a long way from home"? Too right, too bloody right. A gambler, me, so don't weight the dice.'

She finished her drink, still white and troubled. 'I'm sorry, Face, far sorrier than I think you'll ever know. Let's go home.'

We went back to Chiswick together but in silence.

For the most part, we continued to battle with more obvious adversaries. Rog liked the idea of the Dunbar poem to be set against a hospital background, the melody as simple as a traditional air, as poignant as a piper's lament. He suggested a better hospital, a charity institution due for demolition. There were wrought iron balconies designed for the under-privileged consumptive to breathe in the sooty air of industrial London while his betters went to sanatoria in Switzerland. The corridors were tiled like an everlasting public lavatory and the length of the wards was an artist's exercise in perspective. It needed little imagination to hear the nurses' floor-length starched aprons and the boots of the frock-coated doctors as they hurried, ghost echoes, over the deserted acres. The entrance hall boasted a mosaic depicting a substantial lady in Graeco-Roman robes, one arm raised to banish a wispy skeleton while the other arm held forth the lamp of healing to a huddle of ragged children. The whole building was a monument to civic pride, the Victorian lack of architectural understatement, and the inability of charity to keep the dread specter at bay.

Truly, *timor mortis conturbat me.*

The Raindew commercial was a bastard. Dear Pippa was proving a caricature of a difficult actress. She postponed her arrival several times, causing expensive cancellations of studio time, she made demented demands over her costumes and ordered cars to meet flights that she had no intention of catching. Liz was monitoring progress surreptitiously and sneaked a phone call when the office was empty to check the position at my end. We agreed, to our mutual surprise, that our concern was proving unnecessary and she was coping remarkably well.

'Don't become smug,' Liz snapped. 'Sarah hasn't yet had the doubtful pleasure of meeting La Waters in person.'

'I'll bet on her survival,' I said with phony confidence. 'Evens.'

'Risky. Odds on, or no bet. Remember, I know the running conditions and the trainer's report. To say nothing of the height of the fences. It's stamina and pedigree I'm unsure about.'

'A horsy childhood, I take it. What's a girl like you doing in a job like this?'

'Once you've seen one gymkhana, you've seen 'em all. Now, get off the phone and stop wasting my time.'

Pippa's London agent was Jamie Marriot, a gentle bisexual, who had escaped from being an actor and managed cleverly to disguise the fact that he was extremely good at his job. He invited Liz Wilton's new assistant out to lunch, ostensibly to discuss the best way of dealing with Madam's vapors, but his real purpose was to twist her arm without her noticing the pain.

The lunch was a success. The business was dealt with quickly; and Jamie, unaware of Unity's familiarity with him, was flattered by Sarah's interest.

'I made him tell me the story of his life, most of which I knew already, but I wanted to check my data, as it were. Once I nearly betrayed a very private confidence that Sarah could never have explained. I asked him about his clients and when he finished extolling the virtues of each and every one of them, I asked him whether he had Ned Roland and Unity Penfold on his books.'

'But you knew what the answer had to be. Why ask?'

'It's like picking at a sore spot. You can't leave it alone. I raised a funny reaction, all the same. He sat bolt upright and looked at me over his shades. Very trendy, our Jamie. He said, "You're the second person to ask me that and the first was a maniac, an absolute harpy who screamed abuse at me over the phone." "Dear me," I said, "why would she do that?" "She," he asked. "How did you know?" "You said a harpy, aren't they always female?" "Oh very classical. We've got a bright one here." "What did she want?" I prompted. "Haven't a clue, petal. Mercifully, she ran out of money and we were cut off. Who are they, anyway? A double act?" "I don't know," I said. "I was asked about them once. Figments of imaginations, I expect." "Hideous imaginations some people have," he said with a very inelegant sniff. "That virago sounded positively dangerous. But I don't want to talk about her, I want to hear all about you. How are you getting on with dear Liz?" '

Inevitably, one evening the news stands carried the placards announcing that Klaus had finally died in his coma.

'Well, that's that,' she said in a tight, little voice.

'Do you want to go to the funeral?'

'No, that's their Klaus. Mine died last April. I'm all alone now. Not one of them left.'

'Pippa?'

'No, I'm no longer hoping for anything. Jamie convinced me. She won't bring enlightenment. I don't understand how Klaus was allowed to filter through the net. Perhaps because he was so near to death. No, he was my last chance, and he's gone.'

I too could pick at a sore spot. There is an impersonal curiosity, a scientist's itch. It can lead to splitting the atom and ignoring the possibility of the atomic bomb. I'd break the shell to check that the egg was fresh enough to be worth keeping. Beyond this gossip's excuse for interference, I decided it was time to nudge the momentum of events toward a resolution. Do or die. It was time for both of us to climb off the fence. When I was alone, I phoned Susan.

'Hello, Mrs. Penfold, this is Mr. Phillips here.' My inspirational first name escaped me. 'Do you remember, I phoned you a few weeks ago?'

'Yes.' The dry, expressionless voice. She didn't even deign to give her assent the question mark that would indicate any interest in the conversation.

'You told me that I had the wrong number.'

'Yes.' Did she remember?

'Mrs. Penfold, I shall be near Oxford over this coming weekend, I wonder if I might drop by and discuss the matter with you. It is hardly a topic to go into over the phone.'

'I have no daughter.' She had remembered, very clearly indeed. She was very much on her guard, her defenses in full working order. She had expected me to call again.

'Look, I'll be passing on Saturday afternoon. About tea time. Is that all right with you?'

'I can tell you nothing further than I've already told you. It would be a waste of your time.'

'All the same, I would like to meet you.'

'As you wish.'

'I'll be along Saturday, then.'

Silence in reply. Not even a cough. The receiver was replaced gently, as if she'd picked up an intrusive dead leaf and was throwing it away.

'How about a jaunt this Saturday?' I asked at pub time.

'What constitutes a jaunt?'

'A run in the country. Rog will lend me his car. Lunch at a wayside inn, chasing leaves, looking for four-leaved clover, picking up lots of forget-me-nots.'

'What inspired all this?'

'The city palls and I feel winter in my soul. We ought to get away before the gray days start.'

'Where would we go?'

'Mallet's Mystery Tour. All the fun of the fair. You won't know until you're there. All for no additional fee.'

Her smile was tired. 'Fun, if you remember, has the habit of going sour on me. But I'm game, if you are willing to take the risk.'

'I keep telling you. I'm a gambler.'

I spun Rog a yarn about Oxford's dreaming spires and collected the car from him on Friday evening. Actually, I did have a fourth poem to find, a contrast with the Thomas Jordan, the Dunbar and Ecclesiastes. I had been sterile, creatively dead, dredging up nothing but rubble for my hard work. I had sold Rog a specious pup; but, I must admit, that whatever else this excursion might produce, I also hoped that the autumnal splendor around Susan's village would trigger off a responsive chord in me.

We drove out of London on the A.40. She didn't chatter at all, but as we left the concrete behind, she began to relax, leaning back in the passenger seat. I felt her slowly unwind as the tension dropped away and released her from the hundred nags and worries of her office self. She had traveled a strange and narrow road for a long time and she looked about her with wonder at the wider horizon of the Home Counties, pathetically limited though it was.

I turned off the main road as soon as I could. I'm an instinctive navigator with no faith in maps. If I sometimes end up in a muddy farm yard with an angry tractor behind me blocking my escape, then I make up for it later when I find a true and uncharted lane, untrodden by the stumbling feet of day trippers.

We drove slowly through sun-dappled branches of red and burnt orange and found at the end of the lane I had promised a pub as yet untouched by jukebox and fruit machine. The ham in the sandwiches was home-cured and the beer had a heavy flavor not bottled by the big breweries.

'We should have done this before, Face. I've forgotten that there is a bigger world than my own little rut. I should have escaped from the groove before.'

'Stagnation is the next thing to death, lady.'

'You don't stagnate, do you Face? You take off and recharge where the energy is fresher. Before you go this time, teach me how.'

'You know how, by asking the question. But there are two ways. One way is mine—irresponsibility. The other, and harder, way is yours—courage.'

She laughed. 'Flattery won't alter a coward. And, if I am to stagnate, I'd better get fat on it. May I have another sandwich?'

Her face was soft and tender, the little wrinkle of a smile about to break hovered on the corners of her mouth. The embattled stance, the poised tension had gone; she was no longer on the alert for attack. She must have looked like this in the lost days with Ned before the depression soured their lives. I wanted her to look like this always, to fight her way back to the certainty of her own worth, to accept the odd path she was forced to tread. There are those with no aptitude for serenity, but she was not one of them. There was peace in her, if she could find her way to it. It brushed her now, a pledge for the future, a promise. But first I had to destroy it. She had a further bitter trial to endure.

I took her hands in mine and told her where we were going. The peace faded from her eyes and there was a transitory hint of reproach, but it didn't last. Her courage and intelligence saw the inevitability of the confrontation.

'I wish it had been my father. Is she expecting me?'

'No, only a fool called Phillips who babbled about a daughter she denies.'

'My mother is dead.'

'On the other side of the screen. It's worth it, worth the pain and the sorrow. You may find something that will help you to make sense of it. Or a way of coming to terms. Who knows, unless you try?'

The address was the cottage where she grew up. White and drawn, she directed me to the village. When we drew up by the side of a trim, hedge-bound garden, she asked me to drive on to the corner and wait for her there.

I watched her in the driving mirror. She wiped her eyes free of the treacherous tears that had flooded them at the sight of home, then she breathed deeply and shook herself. With head held high, she walked up the path, a gallant lady, and in at the front door.

As I lost sight of her, I knew the image I wanted for my fourth poem.

Part Four

Sarah

She was much older than when she had died, and the skidding illogic of that thought unnerved me and brought in its wake an hysterical giggle. She had died, eaten by her putrid womb, in her forties; now, she was in her sixties, a stranger with whom I had never been close.

She made no move to greet me. The door was open and I walked the well known path through furniture anchored to my past toward the living room. She was sitting in the armchair that I remembered as my father's, as upright as a drill sergeant. Her lavender wool dress reflected the faint smell of furniture polish and evoked memories of the fresh lavender that had crept in from the gardens of my childhood.

I stood awkwardly before her having no words, not even my name, to offer her. I had stopped naming myself a long while ago. At work I used a code, a *nom de guerre*; Face had evolved his charming nickname and we both had fallen into the habit of regarding both Unity and Sarah as alternative solutions to a puzzle we couldn't solve and not as the outer expression of an inner being that most names signify. Eventually a person and a name become inextricable. Not mine.

I bent to kiss her but checked myself. In the face of her age and anger I felt an intruder. 'Mother,' I said shyly, and then felt the tears sting in my eyes. 'I'm sorry that I haven't been to see you for so long. There has been a terrible muddle. I thought you were dead.'

She didn't answer me, but stared at me with the horrified loathing of one inspecting an unpleasant insect. Her lips were clamped shut, accentuating the thin wrinkle lines that ran toward her mouth, which spoke of years of loneliness and emotion held at bay by force of will. Her gray hair was dragged into a faultless bun, and behind the distaste in her eyes I saw fear.

'Mother.'

'Don't you dare to address me by that title.'

'Why not?'

'Because you are not my daughter. It is impertinent.'

I wondered whether her objection was purely metaphorical. In her world, by her calculation, I had indeed neglected her, and by so doing would have forfeited, in her eyes, the right to describe myself as her daughter. Duty was a word that came readily to her tongue. Or was her denial merely a statement of fact?

I said as gently as I could, 'Mother, I'm Unity.'

Her head gave a quick shake of impatience, but she refused to answer.

'Listen, I am Unity, Mother . . .'

'Don't!'

'Don't what?'

'Don't use that name. How did you know, you and your accomplice? How did you know that if the child had lived . . . ? I never told. How did you know?'

'Because I am here. I am Unity.'

'Don't keep up that pretence. I know what you want, you and your young man. When he phoned . . . It was cruel, too cruel. To mock me with the name I cherished. I know what you're after, of course. Clever, very clever. But I knew, you see. I knew that somebody would crawl around me. Trying. It's why I kept quiet while I watched the sharks gather around him. Vulgar men with vulgar words pretending to praise him but despoiling his greatness.'

'Whose greatness? What are you talking about?'

I was still standing before her chair like a child waiting for a scolding. She stared ahead, refusing to meet my eye. I knelt down, trying to force her to see me. 'Mother.'

'Don't pretend that you don't know.'

'Know what? Please tell me.'

'I beg of you.' She drew dignity about her like a shawl and turned slightly in her chair to avoid me. I was so close that I could see the faint dew of perspiration on her forehead and that, although held tightly by the anchoring bun, her hairline held still a delicate wave, a mockery of the marcelled hair of the Thirties when she had the prettiness of health and youth. 'I beg you to grant me the intelligence to understand your motives. I am not a fool, nor senile yet. I suspected some attempt of this sort since I first read the news.'

'But what news?'

'I suppose you will put forward the fiction that you haven't heard of Klaus Narraway?'

'Klaus? But, of course, I knew him. I visited him in hospital just before he died. He was only conscious for a few moments but he spoke to me.'

A spasm crossed her face, rage and pain quickly checked that left a new film of moisture. 'How were you allowed to visit him? From whom came the permission?'

'I told them who my father was. It was enough. Father's connection with Klaus was well known and Klaus was pleased to see me.'

'No!' Her cry tore through her control. 'How dare you traduce us all and drag us into your sordid plot.'

'Plot? This is madness. I don't know what you are talking about. Mother, please. Let us try and understand each other better.'

'By my husband's will, the tragic death of Klaus and his wife leaves me a rich woman. Not that I want the money, I have no needs. But I watched the television and saw the vultures gather. I knew that you and your sort would sniff out the money and follow it to me and then attempt to take it . . .'

'No!'

'But I couldn't think that any scheme could be as elaborate or so cruel. A child . . . Take the money. I don't want it. All I wanted was to keep the memories pure. A futile hope in the world as it is now. When my husband was alive, when we were young, there was meaning, purpose, sense. We had ideals and worked for others less fortunate. My husband brought Klaus from . . .'

I interrupted her, compelling her to listen. An actor's trick, but it worked. 'Berlin in 1938. He came into this room at dusk with Klaus by the hand. Klaus was terrified, exhausted, and when you gave him a glass of milk he kept hold of the glass and wouldn't give it back. He was frightened he wouldn't see it again. My father asked Doreen, the maid, to make sandwiches. He wouldn't eat them because he wouldn't eat ham and didn't know how to ask what kind of meat it was . . .'

She whispered, 'How do you know?'

'*You* told me. *You* would tell me when I was naughty and wouldn't eat. You would tell me about poor Klaus, a starving boy, who wouldn't eat because of a principle. I could never see that boy in Klaus. He was so big and jolly and we would play in the summer house . . .'

She moaned and put her hands over her ears, but I reached up and gently pulled them away.

'Mother, why won't you listen? Father called the summer house "Little Ease" because it leaked and was plagued with earwigs. Klaus said it was a magic tower in which I was imprisoned while I waited for the Prince to come and rescue me. If you were angry with me, he said you were turned into an Ogress . . .'

My words petered out. I was trying to prove a point she was nowhere ready to accept. She still remained sitting bolt upright with her gaze carefully directed away from me, rigid as if in shock. I recognized that her mind had sprung shut to repel the invasion of the disturbing ideas that I was desperate to pursue.

We were caught in one of those silences that haunt casual acquaintances forced into prolonged conversations. We were strangers, yet we were bound by the closest of all blood ties. We had nothing to say to each other because there was too much. All the words in the world would be insufficient to convey fully our mutual predicament.

I knelt back on my heels and covered my inability to find any appropriate approach by examining the room. A host of memories, pleasant and trivial and not, to my surprise, painful, flooded forth from the walls. It was a room in which I had known a placid contentment but not enough joy to evoke the poignant tears of nostalgia. I'd been happy enough to leave it for the more flamboyant less meticulous world of the theater.

The room had changed little. The polished parquet and the brass lamps, long since converted to electricity, shone in the slanting autumnal sunlight. The rugs and curtains were faded with wear, but the oaken beams, embedded in the ceiling, glowed with inner health despite their age. On the mantle, there was a collection of prized bric-a-brac. I became absorbed in these trivia, thankful for a respite from the impossible tension of our situation.

'Oh, Mother,' I said suddenly without thinking first. 'Where is the enamelled clock that Father bought in Salzburg? It had that beautiful rose pattern ...'

She screamed, a harsh, jolting sound, then brushed past me clumsily as she scrambled from her chair in distress. For a second or two she started wildly, looking around her own living room unable to think where to run, to hide. Then she fell back against the chair she had vacated and held on to the back for support.

'Who ... are ... you?'

'I am your daughter, Unity.'

'No, no.' Her frail body shook and her grasp on the chair became a real necessity. 'Unity died. I was five months gone ... it would have been a still birth. They told me it was a girl as they took away my womb and took also any further chance of bearing a child, a son. I had the name ready ...'

I think I said aloud, 'So, it's true. I was never born,' but I wasn't sure. I may have managed to keep it in my head to spare this woman confronted by the grown-up ghost of a dead embryo.

She swayed and I caught her and helped her back to her chair. She watched me all the time now, her eyes following my every movement.

'Sit, Mother. I'll make us some tea. Then I'll tell what I can piece together of this grotesque contradiction.'

I went into the kitchen and put the kettle on to boil while I arranged a tray. All was as I remembered it. She watched me through the open door and said something that I couldn't hear, so I left the kettle and came back to her.

'You know your way around,' she said, and her voice shook.

'I was brought up in this house.'

'No. It is impossible. No.'

We looked at each other in helpless disarray. I think she saw me, looked at me properly for the first time, for she said, 'You look like a Penfold.'

'I am a Penfold.'

'Like my husband's sister. Why? Why?'

I put out my hand to take hers and offer what comfort I could, but she snatched it away. My head throbbed and I wanted her understanding, her recognition of our predicament and an acceptance of me; but, before I could follow up her grudging admission of a family likeness, the kettle boiled and I returned to the kitchen.

I made the tea and carried it through to her. We drank it in silence, her scrutiny of my face never wavering. What she was looking for, I could not guess; but I began to realize that beyond the recognition and the understanding, I wanted love from this woman, who, as I well remembered, withheld love as a punishment and who doled out physical affection as rationed as the rare extravagance of a chocolate bar.

After a few sips, I put down my cup and drew up a stool to sit near her chair. I began to talk. I had to convince her of the roles we had to play in the tragic comedy that had been forced upon us.

'Mother, listen to me please. Give me a few minutes to tell you what I think had happened to us. Try not to interrupt, if you can. It makes little enough sense as it is, and it helps me to think aloud and follow a train of thought. May I go on?'

She nodded slightly once, and put aside her tea. It was encouragement of a sort.

'It's a ghost story, if you like. But the trouble is that one of us is a ghost, not real in the logic of the world. You see, until April, I lived in the certain knowledge that I was born your daughter, that I was christened Unity, and that I was brought up in this cottage. I could recite memories, names, relatives, private jokes. I could describe your bedroom upstairs, my father's clothes and habits. Anything you may ask. Endlessly. But what would that do? If you believe me, we are trapped in a nonsense. If you don't, you will still think I'm a confidence trickster who has done some excellent homework.'

I stopped because I couldn't find easy words to encompass the paradox of her death; but she had become calmer, the hostility had faded from her eyes, and I saw an awakening interest.

'What happened in April?'

I told her as quickly as I could. It was a bald recitation without any emotive coloring.

She smiled slightly with a hint of reproof tempered by indulgence. 'I doubt that you would have made up such a rigmarole as a prelude to theft. You would at least have thought up a plausible story.'

Rather than plunge directly into our hotbed of contradictions, we discussed Klaus. She baulked at his marriage to Barbara. She had known her as a child, her parents had been neighbors of Klaus in Berkshire. She insisted that nothing would drive him to make such a match.

It seemed to me a good sign that she could talk of Klaus in this way. It meant that she was beginning to accept the irrational. Then, when she spoke, she startled me, for her lips moved before they made any sound like a film that is out of sync. Eventually, I made out the words, 'When you came in, you said that I was dead.'

'After I was born you wanted another child. I think you had always hoped for a boy . . .'

She nodded. 'A boy who was to be called Adam.'

'After my father.'

'Yes.'

'You wanted him enough to defy the doctors. They advised strongly for an operation. My birth had been difficult but you wanted Adam.'

'So I was offered a hysterectomy and refused?'

'Yes.'

She said bitterly, 'I remember no choice.'

'But you had me.'

'And that growth in my womb.'

'You died before Father. He missed you very much.'

'Yes, he would have done. But, you see, it,wasn't like that. I missed him. He went first and left me all alone . . . with nothing.'

She rose abruptly and wandered around the room. As she went erratically from one piece of furniture to another, she picked up a few ornaments from the shelves, an antique christening mug, a china snuff box, a framed photograph of my father. Each piece she examined carefully and then rubbed on the sleeve of her dress to polish it before replacing it exactly. It was a habit that I'd seen a thousand times before when she pondered over a problem.

She spoke fast and quietly, her lips still keeping their own time independent of her words. 'It's a crossroads, I see that. An operation that I resented that probably saved my life. It's odd, but it was a choice that I had no part of. A child and an early death. Or this, this barren loneliness and life with no meaning. Then you came here. From where? But you come with your father's eyes and the secret name I had for the dead baby. And memories of a childhood which includes me and from which I am forever excluded. I have no memory. Nothing to ease the emptiness.' She stopped in front of me and I could see the tension in her neck, the clammy skin and the flicker of hysteria in her eyes. She went on in an excited whisper. 'One of us is a ghost. We are from different realities, alternatives decided years ago. But which one of us is a ghost? Which?'

I tried to steer her back to her chair, but she resisted and seized my arm, her fingers digging in my flesh. She repeated, 'Which one of us is a ghost?'

'I am, Mother.'

'Where do you come from?'

'From my own time, wherever that may be. I slipped through a gap and can't get back.'

'But you can't go back. You mustn't. If you go back, then I'd be dead.'

'Yes, I suppose so, but you wouldn't know because . . .'

'I won't, no I won't.' She backed away, terrified. 'I am not dead. No, I don't want to be dead because you say so. I have had so little from life and now you are trying to take away whatever is left to me.'

'I've explained it all badly. Please, don't get upset, I'm only guessing after all.'

'I don't want to die. I don't want to be dead.' She began to sob, great racking spasms that shivered through her. I reached out again to her, but she lashed out at me and turned away to resume her shuffling with the ornaments.

'You didn't see your father die. Did you? I didn't think you could have or you wouldn't threaten me like this. I did. That good, good man. He was still young. A brave man, a good man, but I saw his eyes as he died and all I saw in them was fear. And disgust for the ugliness of his diseased body. Fear and disgust. All that remains of courage and goodness . . .' She was weeping hysterically, her words all but unintelligible. She was holding the christening mug, frail china with rosebuds around the rim and delicate gold tracery. It had been my grandfather's and my father had used it for pipe cleaners, a crop of white spikes peeping over the rosebuds. It was a valued relic, but my mother had lost reason. She threw the mug across the room, and, as it broke, her control snapped and she screamed as if the breaking china had pierced her body.

'Get out. Get out, you wicked, wicked woman with your wicked, evil lies. Go away, get out of my house. I never want to see you again. You speak lies. Destroy even my dreams. Threaten me. Go. Go.'

She collapsed on the floor, kneeling. She bent over and rocked to and fro, her arms crossed over the offending stomach that had betrayed her, and, as she rocked, she moaned like a woman in labor. I made yet another attempt to help her, lift her, offer comfort and concern, but my proximity only made it worse.

'Go. Go. Go. Leave. Me. Alone.' Her words were gasped out in spasms.

'Let me call for help, Mother.'

'Take the money. Take everything. You and the man on the phone. I don't know how you ransacked my mind. You crawled into it . . .'

'Mother . . .'

'No. No. No. You'd kill me. No.' She swayed backward and forward, screaming each monosyllable as if she were being pierced by a sword. 'No. No. I am not your mother.'

Her mind had rebelled. She had been seduced momentarily by the gift of a daughter, but age and fear had driven her to repudiate the gift. Her daughter's name spelled death and she was clinging to life with the desperation of one who has nothing else but the mere fact of breath to hope for. It was the ultimate rejection of life, for death is the price for a birth, our own; but she was beyond such reasoning. I tried again to explain that by some inexplicable accident, some twist in the logic of time, a trick in the dimension of reality, she could still accept me and continue with the life she now led. Since my father had died, she had led a sour existence for years, clinging to regrets. Any disturbance, however slight, would cause an upheaval; and I had invaded her privacy, blundered into the fragile structure of her days and shattered it, causing an earthquake that could prove catastrophic to her mental equilibrium.

It was a bitter thought that I had acted as a John Lang in my mother's sad little life.

'Take the money. Take all that Klaus left. But go away. Away. Get out of my house.'

The parallel with my experience with John Lang was forcibly underlined. I cried too, but softly, a painful acceptance that I had exchanged my mother's love, perhaps her reason, for a small key to the puzzle, a clue to the mystery of my predicament. Indeed, I had not been born.

I made a few more abortive attempts to quench the rising tide of her hysteria and I tried to lift her from her asylum crouch. I'd seen it before in shots of mental wards: the upright fetal position, the folded arms, the regular rocking to and fro, the mind closed to outside stimuli. Nothing I did reached her, nothing could put a stop to her monotonous chant.

'I am not your mother. Go away. Go. Take the money. I don't want to be dead. Go. Get out.'

Not even when I bent to kiss her cheek in a gesture of compassion and farewell did she give any sign of noticing my presence, so far had she retreated from an unbearable truth. I also found the truth appalling, for my second birth had not destroyed her body as my first had done, but had, I was almost certain, destroyed her sanity.

I phoned the doctor. It was the same number I had always known but a new name was mentioned by the receptionist who answered. I explained to her that I was a distant relative who had called on Mrs. Penfold, but unfortunately my unexpected appearance had upset her. I was not at all sure why. As she was begging me to leave, I thought it wise to do so for it was clear that my continued presence in the house was causing her great distress. I would leave the door on the latch and I suggested that the doctor call as soon as possible as Mrs. Penfold appeared to be far from well.

I then picked up the broken pieces of the christening mug and put them carefully in a plastic bag that I found in the kitchen. It had broken into no more than half a dozen pieces; glue and patience would give me one salvaged keepsake of a lost life and a brave father who died in fear.

Face was sitting in a small copse some yards beyond the car. He had collected a spectrum of colors in dead leaves. As I came up, he hurriedly replaced a notebook in his denim jacket and stuck a pencil behind his ear.

'Doing my homework, lady. I have to prove to Roger that I'm not just a pretty face.' When the joke fell flat, he looked at me more carefully.

'Bad?'

'Very bad.'

'Do you want to tell me?'

'Yes.'

'Here, or in the car? We can go where you like.'

'Here. I need fresh air. And I must wait for the doctor, just to check.'

I told him and, as he listened, he made his leaves into a flotilla of ships. When I finished, he blew them away in a miniature gale.

He said, 'We can all get scuppered as easily, at whim. The winds of fate ... We'll wait for the doctor, but I expect she'll be fine. A sedative and a good night's sleep. She'll think she's had a nightmare.'

'I'm afraid it will be a long one. Why doesn't the doctor hurry?'

He changed the subject deliberately. 'So, you weren't born. You were that five-month miscarriage.'

'It would seem so.'

'Science fiction time. Alternative universes. If there's one for each and every possible birth and death, we must be duplicated beyond mathematical reason. To the nth power.'

'Do you believe that?'

'I don't think so. The cogs would slip more often. Mind you, perhaps they do. Perhaps ghost stories are all just that. The transparent nun is alive and well on her side of the screen.'

'But I'm not transparent. You can see me.'

He gave me a speculative look, a wry mixture of appreciation and humor.

'Yes, lady, I can see you. But I'm not all that sure that you can see me.'

A car drew up outside my mother's cottage.

'The doctor. What should I do? Ought I go and see that she's all right, offer help. But what can I say? I have no explanations.'

'Wait and see.'

'I couldn't soothe her, she won't let me near her. I have no excuse . . .'

'Shush. Just wait. You can't go barging in there now.'

We sat and watched the cottage in silence. I shivered in the chill of the late afternoon. A light breeze sprang up and blew into our faces with a patter of leaves like raindrops. With the breeze came a thin, high wail of a woman's voice, old and on the far side of terror. On and on, beyond the power of frail lungs, the frantic strength of a tormented soul. It engulfed us, holding us immobile until it was stopped, sliced clean into silence by the jab of a hypodermic.

I started to run down the lane, but Face held me back. He was pale and very angry.

'Get into the car.'

'I did that to her. I broke her like she broke the china mug.'

'It will do no good.'

'I must do something.'

He opened the car door and pushed me roughly into the passenger seat. He slammed the door shut and yelled, 'Like hell you will. There's been enough meddling.'

He drove wildly, using the car to ride his anger, lurching through quiet lanes and villages in a tempest of violence. I didn't protest. I was past tears and terror. My foot could well be pressing the accelerator. We needed this explosion of speed to purge our guilt for we were inviting retribution while we courted danger. We had made ourselves pariahs and were not part of the world through which we raced.

It was soon over. The storm passed, as brief as it was violent. It passed because we began to accept and understand the extent of our responsibility. He forced the car to a more decorous pace, for we could not have borne the burden of another broken human being in our wake. It had been scarcely half an hour since I'd left my mother, but already the incident belonged to the past, a horrific memory, cut off from our sedate progress through the Saturday afternoon by the catharsis of our speeding overtures to death.

He said bitterly, 'I had to pry. Meddle and indulge my bloody curiosity. It wasn't you, lady, you didn't break her. You were nearly a victim as well, I nearly broke more than her, I could have damaged you. I'm no better than those generals who play battles with toy soldiers and can't see the human misery that is represented every time they topple over a lump of painted lead.'

I let him ease by a bunch of homegoing cyclists and asked, 'Where are we going?'

'To become clean.'

He followed a hound's instinct, scenting out the place he was looking for. He drove us through lanes and darkening trees until we left the tarmac and jolted up a track that edged us up to the crest of a hill. Below us, we saw a wood ablaze with the setting sun, a flaring intensity of the spectrum from yellow to crimson that was echoed again in the reflection that shone in a small, now derelict, ornamental lake. A house behind the lake was hidden in shadow, but it was possible to make out that it was boarded up, too large for a family, yet too small for an institution and not pretty at all, a solid Edwardian mansion that nobody wanted.

He fetched his guitar from the car and led me by the hand to sit with our backs to the sun so that we faced the image of wood and water.

'Don't talk,' he said. 'Not yet.'

He played softly and privately, soothing himself, searching for the peace that had deserted him. The music was not meant for me, it was impersonal, and I was as detached from him as from his music. I was free to watch the colors slowly fading and the waters of the lake turn dull with an assurance and a calm that had not only seemed beyond hope but an hour before, but which had eluded me through the years of senseless depression.

He had indeed found a place in which to become clean.

The first brightness soon faded leaving a long, slow twilight. The breeze was cold but cleansing and I let it scour me.

Eventually, he said, 'Sorry is a remarkably inadequate word. You mustn't take any blame to yourself. I was wrong and it was entirely my fault. I can plead no mitigating circumstances.'

A leaf fell into my lap. 'Look,' I said. 'It chose me to fall down upon. When I was a child, I would spend hours trying to catch the leaves as they blew away. It's surprisingly difficult, but it was meant to bring good luck. Now one falls straight into my lap. Why? Why did it fall on me? Why was I chosen for this silly farce? Why me, Face?'

'The universal question in any catastrophe. There is no answer. Or rather there are so many you can take your choice. Kismet? Destiny? The Fates playing Russian Roulette. The God of Vengeance taking a pot shot? Who knows?'

'Will I ever get back?'

'I would guess not. You've gelled. That transparent nun hasn't jumped the gulf completely. But you're real. Very visible and very tangible.' He laughed softly. 'That is your cue to vanish in a puff of smoke. Who knows, lady? I don't.'

'And Sarah?'

'Is probably at the bottom of the Thames. Or sold to white slavers. From what we've gathered about her, she'd quite like that. Perhaps she's jumped into her own alternative world.'

'Her still-born child?'

'Might be alive and well, another Unity. You're not going to know. Forget it.'

'My boys, Chris and Tim . . .'

'In the thunderstorm? Atmospheric disturbances, electricity floating loose . . . I'd say that anything can happen under those circumstances. You can't spend the rest of your life chasing after thunderstorms. You are going to have to forget it all and start over again.'

'I wish I could.'

We said nothing more in the fading light. He returned to his guitar and picked out a melody and a few chords that sounded atonal and Asiatic to my ignorant ears. The hint of a samisen, an evocative whisper behind bamboo and rice paper.

'I'm going to sing you a song,' he said abruptly.

I and my sorrow walk in the garden and leave no shadow.
I am the mirage of a lost ship
With gallant sail that drowned in a requiem.

I am the shadow behind the dream that faded.
The chrysanthemums ignore me,
The leaves die in glory and do not hear me pass.
The dying leaf mimics a wind-tossed sail,
A reflection in the water.
I cannot see my face when I look in the glass.

The sound died away into the night, but I said nothing, not wanting to lose the moment in words. I recognized the images in the song and knew where they had been found and a deep gratitude flooded through me, for him, for the gift of the sunset and the music, and for the pain and plenty of life itself. Finally, I forced myself to speak, not wanting to appear ungrateful.

'That is what you were writing when I came from the cottage.'

'Yes.'

'Thank you is as inadequate as sorry. That's how I felt, all the time. A sad and invisible ghost casting no shadow, leaving no mark on the world. I didn't even know whose face I saw in the glass.'

'Do you now?'

'I think I'm on the way to finding out.'

'I wonder who it will be,' he said thoughtfully, then broke the mood with a strum of buccaneering chords. 'Heave ho, my hearties! Nearly back on an even keel. By the way, do you mind if I offer that to Rog as my fourth poem?'

'Of course I don't mind. But I thought he was against you writing your own material for this particular program?'

'I'll tell him it's by somebody else. I'll think of a likely name. He won't know, he's not as clued up as he thinks he is. I'll get him all turned on about his pictures. I see a Thames barge, one of the old sailing ones with those brown sails, gliding down the river. Then autumn leaves falling on the lake in Regent's Park or St.

James's. Brown sails and brown leaves on water and a wide-eyed girl.'

'A transparent nun?'

'Not her, she always hogs the best shots. No, I'll find a softer waif caught on the wrong side of the veil.'

'Then what?'

'Then, with luck, Rog will go bananas, making little squares with his fingers and muttering about lenses and angles. When he's all worked up and whirring like a camera, I'll break it to him that the poem isn't a translation from a Zen master, or a meditation from a Californian acid head, or whoever I think up, but only by one barbarian digger. By then, he won't care.'

I laughed in the dark. The sun had set and a thin sliver of moon was climbing slowly out of the trees. He kissed me on the mouth, a long, yet oddly passionless kiss. It was an act in itself, neither a beginning nor an end, an invitation or a farewell.

'Come on, lady, I'm taking you home.'

My first sight of Pippa was on television, a late night chat show. She was a creation, an edifice, miraculously svelte and soignée. I knew so well the tilt of her head, but I didn't know at all the new tilt to her nose, nor the rock hard gloss of her confidence. The interviewer was terrified of her and she knew it. She mocked him, bewitched him, mimicked him and butchered him until the hand clutching the clipboard showed white at the knuckles, and the hand scratching his head was halted in mid-scratch and his whole being was frozen into self-conscious embarrassment.

The studio audience loved her. They were safely out of the way of her barbed tongue; and her outrageous indiscretions about the private lives of her friends made them roar, they and their own friends were cosily hidden away in grateful anonymity.

'Jesus, lady, she makes me nervous just watching her. Were you really buddy with that?'

'She's a monster, a holy cow, but—can't you see?—she's acting it, she's sending it all up. It's a part, a role and she's enjoying it.'

'She's enjoying it all right. She likes to have blood on her nails and a skeleton to rattle. A vampire.'

'No, I mean she enjoys pretending to be that outrageous person. I can still see the real Pippa. I'm sure I can.'

'She's turned that way forever. The wind must have changed. Didn't they tell you as a child not to pull faces? Else you get caught when the wind changes? I think I'll try and borrow a bulletproof vest for you.'

'Really, it's no worse than you acting out the Wild Colonial Boy for the punters. Isn't that what you said you tried when you went busking? Pippa is acting out the Bitch Goddess. She still knows what is real and what isn't.'

'I wouldn't count on that, if I were you.'

I wasn't; but I wasn't put off either, or dismayed by the new Pippa. On one level she was a challenge, one very unruly piece of the living jigsaw that make up the whole of any production from a full scale musical to a thirty seconds commercial. It was my job to complete the jigsaw on this occasion. Liz had said nothing concrete, had issued no ultimatum, but it was made plain by an undercurrent of innuendo that the Raindew commercial was to be the test, the final examination by which my future with the firm was to be assessed. The commercial was in no danger of floundering, Liz made certain of that. I caught her stealthily checking my files, and occasionally, when I was on the phone booking studios or the crew, or talking to the advertising agency, she left the office and I was sure that she was monitoring the call on Trej's switchboard.

A few days after the chat show and the day before shooting, Jamie took me to the Savoy to meet Pippa. He had borne the dog's burden and had survived the tantrums over script and costumes, soothing ruffled feathers all around with the tact and understanding of a good agent with a client whose ten per cent is worth the earning. I was to be alone in the studio, sole representative of Location Services, the advertisers, and surrogate handholder as Jamie was miraculously tied up, as was Liz, and 'wasn't it lucky that Sarah can cope?'

I was looking forward to the encounter for all the wrong reasons. I was, I decided, the only woman in the Western Hemisphere who knew more about Pippa Waters than Pippa knew about herself, and I was prepared to exploit and enjoy this illicit knowledge. From her official biography, I had learned that La Waters had deviated from my Pippa about two years out of Drama School. The early days on the Fringe were much as I knew them but, of course, there had been no fit-up tour of South Wales. A production that had flopped disastrously (I remembered her vivid distribution of blame) had, after all, prospered and had finally appeared Off Broadway. La Waters was about to be born.

Jamie and I were kept waiting for three quarters of an hour before being allowed up to her suite. We drank tea and ate a sinful pastry and Jamie chattered with great animation.

Suddenly he stopped. 'Well, Sarah, here I am making the most gigantic effort to put you at your ease, working myself into a positive lather to stop you fretting, and you are not the tiniest bit flustered. Sitting there like the Mona Lisa on a dull Sunday. I've never taken anyone to see Madam who hasn't been shaking like a leaf at the first meeting.'

'Well, here's one.'

'You are a cool customer and no mistake. What's your secret? I was nearly wetting my knickers when I first had to deal with her.'

'No secret, Jamie. She is not the sort of woman who frightens me.'

'My dear, if it wasn't that Liz would slit my throat, I'd offer you a job in my office right away.'

I laughed. 'No deal. If by this time tomorrow there is a commercial safely in the can, I won't need your job. If there isn't, you won't want me, anyway.'

'If you know that,' he said thoughtfully, 'and you are still unworried, then my offer most certainly does stand, whatever tomorrow brings.'

We were summoned by Pippa's factotum. It was hard to assess his actual function as he appeared to be dresser, hair stylist, secretary, bodyguard and personal maid all rolled into one lean, tanned, camp, American youth. Audience had been granted.

She received us in a skin-tight jumpsuit of white velvet. A garment which no other woman would attempt to wear, or, if foolhardy enough to try, would not have remained unscathed from the contest. Pippa won.

'Come in, darlings,' she crooned from a sofa where she had

carefully arranged herself. 'Bunny, do fix these people a drink. Jamie has a Bloody Mary, and—you do drink, do you dear?'

I knew the trick. The nice, kind, friendly loosening up to get 'em off guard before the rabbit punch. She had spoiled it by being patronizing, but I was presumably too confused to notice. I was, after all, a sitting duck.

'Do speak up, dear.'

'I'll have a Whiskey Sour or some chilled white wine. Whichever Bunny can manage most easily.'

She looked at me sharply, sensing the absence of awe, and she caught the glint of amusement that I couldn't repress. Her action was exactly as I could have predicted. She stopped lounging, sat up and became businesslike. The rabbit punch was abandoned and she had to know me better before deciding on rapier or poison. I had, in that brief second, become a more worthy foe.

'You are Sarah Davies? From Location Services?' She had known my name all along.

'Yes, Miss Waters, I'm very glad to meet you.'

'Pippa, darling. Everybody calls me Pippa. When they are not being insulting. After all, I am public property.'

'Thank you,' I said rather coldly.

She was used to people falling over and purring, saying, 'Thank you, Pippa,' and begging her to use their name even more freely. My cool acceptance and refusal to purr alerted her still more. Jamie and Bunny were looking at me in amazement. The secret is, you fools, I wanted to tell them, is knowing this monster like a sister. I've seen her cry, pick her nose, shiver with flu. I've borrowed her clothes, heard her secret fears, watched her with her guard down. You can't be afraid of somebody you've seen weeping with fatigue in a cold and dusty dawn.

She launched herself into the matter at hand. She went through the script, the shooting schedule, the personal arrangements and so on. It was too easy, and I knew that tomorrow would be a day of reckoning for me, she would be unable to resist getting under my guard. We finished all the business in fifteen minutes flat and then we were dismissed.

'Thank you, Sarah, you've been commendably thorough. I'll see you at the studio tomorrow morning then. I won't be late.

Goodbye, Jamie darling. Isn't it a refreshing change to meet somebody who knows their job?'

Leaving her suite, Jamie asked, 'Do you use hypnotism? I've never seen her as meek as that. A positive lamb.'

'I'll pay for it tomorrow, you know.'

'Of course you will,' he said sharply. 'I'm not fool enough to suppose otherwise. But I'll back you for a win and yesterday I wouldn't have taken a bet at all.'

The director was a youngish man who always made the Raindew commercials. They were not technically demanding and were, for him, a matter of routine. On this occasion he had wisely decided to leave the manipulation of his temperamental performer to the producers represented by me; and, after a preliminary inquiry about her probable behavior, became involved with an unnecessary and intricate discussion with the lighting cameraman.

I was prepared for late arrival, non arrival, a morning temper, even a migraine and a wasted day. She upstaged me. She arrived two minutes before her Estimated Time of Arrival, smiled sweetly at the director and his crew, said nice things about the set, praised the script. And didn't look in my direction once.

It was going to be a rough day, though by the expressions of relief on the faces of the crew, they hadn't realized it yet.

She was dressed and made-up and back on the set in record time. Then, with a charming smile and witty tongue, she set to work. She created factions, drew up lines of battle, manufactured friction. The lighting cameraman was soon enraged with the costume designer, her costumes were impossible to light correctly in that set; the set designer was played off against the script writer to whose ridiculous stage direction the set was designed. The director was pointed and fired at the script writer; couldn't he hear the innuendos in the script? Like Marie Lloyd who, it is said, could read the Hymn Book and make it suggestive, Pippa packed meanings into her rendition of the advertising matter that would have been actionable. The spiral of panic and antagonism mounted higher and higher. The sofa, the height of the chair on which she had to sit, the bunch of flowers on the table, the type of film in the camera, were all thrown into the arena, and the pack tore after these scraps of red herrings and tore them apart. The studio became a mass of squabbles and futile argument. The assistant shouted in vain for quiet, appeals to reason went unheard.

At the peak of this invented chaos, she burst into tears, real watery tears. She tore her dress into unmendable shreds, rushed sobbing to her dressing room and slammed the door in Bunny's face as he tried to follow.

The thud of the slammed door acted as a mute. The studio was silent and sheepish in the wreckage.

I had been sitting and waiting alone by the wall. Before the director could collect enough wits to appeal to me, I stood up and said, 'There's nothing to worry about. I'll have her back on the set within half an hour at the most. Tidy up and sort out whatever you have to sort out and be ready to shoot at 11:30. I reckon she'll do it in one take. She can, you know.'

A ripple of disbelief answered me. Bunny said petulantly, 'She won't talk to you. She won't even let *me* in, for heaven's sake. No way will you get in through that door.'

I knew better. This was her victory and she wanted to gloat. I knocked loudly on the door.

'Pippa, will you let me in, please?'

She recognized my voice, no slouch Pippa, but then, she had been waiting for me. The door opened at once and I was allowed to enter. As I turned to close it behind me, I saw Bunny flounce off in a pet.

We stood looking at each other. The tears were still running down her cheeks. I wasn't impressed. It was a trick she had used for years, fetching pathetic streams of water from her eyes. She had once wangled a free meal for us by doing just that for a susceptible landlord in a pub.

I grinned. 'You did that on purpose, didn't you? You knew exactly the right moment and the right pressure and when to apply it. Now, I want to know why?'

She was undecided. I should have been in a blind panic by now and I wasn't; but she hated to abandon a good fight. For a moment, she looked dangerous and I regretted the grin; but then, she too grinned and, though she didn't know it, my Pippa was back.

'What the hell is wrong with you, Sarah Davies? Don't you need to keep your job?'

'I lose a damn sight more than my job, if I don't make sure that this commercial is shot today.'

'Then why in hell play so cool?'

'Why do you play so rough?'

'Fools scare very easily. It stops me dying of boredom in a very boring occupation. Acting is a very dull profession. My shrink says that I suffer from compensatory sadism. I daresay he's right, given his ludicrous jargon. I get a real buzz from seeing how quickly I can make people cringe.'

'I'm not cringing.'

'No. And you won't play my game either. Why not?'

'I can read the moves you are going to make.'

'So very few can, it makes a refreshing change. Actually, it just encourages me when they all play up to the myth. Bully me, call my bluff and I'm putty.'

'Then re-do your make-up and I'll send Bunny for the alternative costume. It's the better one, anyway. That's why I held it back.'

'It is also why I was careful to tear this one.'

We laughed together. No, not like old times for she didn't know me at all. There was no lifting of the veil for Pippa. Perhaps because she was so firmly rooted in life, at the very peak of her powers, whereas Klaus had been dying, losing grip on his own reality.

I went to the door to summon Bunny. She called after me, 'Hey you, Sarah, don't go. Stay and chat while I repair my maquillage.'

'You didn't do it much harm.'

'Of course not, darling.' She dabbed at her face, peering in the mirror and humming slightly as she always had when she concentrated on her appearance. No sign left of the Bitch Goddess. It was indeed a plastic creation, but I had taken a considerable gamble on my own judgment and I shuddered at the risk now that the danger was over.

We chatted easily while Bunny tutted and aahed over the costume. I asked her about her days at Drama School. I was turning into a facile liar. I claimed, as my alter ego certainly had, an acquaintance with several of her contemporaries there. We exchanged news and gossip and among the general barrage of names I threw in the two that were missing.

'Never heard of them. Were they in my year?'

I shrugged. 'Perhaps not. They've dropped out of the business, anyway. I think I met Unity once because I am sure that it was she who told me about your flat in Gower Street.'

'Oh, it was bliss. The vandals were about to knock it down. I wonder if they have. They ought to put a plaque instead. "Pippa Waters slept here—with practically anybody." '

'I remember Unity told me that there was a craze for playing "Botticelli" at Drama School.'

'Christ, yes. I'd forgotten. We nearly drove ourselves schizo. Those were the days. My God, to think that the height of fun was a couple of beers and word games. How delicious to be so naive. Now, it takes some very expensive champagne and at least two pretty young men . . .'

I interrupted, not wanting to be diverted. 'There was another game called "Titles." '

She pouted at her reflection in the glass and patted her immaculate hair.

' "Titles"? Do I remember a game called "Titles"?'

' "The Guelph who was a Ghibelline," ' I prompted.

'But yes.' She laughed. 'I remember one. "Dogger, Fisher, German Bight." Very nautical. Wasn't it a musical?'

'From the shipping forecasts.'

She suddenly frowned and looked at me steadily from the dressing table mirror. I was behind her, but she didn't turn her head and her reflection stared at me with a faint tinge of hostility. I wondered whether the veil had lifted at all. Finally, she said, 'You are a very freaky lady. You know too damn much about me. I had that dream a long time ago. Before I went to the States. It was very vivid, which is why I remember it. The games. The titles. But I never told anybody and it's only just come back to me just now.'

I said, as casually as I could, 'My grandmother is Scottish. I'm prone to strange insights. It must be a relic of the Second Sight. Half the time I don't realize I'm doing it. Sorry to intrude on your dreams.'

Bunny had come forward to supervise the last touches. I asked softly, 'Can you remember anything else about that dream?' But she merely grunted dismissively. She was absorbed with Bunny, putting together the faultless, money-spinning bundle that was Pippa Waters.

'Sorry darling, it was an age and a half ago.'

She stood up and she and Bunny began a careful inspection. When they were both satisfied, she said, 'O.K. ladies. Let's get this show on the road. Wagons Roll!'

It was shot and wrapped up by lunchtime. When I went back to her dressing room to say goodbye and thank her, she said, 'If you ever hit the West Coast, why don't you drop by and visit? I like you and that's rare. I don't use them myself, but we might have become friends in another day and age.'

Pippa, in another day and age, we were.

Back in the office, Liz was offhand and not interested in my report of the day's work. She must have had a spy in the studio and known the saga already for her behavior made it apparent that she was delighted with my victory. Toward the end of the afternoon, she murmured angrily about negotiating a proper contract for me the following day, if she could find the time.

'Thank you, Liz. I'm very glad that it's worked out like this.'

'Hm. And you'd better hire a shorthand typist that we can share. It's about time that we had some competent secretarial help here for a change.'

Back at the flat, Face was absent and there was no indication, no note or message, to tell me where he had gone. He had not shown up at Wardour Street to meet me, but I wasn't surprised for his own work was pushing him hard. It amused him that he, a barbarous Aussie, knew London better than the effete and protected Roger who was native-born, and he planned to show Rog the seamier side of the city. Today must have turned into the outing that Face proposed on the pretext of looking for Thames barges. They could have been found any day *in situ* at the tourist trap of St. Katherine's Dock; but Face had plotted an adventure trail through Limehouse and the West India Docks that was to end in a pub called 'The Gun' in the Isle of Dogs.

I assumed that this expedition had taken place and that it had mutated into a working session or a pub crawl. I was childishly disappointed. I wanted him to share my sense of success and the vindication of my faith in the Pippa under the plastic; and he had uncharacteristically absented himself. Or was it out of character? I had been too self-obsessed to delve very deep. I had cast him as my protector, asked much and given little, forced him into a straitjacket of forbearance as formidable as my mother's. I had no rights, no claim on his time or his company; and yet I wanted a celebration, however trivial, and the lack of it left me dissatisfied and fretful.

The reminder of my mother burned. I had phoned the doctor from the office the Monday after our excursion to Oxfordshire and had been told by the receptionist in formal and uncommunicative tones that her condition was satisfactory, a medic's platitude that can mean anything. Illogically, I felt that Face's desertion was a punishment for my dereliction of duty and I dialed the doctor's number. By some lucky chance, I caught him at the end of the evening's surgery and he came to the phone himself.

'Ah, yes. I understand that you are related to the late Dr. Penfold.'

'Er . . . yes.'

'Mrs. Penfold seems to have been very confused by your visit.'

'I'm sorry. I feel very guilty. I had no idea . . .'

'If it relieves your mind, I must tell you that this is not the first time she has suffered a temporary breakdown. And I assure you that I have no doubt that it is positively temporary. I am certain that she will be sufficiently recovered to return home very shortly.'

'Thank you, doctor.'

I went to bed early. My euphoria had dissolved into a mush of self-pity and tears.

In the morning's light, I felt stronger, though Face's continued non-appearance disturbed me. I recognized with a pang that I had no right, when he did show up, even to ask for an explanation, still less to make the demand for an apology that my bruised pride wanted. However, work called and there was no time for introspective regrets.

As I passed Trej on the way to my office, she said, 'I saw your
friend last night. He was having a wild time.'

Again the possessive, shameful pang. 'Good,' I said casually,
'where was this?'

'At a party in Hampstead. He was playing his guitar, knee-deep
in women. All fighting over him. I had to stab a few myself, just
to say hello.'

'Whose party?'

'No idea. I was taken there and lost my escort within minutes,
so I never found out.'

She was waiting for a reaction from me, so I said, 'He's been
working extremely hard. He's due for some fun and relaxation.'

'He was finding both last night. Was he ever!'

'That sounds like a good thing, then,' I said, as evenly as I
could. 'I'll take the mail through, if you've finished sorting it.'

Negotiations with Liz were commenced at once and quickly
settled, as I was offered far better terms than I thought I deserved.
My so-called achievement had been no more than a conjuring
trick, after all. But, if Liz had confidence in me, I recognized that
it would be a sufficient spur to justify my employment. I wondered if Jamie had hinted that he had put in a bid for my services,
because Liz was binding me to her with a generosity that I'd be a
fool to pass by. She then handed me a workload that would sink
a Greek tanker, and under the pressure of coping with it, I forgot
about Face; a fact which, when it came to my notice, cheered
me greatly. It was yet another sign of a belated growing-up that I
could concentrate on the job in hand and forget about emotional
vicissitudes.

He said little about his outing when we met that evening as
usual, other than that yesterday had ended in a party and that
rather than struggle home he had kipped down where he could.
I asked no questions and he was a delighted, if overdue, audience
for my round-by-round account of the Battle of La Waters, and
he was impressed by my contract with Location Services.

We were having a drink in our usual pub. We had ventured
back after my encounter with Martin and Louis to find that they
had left the field to us.

Face said, 'We'll eat out tonight. Somewhere smart and very

expensive to celebrate your victory, the successful vanquishing of lady dragons of all complexions from Liz Wilton to Pippa Waters, not to mention Jamie Marriot. And also . . .' He stopped with an apologetic smile.

'And what? Speak up, I can take it.'

'No tact, me. The wrong time to harp back. But I mean survival. Your victory over life in general. Look back a few months and take a good look at what you've achieved. An assured future, a job that you are good at and that pays well. Laughter and confidence. You were such a hopeless, copeless lady, that I'd not have reckoned much for your chances.'

'Nor I. It's good to wake up in the morning with hope instead of misery. I should have tried it before when there was a reason.'

'Nearly seven months,' he continued, 'is a long time. Time to go around the world without an airplane. Learn a new language. Just about give birth to a new life.'

'It would be premature.'

'Yes,' he said into his glass. 'A year and a day is the usual time.'

I ignored the implication. 'Where shall we eat? You choose and I'll pay. A fair exchange for a rich and liberated lady like myself.'

'Sheekey's? Wheelers? Manzi's?'

'Fish restaurants.' My tones were harsher than I intended, but he was hammering the implication too hard this time. ' "Fish dinners will make a man spring like a flea," is that it? No, Face, not yet. Please not yet.'

He repeated his comic mask of apology. 'Lady, I waited till you passed your driving test. The crisis is over and I've free choice again.'

I went cold. 'You are going to leave, then?'

He laughed. 'Good God, no. I'm not issuing an ultimatum. Stating a few alternatives. Testing the wind before releasing the straws. "The Seeing Eye" will be recorded about the end of this month. 28th or 29th, so Rog tells me. After then, I don't know what. Perhaps I'll go walkabout a bit. Take a little saunter to some sunshine. December is a bleak month for this old slattern of a city.'

I looked hard at him, but his expression was cheerfully negative. He too was hedging a few bets. I knew my feelings for him well: warmth, gratitude, friendship, even love; but not desire, not yet.

I answered him obliquely, following my own trail. 'John Lang still invades my dreams with his maggot fingers.'

He nodded an understanding. 'Let's eat Italian. I'll take you to that restaurant where Rog took me and I'll point out to you all the telly producers, publishers and agents. But only if you promise to gawp like a tourist.'

Supper was relaxed and easy. Only a few strands, disturbing and elusive, were woven into the fabric of conversation and we both worked hard to pull them out. I told him about my new projects.

'In fact, I go to Gloucester tomorrow.'

'Like Dr. Foster in a shower of rain?'

'I hope not. I'm going house-hunting. One is needed for a location, an empty period house with a well kept garden. Though show me any garden in November that looks well kept . . . However, Liz knows of a house, an old manor, and I'm to vet it. If it's suitable, I'll have to get the mains services laid on—gas, electricity and water. And phones. God bless the Post Office.'

'How will you get there?'

'I've been elevated to become a licensed borrower of the firm's car.'

'Wow, I'm impressed. How long will you be away?'

'Mice wanting to play, are they?'

'Too true. But you're no cat.'

'You've never seen me scratch. I'll drive down tomorrow afternoon and probably meet the solicitor on Thursday morning. His firm acts as trustees for the manor. If all that works out, I expect I'll be back on Saturday morning, but if I have to find another house I'll have to do the rounds of estate agents and I could be well over a week. Plenty of time for you to get up to no good.'

'What, me? I wouldn't know how.'

'Not what I heard from Trej.'

'Oh yes. She was at the party last night. She's only a doxy.'

'And I am not?'

'No. Be thankful for it. If you are still uncertain, look up the dictionary definition and think about it in Gloucester. Cathedral towns are good for contemplation, lady.'

His tone put an end to that conversation and an invasion of such obvious BBC types made us giggle. Some Hollywood tycoon had ordered the batch from Central Casting as background to his meaningful movie about the Decline of the British Empire.

Next morning I packed some clothes. My wardrobe had grown and improved over the months; Sarah's cheap synthetics had been disposed of, and I had conquered Unity's addiction for jeans and little else. I was taking a pride in my appearance and chose carefully the right image for the job I had to do. Face helped me trace a route from road maps we found in the flat. It went uncomfortably close to my mother's village, but he was adamant that it would be foolish and destructive to chance another encounter.

At the office, Trej booked me a room at The White Hart Inn and made an appointment for 9:30 the following morning with Mr. Wells of Stephens, Walker and Wells, Cathedral Row. Then I went with Mark-or-Mike to collect the car. He explained its peculiarities to me with love, for he treated it with a tenderness born of necessity. He used it often and made me feel that I was committing piracy.

I set off early as I intended to reach Gloucester before dark, if I could. The nights were drawing in since October died and I hadn't driven a car for many, many months. It would have been wasteful to end all my new hopes in the accident ward of the local hospital.

I soon came to terms with the car and began to enjoy the drive. It was a windy day, stripping the last of the trees naked in the fitful sunlight that glinted occasionally through shifting gray clouds. The air smelled soggily of the approach of winter, the cold mustiness before the true frosts come. It reeked of dead leaves, brown earth and bonfires; and tomorrow, I realized, was November 5th, Guy Fawkes Night. Bonfires, a straw-filled Guy, soup and hot sausages and Ned letting off the fireworks to delight the boys. How they loved Guy Fawkes . . .

Tears blinded me and I had to slow up. I slipped into the slow lane amid angry hootings. I cleared my eyes and drove slowly, forcing my thoughts to probe the wound, to test how much it had healed, instead of my usual trick of pushing the painful memories to one side with busy details of work. It hurt, it was still very sore, but I could bear it, suffer it without analgesics. Even a Bonfire Night without Ned and the boys could be borne for I had traveled a long way from the woman who had fed on her own sense of incompetence fostered by self-pity. Last year, I had cried because I had imagined that I'd let them down by making an inadequate Guy. The Guy was perfectly fine, but my tears had nearly spoiled the evening until it was rescued by Ned. This year, I was crying because they had inexplicably vanished behind the veil; but the woman who was left behind would not now cry over an ill-made puppet.

The White Hart Inn must have flourished during the latter half of the eighteenth century and gently declined ever since. It seems to have had a brief revival during the Twenties of this century for its classical façade opened into a foyer decorated with Art Deco dados, and the menu displayed in the austere porch was improbably elaborate and written in snob kitchen French.

On the steps of the porch, two grinning urchins sat beside a sack with a cloth head and wearing a tattered jacket. They chanted continually, whether there were passersby or no, 'Penny for the Guy. Penny for the Guy.'

Chris and Tim had ventured forth last year with two sticks wrapped in a cloth by Ned. They had met unscrupulous competition from wilier guttersnipes but had returned with shining eyes, fingers numb with cold and 14½ pence. I gave the urchins a tenpence piece each, and the chanting ceased while they examined and compared their booty.

I dined alone and rather gloomily, less sanguine than when I was starting out on my drive through the stormy afternoon. Hotels are lonely places out of season and I'd have welcomed a working companion, or even more gossip-prone sales reps than those with whom I shared the lounge and ghosting television set, which they had firmly anchored into the wrong channel. I became low enough to be forced into lecturing myself about the progress I had made. I was barely past halfway in my mourning and I was asking over much. All the same, I wished I wasn't going to spend Bonfire Night alone in a gloomy hotel.

I presented myself at Stephens, Walker and Wells, at 9:30 the following morning. The offices were straight from Trollope. With their view of the Cathedral and the vague air of belonging to a more spacious and gracious age than ours, I assumed, since my appointment was with Mr. Wells, that Messrs. Stephens and Walker had long since departed to some Barsetshire heaven and that Mr. Wells was the elderly grandson of the original partner.

The girl in the office confirmed my guess when I announced myself as the representative of Location Services.

'That'd be Miss Sarah Davies, would it?' she asked with her West Country burr. 'I'm ever so sorry, but I don't think you'll be able to meet Mr. Wells. He's been a bit poorly, but then he's getting on a bit, so what can you expect? Now, let me see, one of the junior partners was to help you.' She consulted a list. 'Oh yes, here it is. Young Mr. Edward it is. He's engaged at the moment, but if you'd like to wait in his office . . .'

She might sound slow but she was well trained. Young Mr. Edward was late. She showed me into his office and left me to wait. It was a large room, littered with the paraphernalia of a profession that regards paper as sacred, but it had an elegant bay window that overlooked the Cathedral Green. There was another profession which dealt with sacred matters, but the clergy of the Church of England had an appreciative eye for material beauty. They always nabbed the best accommodation and treated it with proper respect.

I was deep in a gently melancholic contemplation of the view so that I didn't hear him enter the office. The familiar and beloved voice spoke behind my back.

'Miss Davies, I really must apologize for being unforgivably late . . .'

I leaped to my feet and turned to look at him. My arms reached out to touch him and I saw him back away, startled, as I gasped, 'Ned, oh Ned, where have you been?'

The shock on his face which held no recognition pulled me together. I tried to gather my scattered wits and stood still, white and trembling, an odd spectacle of a business woman. He too seemed disturbed. His face was flushed and he made small, meaningless dabs at me as if they would alleviate my distress.

'I am so sorry for giving you such a fright, Miss Davies. I must apologize. First, I'm late. No excuse. And then I creep up behind you and give you a shock. I really am most frightfully sorry. Can I do anything? Call the girl?'

I sat down heavily. 'No, I must apologize as well. I'm not usually such a bundle of nerves. You look and sound remarkably like . . . an old friend of mine.'

'Nevertheless, I'll ask the girl to make us some tea. Dear me, what an inauspicious start to a day's business.'

He bustled out, thankful to escape I realized, and it gave me a chance to recover. On his desk stood a small wooden plaque: E. R. Taylor. Young Mr. Edward, very Trollopian. I had blundered into the place where Edward Roland Taylor had remained, never translated into Ned Roland.

He came back cautiously into the office and appeared reassured by my more normal behavior. He was carrying a tea tray with which he busied himself at the desk. I took the chance to examine him more carefully. It was certainly Ned, but Ned playing a character part. My Ned would have loved the careful hair cut, the old-fashioned navy blue suit, the tie pin and the black, highly polished leather shoes. I could imagine him taking a craftsman's delight in the choice of spectacles, signet ring and clocked socks. As I watched Edward Taylor pour the tea, I was expecting him to throw aside the specs, rumple his hair and say happily, 'That's the right way, don't you think, Newt? Not overdone, but just slightly over the top. A country solicitor, ten years behind the times and complete in every detail.'

But he was not going to throw off the disguise. These clothes were not a joke. He didn't know that my name was Newt. He was going to be a far greater challenge than Pippa, for this time my heart was breaking.

He handed me a cup of tea and smiled the tentative smile that hoped I wasn't going to prove a difficult client. I forced myself to play my part. It was easier than I would have dared to hope, but I had, I realized, had seven months to rehearse it. I smiled back bravely and said, 'I must apologize again, Mr. Taylor. Ned, the friend whom you resemble so closely, died last April. You can imagine the shock. My mind was far away, admiring your lovely view of the Cathedral.'

He brought his cup with him and drew up a chair so that we sat facing each other like guests at Mrs. Proudie's tea parties.

'Don't mention it, Miss Davies. The mind plays odd tricks and a bereavement is a very shocking experience. Now, I'll tell you a little secret. You gave me quite a fright as well . . . but no, I mustn't waste your time with my silly stories.'

'Please, do go on, Mr. Taylor. I am most interested,' I said, as moderately as I could manage as we acted out our parts in this lunatic tea party. 'Do tell me about your fright. I am a great believer in the odd insights we often have about complete strangers.'

'Alas, it was nothing like that. The truth is that I've been looking forward to this meeting. You represent a world that I once . . . ah, lost dreams. I wanted to go on the stage myself. How trite that sounds. But I used to be told that I had a modicum of talent. I was the mainstay of the school dramatics, and, even now, I'm no mean member of our local amateurs. I had such dreams. I was going to call myself Ned. Ned Taylor, so much more dashing than Edward. But my parents, you know. An only son. They wanted to see me settled. Ah well, a very dull story, I'm afraid. You must hear it as often as I hear my clients believe their own lies.'

'Not so dull or trite, Mr. Taylor. I understand better than you know.' I said, but he didn't pick up on my comment, only on my use of his name, for he said, 'Please, call me Edward. After such an unconventional introduction we really can't go on being formal. And we shall be seeing a lot of each other during the next few days, I very much hope.'

'Thank you, Edward. Please call me Sarah,' I said. And wondered why I was still sane.

He beamed. 'Thank you. Sarah is one of my favorite names.'

I smiled prettily at the compliment. For one bizarre moment, I decided that we had been engaged to play opposite each other in a play and that we were acting out this ridiculous scene cast as Sarah and Edward and that I had slipped so completely into my interpretation of the role that I had dreamed up the whole complex history of the plot. Any minute the scene would finish and we would return to our proper selves and assess our performances. We were both giving exceptionally fine characterizations, the sense of reality was overpowering.

He put down his cup and stood up. 'Have you finished your tea?'

I nodded.

'Well, if you've fully recovered and you're feeling game, perhaps we'd better go and take a look at the Manor. My car is outside, ready and waiting, Sarah.' He opened the door and ushered me through with a flourish. He stopped on the steps and looked critically at the sky. 'No rain and we might even manage to produce some sunshine for you. Quite a jolly day for a run. I always think I'm a lucky chap if I can combine business with pleasure and today is clearly my lucky day.'

Those inane phrases were the product of a life spent in growing up to be a pillar of the community in a country town. He must hover on the periphery of Cathedral politics, local government, the planners and developers, the farmers, and the Jaguar and cavalry twill set. They would all require a solicitor and the one they chose to handle their business would need to be a social chameleon, an easy task for an actor *manqué*. Edward would be startled to know he used the same skills as Ned.

The Manor was perfect inside. Stephens, Walker and Wells held it in trust for the orphaned offspring of the previous owners who was about to enter his majority. Since the last tenants had left, three years previously, they had used it as a source of income for the estate with short and occasional lettings, for they wanted the new owner to make his own choices when he came of age. They had kept it in good trim. It had been recently decorated and the mains services could be, Edward promised, reconnected within a few days. I was certain that the promise would be kept.

The only problem was the garden. It had been left to grow wild during the summer and the lushness had decayed into a dank jungle that not even a squad of gardeners could make attractive.

We strolled through the grounds discussing the matter.

'The best we could hope for in early November,' he said, 'is to make it look tidy. Cut everything back, burn the leaves, dig over the flower beds. But it will look very bleak.'

I agreed. 'I doubt if I'd fare better anywhere else. Film makers always want the moon. Nobody in their right mind would demand an attractive garden in November on a location. In a studio perhaps one might use some poetic license, an allowable cheat.'

He said wistfully, 'It must be a very exciting life.'

'Exciting but not always agreeable, I'm sorry to say. I think you have the better deal in life, Edward,' I added, trying the name on my tongue.

He smiled at me with real warmth. 'It's generous of you to try and console me. I suppose I'll always harbor a host of might-have-beens.'

'We all do.'

We were walking past a weed-choked goldfish pond. He had picked up a fallen branch and was using it to hack at the weeds and explore behind the overgrown briars. He turned over a water-lily leaf and squatted to examine it, a gesture so typical of Ned that it was hard not to claim him.

'This must look very pretty in the spring,' I said instead. Under these banalities I was conducting a unilateral dialogue of dissolution.

Suddenly, he dropped the stick and dived into the briars with suicidal abandon. He emerged dishevelled and triumphant, holding out to me what appeared to be a small, round stone.

'Look,' he said happily. 'He was about to hibernate. I've rescued him from the billhooks of your minions.'

'A tortoise.'

'Yes, and he's a beauty. He must have lived wild for a few years. They can survive, you know, if they can find a compost heap, or dead leaves that ferment and retain the heat. They can dig beneath the frost line too. If they are lucky and it's a mild winter.'

'You know a lot about tortoises.'

'My parents had one. I loved it.'

'Called Speedy,' I said without thinking.

'How did you know?'

'They often are, aren't they? Like short men are called Lofty.'

'I suppose so.'

The head and flippers were neatly tucked away in an economy of space. Edward stood with untidy hair and specs awry, a streak of mud down one cheek. The solicitor had been sponged away like make-up, leaving, not Ned but nearly, a warm, compassionate man with a clown's face that changed with his mood.

He must have sensed my sympathetic scrutiny, for he grinned
boyishly. 'I look a terrible mess, I expect. And I seem to have won
a tortoise. I'd better take him home.'

'You must have sharp eyes.' I knew he had.

'I have. I use the specs rather like a stage property.' He dared
me to laugh, though he was smiling at himself. 'I have a rather
ludicrous face and I think that the specs make me look more serious. Add weight to my image. Don't you think?'

'Absolutely,' I said seriously. Oh Ned, I want to share this with
you. 'It's a very good idea.'

'But I must wash. And I think we are ready for a spot of lunch,
don't you, Sarah? There's a young couple who've opened a restaurant in a barn nearby. Clients, actually. They are always begging me to patronize them. I haven't any idea if their food is any
good. Would you care to experiment with me?'

'I'd love to.'

'Jolly good.' Behind that automatic courtesy, I heard a real
pleasure. 'Then we can settle all this tedious business as quickly
as possible and enjoy ourselves afterward.'

Over lunch I relaxed further. I was becoming used to this
stranger to whom I had been married for ten years. He didn't
know it, but I had lived with him, slept with him, borne his children . . .

'The tortoise,' I said slyly, 'will be a great treat for your
children.'

'I'm afraid that I have no children. I've always wanted them,
though. I think I'd make a good father.'

'Yes, I think you would. What about your wife? Does she want
children?'

He shook his head. 'My wife died in a car crash three years ago.
She was, I'm sorry to say, a very slapdash driver.'

'I'm sorry. What a tactless question. I didn't mean to pry. How
very tragic for you.'

'One gets over it with time.' He put his joke specs on the table-
cloth, then looked at me mischievously. 'Now you've broken the
ice, I can ask some questions I've been longing to ask but didn't
dare. Why does a Miss Davies wear a wedding ring?'

'It's quite common in my business. Women tend to keep their

own names for work. But I'm not married. This ring belongs to my grandmother.' I lied so easily that I knew I was beginning to believe in my own fictions.

'Now, how could an attractive woman like you escape marriage?'

'I never found the right man is the correct answer, isn't it? The real answer would take the story of my life.'

'Ned?' he asked.

I was agitated. I had forgotten the scene in his office. I said nothing.

'Ned,' he repeated. 'The man who looks like me.'

'Yes, I suppose you could say that he was one of the reasons.'

'He must have been a very lucky fellow indeed to have commanded such devotion from such a very lovely lady.'

He was attracted to me, flirting with me in his ponderous, clumsy fashion. My own husband was making a tentative bid for my favors. I was touched and terrified. The temptation was to break down and tell him everything, tell him the story of his years at Drama School, his success as an actor, the richer, deeper person he had become in less circumscribed surroundings. I wanted to tell him about our marriage, our love, tell him things about himself that he couldn't deny. I wanted to tell him about the boys, share again the joy in Chris and Tim . . .

But I couldn't. I couldn't hurt him that much. I couldn't watch the pain and distress in his eyes, the suspicion that I was, after all, a dangerous neurotic, that I could be cruel enough to taunt him with his wifeless, childless existence, invent a chimerical family and then be unable to follow up this fable by producing Chris and Tim, our boys who had never been born . . .

Ned had always hated the inexplicable and the indefinite. He liked order and hated ambiguity. He used to be angry if the boys were frightened by ghost stories. Even in the free wheeling world of the theater he had carved for himself a safe career.

I couldn't tell him, now or ever. I saw him smiling at me across the table and I was filled with longing, a nostalgia, not for him but for the man whom I'd left behind the veil. In this dimension, we were the same people, we were still mutually attracted, that much couldn't change; but we had nothing left to share, the diversity of our experience of each other left no common ground on which to build.

'Sarah, you've gone miles away. Where have you wandered?'

'Into times past.'

'Did I tread on a corn, speaking of Ned?'

'No more than I by asking about your wife.'

'Do you know,' he said cheerfully, 'I suddenly feel very odd and frivolous. It must be your influence. I have the feeling that you are going to bring me luck.'

'You don't know me. I am not a luck bringer.'

'I know what I can see. A handsome, sensitive, efficient woman. A rare treat for me, I assure you. I say, would you like a liqueur to round off this surprisingly well-cooked meal? It would be appropriately festive.'

I wanted to scream, to force him to acknowledge me and put aside his disguise. Instead, I smiled at him demurely, walking a careful tightrope between too blatant an invitation and the cold snub that would bring a pain I had no wish to inflict.

'I'd love a liqueur, but what is there to be festive about?'

'Meeting you.'

I laughed. 'Are you usually so reckless? Not a very good advertisement for a lawyer.'

He took my hand, which was lying on the table. 'Sarah, tonight is Bonfire Night. I've been invited to a rather jolly party. In fact, I've been co-opted to light the fireworks. It's rather a hobby of mine. The hosts are old friends, dear people. They have three kids and there'll be roast chestnuts and excellent hot punch. Please come with me. I'd like that.'

The choice was mine. I could spend the evening with Ned and watch him let off the fireworks, after all. We would laugh and get mildly drunk on the spiced punch, and later we might wander away from the others and kiss . . . the first time for him. For me, times without count. Perhaps I could win, or regain his love. Perhaps I could win his devotion all over again, wean him from his impersonation to become the man I knew.

I couldn't do it. I couldn't live like that. I couldn't love, perhaps marry—for Edward would insist on that I was sure—a man with whom I had already shared a decade of memories. Ten years ahead, the mother of ghost children . . . Memories that he would never share.

I looked at his dear, loved features and knew that it was impossible. The lie, the duplicity would defeat us both. I had traveled far since April. Then, I would have settled for the lie, settled for an amnesiac husband with a ten-year discrepancy in our anniversaries.

'Edward, how kind of you. An enchanting invitation but, sadly, I must decline. I'm due back in London the very minute we complete our business. The contents of my In Tray would make you shudder.'

My polite refusal churned on. I was on automatic pilot, half appalled at what I was doing, half relieved, aware that I could now embark on a future freed of clinging regrets for the past.

He expressed disappointment and was briefly saddened; but I had nipped the bud cleanly before it began to flower and there was little harm done. By pleading pressure of work, I had lifted my rejection away from personal considerations and that is always more acceptable.

We completed our business and said a formal goodbye. We'd meet again during the shooting; but the moment had gone, the choice had been made and accepted. If Edward parted from me with any regret, it soon vanished as he went toward his happy evening. And, as for me, my mourning was over. It was impossible to mourn for a man who is not dead and who has just asked you out to dinner.

I went back to the hotel and booked out. Then I phoned the flat at Chiswick.

'Face? This is Sarah. I'm on my way home.'

He whistled. 'Well, what d'you know? I thought you weren't coming back till Saturday.'

'No, it's all sorted out here. Everything. I promise you, everything. I'm starting off now. And, Face, I think I'd like a fish dinner when I get back.'

He whistled again and I knew he was smiling.

'So, I'll be back around nine.'

'Hey, lady.' He hesitated. 'Hang about. I ought to tell you something. Trej is here with me.'

I thought about it, then I laughed, a full acceptance of the delicious irony of living.

'Then she'll have to go. Get rid of her.'

I was about to replace the receiver when I heard him shout.

'Hey!'

I picked up the phone.

'Yes?'

'Drive carefully, Sarah Davies.'

But there was still one more thing I had to do before I went back
to Face, one final entry for the account book. I made a detour
coming back so that I drove into town from the north, and I made
my way through the havoc of Guy Fawkes Night along the Finch-
ley Road toward the Park. London was under a riotous attack, a
blazing pink and green Blitzkrieg. The air was filled with raucous
colors, explosions, shrieks, vivid whoops and gasps. Flames blos-
somed from every garden, car park and street corner.

What I had to do was both indulgent and necessary. I parked
Location Services' precious car by the Roundhouse, and walked
slowly over the bridge. I reveled in my newfound freedom from
regret, my sense, at last, of being whole again.

Number 4 was there. I knew it would be. Ned was in the
garden building a bonfire for Chris and Tim. My heart ached for
the boys, yet I saw that they were happy. They were clinging to
their mother, one on each side, clutching an arm apiece, heads
ready to turn and bury their ears in her side if a rocket should
burn too fiercely, or a spark fly too near.

I watched her. And, yes, I recognized her. I had studied the
photos of her often enough in Laura's flat. I knew so well those
tricks of stance and gesture that I had so wildly repudiated
as alien to me. It was just, I must own, this quirk of fate. Sarah
fitted as well into the stability of Unity's life as I did now in the
challenging sphere where my rebellion had carried me. Square
pegs for square holes. We had usurped each other's lives in alternate realities. I wondered how smooth or rough the transition
had been for her, how quickly Ned and the boys had welcomed a
more contented spirit in their midst. Certainly, the four of them
seemed happy now. They were complete. I was the outsider, the
intruder, looking in at them, forever exiled.

I knew it would be the last time that the veil would lift. The last time I'd be able to cross the flimsy fabric that divides us between choice and choice, between ifs and buts. After this I would remain in the new reality, the gap I filled in the tapestry of a world I had floundered into last April, a world where Klaus died, Pippa prospered, and Ned remained in Gloucester.

Beyond that veil, in that other world where Ned and the boys romped around a bonfire with Sarah, did she have any awareness of me? As if in answer, she looked up from the fire across the street to where I was standing on the dark side of the pavement. For a while I was worried that she wouldn't see me, that even at this moment I had mistaken the nature of the veil. But then she smiled. A warm smile of recognition and greeting.

But, as we looked at each other across a street busy with shadows, the veil dropped gently and finally. The house, the garden, and the bonfire all faded, the lines blurred and the colors smudged. All was being gathered together and pulled from my sight like a badly painted backcloth.

I watched them go. Watched the last of my sons, my once-loved husband, my surrogate self, being tweaked from one stage set to another with no more ado than puppets in a toy theater are jerked here and there by the whim of a child puppeteer. I suppose that we, none of us, are more than toythings. Sarah and I were luckier than most. We had been allowed to catch a glimpse of the strings.

The street was quiet and empty. The fire and the shadows had vanished with the house.

Gone. The boys had gone forever. No thunderstorms, no odd tricks of perception would ever bring them back. I had no tears. Not for them: they were happy; any sense of change would only be felt as having been for the better. Nor for myself: there was no time for self-pity in my busy future.

As I walked to the car, I found I was humming one of Face's tunes:

> For health, wealth and beauty, wit, learning and sense
> Must all come to nothing a hundred years hence.

www.ingramcontent.com/pod-product-compliance
Lightning Source LLC
Chambersburg PA
CBHW030830020726
47499CB00006B/2148